Fresh Blood²

edited by Mike Ripley
& Maxim Jakubowski

BLOODLINES

THE DO-NOT PRESS

First Published in Great Britain in 1997 by
The Do-Not Press
PO Box 4215
London SE23 2QD

A Paperback Original

ISBN 1 899344 20 9

British Library Cataloguing in Publication Data. A catalogue record for
this book is available from the British Library.

Printed and bound in Great Britain by The Guernsey Press Co Ltd.

Fresh Blood²

BLOODLINES

Fresh Blood 2: **Contents**

Mike Ripley

Foreword

The first *Fresh Blood* anthology was, in effect, seven years in the making, celebrating as it did the new wave of British crime writing which emerged around 1989 and was then followed by a 'second wave' of new talent in 1995.

Of that initial first flowering, writers such as Michael Dibdin, Philip Kerr, John Harvey, Sarah Dunant, Ian Rankin and others, are now well established as top-flight practitioners of their trade. From the more recent second wave, Stella Duffy, Nicholas Blincoe, Colin Bateman, Jeremy Cameron and Lauren Henderson have rapidly earned respect and success.

Crucially, there has not, this time, been a four or five year gap between the second and third new waves. In 1996 and 1997, more new writers have taken to crime and done so with frightening skill and aplomb. Some – Phil Lovesey, Christopher Brookmyre, Ken Bruen, Carol Anne Davis and John Tilsley – are represented here in *Fresh Blood 2*. Many more, I am delighted to say, will have to wait to see if there is a *Fresh Blood 3*.

Certainly there is enough talent out there, plotting, scheming, observing. There is no indication that this 'third wave' is ebbing. Check out the recent first novels of Peter Guttridge, Tony Frewin, Paul Johnston, Manda Scott, Gaby Byrne, Emlyn Rees, Greg Williams, Jerry Raine and Jon Stock, to name but a fistful. I rest my case.

But what is fresh about 'Fresh Blood' and how new is the 'new wave'?

Is it a question of 'realism' being injected into the crime story? Only partly. Even the most traditionally-crafted detective story – with conventional policemen and women and, usually, a closed circle of murder suspects – can go into the most graphic detail these days. Autopsies and forensics are no longer taboo subjects and the era when victims were dispatched by a neat bullet hole between the eyes is long gone.

If there is a greater degree of realism in the new wave of British crime fiction, it probably comes in the accuracy of dialogue and the depiction of social pressures and problems in today's Britain. It is, after all, a Britain which is becoming increasingly urbanised (and paranoid!), which is multiracial and multi-cultural and where drugs, videos, music and even fashion can dictate crime and the consequences of crime. Crime is an equal opportunity employer and the crime story can no longer be exclusively written to conform to any set of 'rules' or moral guidelines.

The great American *noir* writers of the '40s and '50s showed that crimes could be committed in fiction, as many are in life, for sad, pathetic reasons *and be successful* – though not necessarily for the perpetrator. The British detective story in its classic form, has long upheld a moral code that crime must not pay, yet we all know it can and does in a thousand different ways, large and small, on personal, social, economic, corporate and political levels.

The new wave of British crime writers recognise that crime happens. It is how people are affected by it which is interesting, whether there is a neat moral solution or not – and usually there is not. This element, perhaps, is the most realistic aspect of all.

Over fifty years ago, that brilliant crime writer and *Daily Telegraph* reviewer Anthony Berkeley predicted that the days of the pure puzzle novel – the classic *whodunnit?* – were numbered. It would no longer be the *who?* or *how?* of crime which was important to the novel, but the *why?*

Few would dispute that he has been proved right, although few could dispute that when the puzzle element is performed by magicians such as Colin Dexter or Peter Lovesey or PD James, it is done magnificently well. But in the main, the modern crime novel concerns itself with motive and the psychological fallout of crime.

Where the British new wave have taken this one stage further is that not only is the puzzle element no longer predominant, but in many cases, neither is the crime.

The stories in this collection deal with crime of course, and are populated by thieves, murderers and lots and lots of victims. All are, one way or another, on the edge – sometimes a very personal edge. Crimes happen to them and around them and they get sucked in. How they escape – or fail to escape – is at the heart of the matter.

*

Since the first *Fresh Blood* collection was commissioned, two trends have emerged in crime fiction which would, I suggest, support the theory that a sea-change in attitude is taking place.

The first is the deliberate and commendable move by many publishers to promote good fiction with a criminal element outside the straight-jacket of a fixed crime 'list' or imprint or house style.

With inventive design and attractive jackets, crime novels can reach an audience far wider than the mystery aficionado and come to the attention of readers who would not naturally seek out a Crime shelf in a bookshop.

The themes, styles and attitude of British crime writing are broadening and genuine efforts are being made to market good crime stories to a broader-based audience. An audience which will, hopefully, expand. Notable examples would have to include the stunningly-presented novels of Colin Bateman, James Hawes and Christopher Brookmyre, none of whom were specifically marketed under the soporific catch-all of 'crime and detection'.

The newer, independent publishing houses have had much to do with this and names such as 4th Estate, Serpent's Tail, No Exit Press and our own beloved (The) Do-Not Press now rub book spines alongside the corporate giants. Forced to rely on imagination rather than mass marketing, they have led and many are thankfully following.

The second emerging trend is a mark of the growing confidence of new British crime writers in that more and more are willing to take the risk of setting their novels in America, the spiritual home of the hardboiled style which has influenced them.

This was once a dangerous path indeed. A British writer trying to beat the Americans at the own game would himself become fair game and British novelists attempting to write American private eye stories have provided in the past (and not too distant past) some of the most embarrassing examples of the genre.

But within the 1990s, Brits such as Philip Kerr, Michael Dibdin, John Tilsley, Tim Willocks, Maxim Jakubowski and Lee Child have successfully, often brilliantly, set books in America and these are by no means copycat or parodies of the home-grown product.

*

The authors on show here in *Fresh Blood 2* were all invited to contribute stories based on their published work and general attitude to crime writing. Some might say *bad* attitude!

All human life – and quite a bit of death – is here.

Ken Bruen and John Baker, both in very different ways, show us the dysfunctional side of family life. Charles Higson and Phil Lovesey take us, respectively, into the heads of a thief and a murderer. Mary Scott and Carol Anne Davis both offer ghastly solutions to their protagonists' dilemmas and obsessions.

Lauren Henderson and Christine Green deal, in their own ways, with the problem of unrequited love, while four contributors take the scalpel to varied types of underworld. John Tilsley adopts the cause of the rootless drifter in modern America; John L Williams turns a compassionate eye on the underlife of the hustlers of Cardiff;

Christopher Brookmyre, riotously, exposes the Edinburgh under-world and that of the Edinburgh Fringe Festival; Iain Sinclair takes us powerfully and surreally through one of London's criminal legends.

As for the editors, Maxim introduces a new character who certainly looks like she has the legs for further appearances in the future, and I tell a joke, though not quite as it was told to me.

A special word should be said about the contribution of R D Wingfield, creator of Inspector Jack Frost and the first fictional policeman I ever came across who fiddled expenses, forged time-sheets and cracked very black jokes (thus proving to be the most realistic one I had ever encountered).

Rodney's tale and the build up to it contains all the elements of a classic crime story: blackmail, greed, psychological warfare, harassment, revenge and death. Personally, I think it is in very poor taste, but after reading it you'll agree that I would say that, wouldn't I?

Mike Ripley, October 1997

Christopher Brookmyre

Notes

Author's prefaces should, without exception, be ignored. You're still reading.

This means that either you won't take a telling or you remain unconvinced. Allow me to pick up the gauntlet.

Authors use a preface for one of two purposes: lying to you or insulting you. In the case of the former, the author will fib freely about his/her intentions, inspirations and aspirations for what they have written, invariably trying to make the whole undertaking sound more worthy and grand. In the case of the latter, the author will attempt to explain to the (presumed stupid) reader what his/her story *really* means, thereby conveying that the work is in fact far more worthy and grand than the idiot who is reading it could possibly appreciate.

Bampot Central is just for fun. Please do not analyse it. There is nothing worthy or grand to be found within its pages.

Of course, I could be lying.

Bampot Central

by Christopher Brookmyre

There was a six-foot iguana swaying purposefully into Parlabane's path as he walked down High Street. It had spotted him a few yards back and instinctively homed in on its prey, recognising that look in his eye and reacting without mercy. Some kind of sixth sense told cats which person in any given room most detested or was allergic to their species, so that they knew precisely whose lap to leap upon. A similar prescience had been visited upon spoilt Oxbridge undergrad hoorays in stupid costumes dispensing fliers for their dismal plays and revues. It was for this reason that a phenomenon such as the Fringe could never have thrived in Glasgow. In Edinburgh, most locals were stoically, if wearily, tolerant of such impositions; though in the west, dressing up as a giant lizard and deliberately getting in people's way would constitute reckless endangerment of the self.

'There's no getting past me, I'm afraid!' the iguana chirped brightly in a stagy, let's-be-friends, happy-cheery, go on, please stab me, you know it'll make you feel better tone of voice. 'Not without taking one of these!' it continued, thrusting a handful of leaflets at him.

Parlabane had put on the wrong T-shirt that morning, forgetting that his errands would unavoidably take him through places residents knew well to avoid during the Festival (or to give it its full name in the native tongue, the Fucking Festival). He was wearing a plain white one, which was nice enough but vitally lacked the legend 'FUCK OFF – I LIVE HERE', as was borne on several others at home. His August wardrobe, he liked to call it.

'Keeble Kollege Krazees present: Whoops Checkov!' the leaflet announced. 'An hilarious pastiche of Russian Naturalism! Find out what Constantine really got up to with that seagull!' Followed by the standard litany of made-up newspaper quotes.

'Come along tonight,' solicited the iguana. 'It might even cheer you up a bit!'

Parlabane swallowed back a multitude of ripostes and summoned up further admirable self-control by keeping his hands and feet to himself also. He breathed in, accepted a flyer and walked on. Remain calm, he told himself. He was over the worst of it now, having passed the Fringe Society office. North Bridge was in sight.

It was his friend's son's birthday the next week, and the gift Parlabane wanted to get him was only on sale in a small toy shop on the High Street. If it had also been on sale at the end of a tunnel of shite and broken glass, he'd have had to think long and hard about which store to visit during this time of year; as it was he'd had no such choice. The gift was a poseable male doll in a miniature Celtic kilt. The intended recipient lived in Los Angeles and would have no inkling of there being any significance to the costume, knowing only from Parlabane's attached note that the doll was to be named Paranoid Tim and must be subjected to every kind of abuse David's little mind could dream up.

He looked down at the pavement, carpeted as it was in further leaflet-litter, mostly advertising stand-up gigs by the A-list London safe-comedy collective, the ones who had each been bland enough to get their own Friday night series on Channel Four. He wondered whether anyone doing stand-up these days wasn't 'a comedy genius', and daydreamed yet again about Bill Hicks riding back into town on a black stallion and driving these lager-ad auditions into the Forth to drown.

Maybe he should have just sent the kid a card and a cheque, he thought, eyeing a nearby mime with murderous intent. But what the hell, he'd bought it now, and whatever he sent wouldn't spare him the next ordeal he had to face that day: a trip to the Post Office.

He picked up pace going down towards Princes Street, as the unpredictable crosswinds made North Bridge an inadvisable pitch for leafleting. The route was therefore comparatively free of obstacles, save for a gaggle of squawking Italian tourists staging some kind of sit-in protest at a bus-stop. Parlabane approached the St James shopping centre with a striding, let's-get-this-over-with gait, all the while attempting to take his mind off the coming horrors with another calming fantasy involving the three female flatmates from *Friends*. This time he was disembowelling them with a broadsword, the chainsaw decapitations having grown a little tired.

It was too simplistic to lay the blame at the feet of the Tories' Care in the Community policy. There had to be something deeper, to do with tides, leylines and lunar cycles, that explained why every large Post Office functioned as an urban bampot magnet, to which the deranged couldn't help but gravitate. From the merely befuddled to the malevolently sociopathic, they journeyed entranced each day, as though hypnotically drawn by the digitised queuing system. Parlabane remembered those Les Dawson ads a few years back: 'It's amazing what you can pick up at the Post Office.' Yeah. Like rabies. Or maybe anthrax.

He bought a self-assembly packing box at the stationery counter, then after ten minutes of being humiliated by an inert piece of cardboard, returned to purchase a roll of Sellotape and wrapped it noisily around the whole arrangement until Paranoid Tim was securely imprisoned. It looked bugger-all like a box, but the wee plastic bastard wasn't going to fall out, which was the main thing.

Then he joined the queue.

There were three English crusties immediately ahead of him, each boasting an ecologically diverse range of flora and fauna in their tangled dreads. They were accompanied by the statutory skinny dog on a string, and were sharing round a jumbo plastic bottle of Tesco own-brand cider and a damp-looking dowt. The dog wasn't offered a drag, but it looked like it had smoked a few in its time, and probably preferred untipped anyway.

Behind him there was a heavily pregnant young woman, looking tired and fanning herself with the brown envelope she was planning to post. And behind her were a couple of Morningside Ladies muttering about whichever Fringe show had been singled out for moral opprobrium (and a resultant box office boost) this year by Conservative Councillor Moira Knox. He'd got off lightly, in other words, and the queue wasn't even very long. The ordeal was almost over.

Except that at the post office, it's never over till it's over.

He caught a glimpse of a figure passing by on his right-hand side, skipping the queue and making directly for the counter. Parlabane was following the golden rule of PO survival – never look anyone in the face – but was nonetheless able to make out that the person was wearing a balaclava. His heart sank. It was the number one fashion accessory of the top-level numpties, especially in the height of summer, and this one looked hell-bent on maximum disruption.

Then from a few feet behind him he heard an explosion, and turned around to see fragments of ceiling tiles rain down upon the betweeded Morningsiders. Behind them was a man in a ski-mask holding a shotgun.

'RIGHT, NAE CUNT MOVE – THIS IS A ROBBERY!'

Parlabane turned again and saw that the balaclavaed figure at the counter was also holding a weapon.

Screams erupted as the people milling around the greetings cards and stationery section at the back animatedly ignored the gunman's entreaty and began pouring out through the swing-doors.

'I SAYS NAE CUNT MOVE!' he insisted, discharging another shot into the tiles, this time covering himself in polystyrene and plaster-dust. He wiped at his eyes with one hand and waved the shotgun with the other, running to the door to finally cut off the stream of evacuees.

'Lock the fuckin' door Tommy, for fuck's sake,' ordered the balaclava at the front counter.

'I'm daein' it, I'm daein' it,' he screeched back. 'An' dinnae use ma fuckin' name, Jyzer, ya fuckin' tube, ye.'

'Well whit ye cawin' me mine for, ya stupit cunt?'

Jesus Christ, thought Parlabane, watching the gunman on door-duty usher his captives back into the body of the kirk. It was true after all: the spirit of the Fringe affects the whole city. The worthy ethos of amateurism and improvisation had extended to armed robbery. Must have been Open Mic Night down at the local Nutters & Cutters, and first prize was lead role in a new performance-art version of *Dog Day Afternoon*.

From the voices he could tell they were young; but even if they had remained silent it still wouldn't have stretched his journalistic interpretative powers to deduce that they were pitifully inexperienced.

He rewound the action in his head, doing his Billy McNeil replay summary. Three seconds in, Mistake Number One: Discharging a shotgun into the ceiling to get everyone's attention, like simply the sight of the thing wasn't going to raise any eyebrows. There were several hundred people outside in the shopping mall, and a large police station two hundred yards away at the top of Leith walk.

Four seconds in, Mistake Number Two: Charging into the shop and leaving umpteen customers behind you, out of sight, with a clear exit out the front door, through which they rush in a hysterical panic.

Seven seconds in, Mistake Number Three: Blowing another hole in the roof, then turning your back on the remaining customers while you chase after extra hostages that you won't need.

Eight seconds in, Mistake Number Four: Telling everybody your first names.

Ten seconds in, Mistake Number Five: Finding yourself with at least ten customers plus staff as prisoners. One or two is usually plenty.

In a moment of inspiration, gunman Tommy began rearranging the queuing cordons and ordered everyone behind the rope.

'Stay there an' dinnae move, right?'

The customers were uniformly terrified, with the exception of Parlabane, who was just in far too bad a mood to entertain any emotions other than fury and hatred. Decadence is often born of boredom. Nihilism even more often born of a walk through the Old Town in mid-August.

'Wouldn't you prefer us to sit down?' he offered, figuring these guys were going to need all the help and advice they could get.

Tommy thought about it. He looked like he'd need to do his working on a separate sheet of paper, but he got there eventually.

'Eh, aye.'

Jyzer was busy making Mistake Number Six, pointing his weapon at a young teller and ordering her colleagues to stay in their seats, where they could each press their panic buttons just in case the two resounding shotgun blasts hadn't been heard first-hand at Gayfield Square polis emporium.

'Jesus Christ,' Parlabane sighed, the words slipping out before he could stop himself.

'Shut it, you,' Tommy barked. 'You got a problem, pal?'

Yes he did. He had a problem with the fact that the chances of these two eejits shooting someone through incompetence-generated panic were increasing by the second. He considered amelioration the wisest policy right then.

'Eh, no problem,' he said. 'But I was wondering... I mean, it's just an idea really, but maybe you should move the staff over here beside us, you know, so there's just one group of hostages to keep an eye on, and your china can get on with posting his airmail or whatever.'

'Christ, mate,' said one of the crusties, 'why don't you offer them our bloody wallets as well while you're at it? I mean whose side are you on?'

'Fuckin' shut it, you,' snapped Tommy. 'An' it's no airmail, it's a fuckin' robbery, right?'

Parlabane held his hands up and shrugged. Whatever.

Jyzer, who by superiority of one synapse was the brains of the outfit, had cottoned on to Parlabane's thinking and gestured the other tellers to file out from behind the counter. Then he ordered Tommy to collect everybody's wallets, proving that he was broadminded and open to suggestions from any of the hostages.

'Sheer fuckin' genius,' Parlabane muttered to the crusty, who wouldn't meet his gaze.

Tommy backed away, eyes flitting back and forth between the growing pile of wallets and purses and the front doors, outside which a crowd had gathered.

'Oh, I just knew something like this was going to happen,' muttered one of the Morningsiders to her companion. 'I just knew it.'

'Me too Morag, me too.'

Parlabane had suffered enough.

'Well it's a pity neither of you fucking clairvoyants thought to tip anyone off, then, isn't it?' he observed.

'Now, son, there's no need for that.'

He looked away. This was the quintessence of British 'respectability'. There were two brainless arseholes holding them prisoner with shotguns, but they could still get upset about the 'language' you used.

Jyzer's initially quiet dialogue with the remaining teller was beginning to gain in volume. Parlabane hadn't caught what Jyzer was asking for, but he wished to hell the stupid lassie would hurry up and give him it, especially as there were now two uniformed plods peering in the doors and hustling the onlookers back. He looked at his watch, figuring the Balaclava Brothers had a few more minutes before an armed response unit showed up to raise the stakes.

'Look, I ken ye're lyin', awright? We've had information. We ken they're in there. Insurance bonds, fae Scottish Widows. They come through here the last Monday o' every month. So fuckin' get them or I'll fuckin' blow ye away.'

The girl had tears in her eyes and was struggling to keep her voice steady. 'I swear to God, I've never heard of any… insurance bonds coming through here. In fact I don't think I've ever heard of insurance bonds full stop.'

'Look, don't gie's it. Last Monday o' every month. Scottish Widows. It should say it on the parcel.'

'But this isn't a sorting office. The only parcels coming through here are the ones folk are sending. They go straight in the slots over there, or in the basket through-by. Please, I'm not lying. You can come through and look.'

'I fuckin' will an' aw,' he said, walking around to the counter's access door. 'An' if ye're lyin' I'll fuckin' mark ye, hen. I'll no be a minute, Tommy,' he assured.

'Insurance bonds?' one of the tellers asked of a colleague.

'Naw, I've never heard of them either.'

'Wouldnae come through here anyway, would they?' queried another.

'D'you think they've got the right place?'

'Fuckin' shut it yous,' Tommy ordered again. 'We've had information. We ken whit we're daein' so sit nice an' it'll aw be by wi' soon, right?'

Parlabane sighed again. Insurance bonds. Jesus Christ almighty. It just got better and better.

'What's an insurance bond, Tommy?' he asked calmly.

'I tell't yous aw tae shut it I ken whit insurance bonds are, right?'

Parlabane made a zipping gesture across his mouth. There was a suspicion growing inside his head. It had germinated early on in the proceedings, but the last few moments had poured on the Baby Bio and it was seriously starting to sprout.

They sat in silence, apart from the occasional yelp from the crusties' skinny dog. Tommy's eyes looked wide and jumpy through the holes in his ski mask.

'Fuck!' came a furious, low growl from the back office. 'Fuckin' Jesus fuckin' *fuck!*'

The girl stumbled nervously out to join the hostage party, followed by Jyzer, whose woolly mask could not conceal that he was little at peace with himself.

'So, d'ye get them?' Tommy asked.

Jyzer took a slow breath to calm his rage. It didn't quite make it.

'Naw I never fuckin' got them ya stupit cunt. Fuckin' Scottish Widows must've changed the delivery day or somethin'.'

'Aye, awright, dinnae take it oot on me.'

'Well stop askin' fuckin' stupit questions.'

'But what are we gaunny dae?'

'Shut up, I'm tryin' tae think.'

Parlabane looked to the front of the post office. One of the uniforms was pointing in and talking to someone out of sight down the mall. Three men in matching kevlar semmits filed into place in front of the sports shop opposite, taking up crouching positions and raising automatic rifles.

Parlabane swallowed. Not everyone was going to be home in time for tea, he feared.

'Giros!' Jyzer announced. He turned to the teller who had most recently joined the ranks of the illegally detained. 'Giro money. Pensions nawrat. Hand it ower.'

'I don't think that should be your number one priority right now,' Parlabane said, pointing at the front window.

'Who asked... aw fuck.' Jyzer took a step back, like that extra two feet would put him out of a bullet's projectile range.

'This is the police,' announced a hailer-enhanced screech. Whatever it said next was lost as Jyzer finally showed a spark of dynamism.

'Right.' he stated. 'Staun up, aw yous. An' line up across the shoap, facin' away fae the windae. That's it.'

They got to their feet unsteadily, most of them turning their heads to cast an eye upon the assembly outside. Jyzer and Tommy stepped behind their human shield, out of the police marksmen's sights.

'Terrific,' muttered one of the crusties. 'Now we're the filling in a gun sandwich.'

'Noo, go an' get us aw the cash in the shop,' he commanded the teller, handing her the sports bag that already contained their wallet harvest.

'We have all exits covered,' resumed the loud hailer. 'Please put down your weapons, release your hostages and come out with your hands on your heads.'

'Come on,' said Parlabane tiredly. 'Do what the man asked. He said please, after all.'

'You think we're fuckin' stupit, don't ye?' Jyzer observed, accurately. 'Smart-arsed cunt,' he added, hitting a second bullseye.

'Well, maybe you'll prove me wrong by explaining how you were ever planning to get out of here, with or without your, ahem, Insurance Bonds.'

'Stop windin' him up, mate,' warned the crusty who had earlier proffered the highly constructive wallet suggestion.

'I'm not winding him up. I'm just curious to know the secrets of how true professionals work.'

'Want me tae slap the cunt, Jyzer?' Tommy offered.

'Just keep the heid and keep your hauns on the gun, Tommy. Dinnae let him distract ye. He's up to somethin', this cunt.'

A telephone started ringing on the other side of the counter as the teller returned with the sports bag, presumably now containing cash and very possibly a dye-charge, seeing as Jyzer had made Mistake Number Fuckknows by leaving her alone to fill the thing.

'Get that,' Jyzer commanded. 'No you,' he added, as Tommy made to reach for the receiver.

'It's for you,' she said. 'The police.'

He gestured to her to rejoin the human shield, taking hold of the bag as she passed, then picked up the phone. Tommy stayed in place, sweeping the gun back and forth along his line of vision like it was a searchlight. The crusties' skinny dog ambled lazily over to him, yawned once and began half-heartedly shagging his leg.

'Get tae fuck, ya wee shite,' he hissed, kicking out at it to shake the thing off, his eye relaying between his prisoners and his foot. 'Fuckin' dirty wee bastard.'

'TOMMY!' Jyzer barked, placing a hand over the mouthpiece, 'will ye fuckin' keep it doon – I'm on the phone here.'

'Aye, awright Fuck's sake,' whined Tommy, hurt.

Jyzer shook his head and took his hand off the blue plastic.

'Sorry, what were ye sayin'?' he resumed.' Naw, naw. You listen. Fuckin' just shut it an' listen ya polis cunt.'

The Morningside contingent tutted in stereo either side of Parlabane.

'Before we even have this conversation, I want to be lookin' oot that front windae an' seein' *nae* polis, right. Nane. Get them away fae the front o' the shop then phone us back.' He slammed down the handset with an obvious satisfaction. Parlabane suspected the sense of accomplishment would be short-lived, but was admittedly impressed at this first sign of Jyzer having any idea what he was doing. In fact, he had noted with some surprise that neither of the pair had shown much sign of panic at the arrival of the ARU, and started to wonder whether their grossly conspicuous entrance had been less of an obvious blunder than he had first assumed.

Jesus, these heid-the-baws couldn't have a *plan*, could they?

He looked back over his shoulder, Jyzer and Tommy peering

between the arrayed hostages. The marksmen got to their feet and moved out of sight left and right, as if exiting a stage. Parlabane figured it a safe bet they'd be returning for the fifth act.

The phone rang again.

'Right. Very good. Well done. Noo here's what we want. Naw, naw, shut it. We aw ken what *you* want: you want the hostages oot an' us in the cells so's ye can boot fuck oot us. Well, the bad news is you cannae have baith, right? So there's gaunny have to be a wee compromise. You can have maist o' the hostages in exchange for a helicopter. We want it on the roof o' the St James Centre in hauf an 'oor. We'll be takin' wan hostage wi' us, an' we'll tell the pilot where we're gaun wance we're on board.' He slammed the phone down again.

'A helicopter?' Parlabane asked. 'What, has Fife no' got an extra-dition treaty?'

'Fuckin' shut it.'

'Another rapier-like come-back.'

'Right,' Jyzer declared, suddenly pointing his shotgun at the preg-nant woman. 'Step forward missus, ye're comin' wi us.'

'No her, Jyzer,' Tommy dissented. 'She's dead fat. She'll be slow.'

'She's no fat, she's fuckin' pregnant, ya n'arse. The polis'll no mess aboot if we've got a gun tae a pregnant burd's heid.'

The pregnant woman began to whimper, tears running from terrified eyes. She put a hand out and grabbed Parlabane's shoulder to steady herself.

'Not a good idea, guys,' he stated.

The phone began ringing again.

'I thought I tell't you tae shut it,' Jyzer said, thrusting the gun into Parlabane's face.

'Look at her,' he demanded, staring into Jyzer's eyes. 'She's ready to burst. Do you want her goin' into labour during your dramatic getaway?'

Jyzer looked at the woman, sweating, tearful, and imposingly up the stick.

'Know somethin'?' he declared. 'You're absolutely right. We'll take you instead.'

Parlabane, who was firmly of the belief that no good deed ever goes unpunished, had been expecting this. He shrugged, put his parcel down and took a step forward, trying not to dwell on the potential indignity of surviving several professional attempts on his life only to be plugged by some shambolic half-wit down the post office.

Bugger it. Just as long as getting killed there didn't mean you went to Post Office Hell.

Jyzer picked up the phone again while Tommy gestured

Parlabane to walk ahead of him through to the area behind the counters. The skinny dog gave another yawn as they passed, then trotted over to Jyzer and began humping his shin, its pink tongue lolling out of the right-hand side of its mouth.

'Naw, naw. We'll let the last hostage go wance we've arrived at. AYIAH! Get tae fuck ya clatty wee cunt... naw, no you, officer. Dug was tryin' tae shag me leg.'

Jyzer eyed the crusty who was holding the other end of the string. 'Heh Swampy, that thing touches me again an' I splatter its baws aw ower this flair, awright? Naw, no you officer. Aye that's right, *aw* the hostages. Once we're up an' away, we cannae shoot them, right? So they're aw yours – but no' until we're up an' away. An' we're no comin' up until the chopper's there. If we come up the stairs an' there's fuck-all, it's gaunny be a fuckin' bloodbath, right? Cause ye'll no have gie'd us any choices – we'll have to shoot oor way oot. Noo, next time this phone rings it better be tae say wur transport's arrived.'

He put the phone down again.

'Are we gettin' a helicopter, Jyzer?' Tommy asked.

'Don't be a fuckin' eejit, Tommy. They're just stringin' us alang, same as we're stringin' them alang. C'mon.'

They backed into the passage leading to behind the counters, Tommy keeping a gun on Parlabane, Jyzer still training his on the hostages.

'Nane o' yous move,' he called out, stopping at the door that led into the storeroom at the rear of the counters. 'We'll be watchin'. Stay where yous are. You might no' see us, but we'll still see you. Dinnae try anythin'. Just cause ye cannae see us doesnae mean we're no there.'

'I'm sure they bought that,' Parlabane said, nodding, as they retreated into the store-room. 'I don't think it would have crossed their minds at all that you might not be watching them. I mean, if you'd overstated your case it might have raised suspicions, but...'

'Fuckin' shut it,' grunted Jyzer, nicking back and popping his head round the door to check his prisoners weren't making a swift but orderly exit.

'More Wildean badinage. Do you mind if I write some of these come-backs down?'

'You'll no' sound so smart talkin' through a burst nose, smart cunt, so I'd fuckin' wrap it if I was you.'

'And if you burst my nose you'll be leaving a nice fresh trail of blood along your escape route; that's if you fuckin' clowns have got an escape route.'

'We've got mair ay a plan than *you* think, smart cunt.'

'Course you have. You're fuckin' professionals. Tell me again about these insurance bonds...'

Jyzer back-handed Parlabane across the jaw, which was very much what he'd been hoping for. Unfortunately the blow came on the wrong side, so he had to execute a largely unconvincing 180-degree stumble before getting to his intended effect, which was to fall down heavily against the door so that it slammed loudly with his back propped hard against it.

Despite Parlabane's abysmally obvious pirouette, it still took Jyzer a few moments to suss the potential problem, by which time the sound of breaking glass was filling the air as the police broke into the front shop and began ushering the hostages out.

'Fuckin' cunt. Fuckin' cunt.'

Jyzer kicked viciously at Parlabane until eventually he rolled clear, then threw the door open to see his prisoners fleeing and the armed cops kneeling down to take aim. He slammed it shut again and pushed a table up against it, then backed into the room, indicating to Parlabane to crawl over against the wall to his right. Jyzer knelt down a few feet away, the gun pointing halfway between his prisoner and the door, his eyes shuttling between both targets.

'We've still got a hostage in here,' he shouted. 'Any o' yous cunts tries this door and we'll do 'im, right? We still want that fuckin' helicopter.'

'OK, OK, everybody stay calm,' appealed a voice from the other side of the door. 'Everybody just calm down. I'm pulling my marksmen back to outside the shop, so don't panic and do something we'll all regret.'

'I wouldnae regret shootin' you, ya cunt,' Jyzer hissed at Parlabane, who just smiled.

'Sorry Jyzer, but in case you've no' worked it out, the *last* thing you can do is shoot me – I'm your only hostage. Soon as I'm out of the equation, it's you versus the bullets. That's unless you professionals can take out a team of trained marksmen with your stove-pipes there.'

Frustration was writ large in Jyzer's eyes. He clearly wished he could blow Parlabane away, or at the very least, finally silence him with a telling oneliner. He settled for:

'Fuckin' shut it.'

Then he called out to the cops. 'We're aw calm in here. Yous keep calm an' aw. An' get on wi' gettin' that helicopter.'

Tommy was hectically hunting through drawers and cupboards, having tried the handle on the only other door in the room.

'I cannae find the keys, Jyzer,' he gasped in a loud whisper.

'Well they've got tae be here somewhere. Keep lookin'.'

'Couldn't possibly be on the person of one of your erstwhile hostages?' Parlabane suggested.

'Aw fuck,' Tommy sighed.

'Keep at it Tommy, there'll be another set somewhere. Dinnae listen tae that cunt.'

'What were you wanting from the stationery cupboard, anyway?' Parlabane asked. 'Checking there's no eh, insurance bonds mixed in wi' the dug-licence application forms?'

'Would ye fuckin' shut it aboot the bonds. They were meant tae be here. Scottish Widows changed the delivery. They're worth thousands. Nae ID needed. Good as money.

'That's right, they're transgotiable,' Tommy contributed.

'Shut it Tommy, that's no the word. Keep lookin'. An' as for you, bigmooth, that's no' any stationery cupboard. Behind that door's the thing that's gaunny make you eat every wan o' your smart-cunt words.'

'What, proof that Madonna's got talent?'

'Naw. That door leads tae the underground railway. Belongs tae the Post Office, for sendin' stuff back and forward. Runs fae here doon tae the main sortin' depot at Brunswick Road, which is where we've got a motor waitin'. They'll still be coverin' the exits up here while we're poppin' up haufway doon Leith Walk. And wance we're there, you'll have out-lived your usefulness, "lived" bein' the main word. Aye, ye're no so smart, noo, are ye?'

Parlabane shook his head, squatting on the floor against the wall.

'Underground railway?' he asked, grinning.

'Aye.'

'I've got two words for you, Jyzer: Insurance bonds.'

'An' I've got two words for you: fuckin' shut it. Tommy, have ye fun' thae keys yet?'

'Sorry Jyzer. I don't think there's a spare set.'

'Fuck it,' Jyzer said, getting to his feet. 'You watch him Tommy.' Jyzer walked over to the locked door and pointed his shotgun at the metal handle.

'No don't do that!' Parlabane shouted, too late.

Jyzer pulled his trigger and blasted the handle, then reeled away from the still-locked door, bent double and groaning.

'AAAAYAAA FUCKIN' BASTARD!' he screamed, falling to the floor, blood appearing from the dozens of tiny wounds where the pellets had ricocheted off the solid metal and back into his thighs, hands, wrists, abdomen and groin.

'STAY OOT!' Tommy shouted to the cops behind the door. 'STAY OOT. The hostage is awright. Just a wee accident in here. Just everybody keep steady, right?'

'Let's hear the hostage,' called the cop. 'Let's hear his voice.'

Tommy, looking increasingly like the least steady person on earth, waved the gun at Parlabane and nodded, prompting him to reply.

'I'm here,' Parlabane shouted.

'You OK, sir?'

'Do you really want me to answer that?'

'I mean, are you hurt?'

'No. But Jyzer here just learned a valuable lesson about the magic of the movies.'

'What?'

'That's enough,' Tommy interrupted, scuttling over to check on his writhing companion. 'What's the score wi' that helicopter?' he called.

'I think an air ambulance might be more appropriate,' Parlabane said.

'Fuckin' shut it,' Tommy hissed. It was the only part of Jyzer's role he had been so far able to assimilate.

'It's over, Tommy,' Parlabane said quietly. 'Your pal's in a bad way, there's polis everywhere, and I'm afraid you're three hundred miles from the nearest underground postal railway, which is in London.'

'It's no'. There's wan here. We've had information.'

'Is everybody OK in there?' asked the policeman.

'STAY OOT!' Tommy warned again, his voice starting to tremble. 'The situation's no' changed. Stay oot.'

Jyzer continued to moan in the corner, convulsed also by the occasional cough.

'There's no such things as insurance bonds, Tommy,' Parlabane told him.

'Shut it. There is.'

'Where did you get this "information"?'

'That's ma business.'

'Did you pay for it? Is someone on a percentage?'

'Naw. Aye. The second wan.'

'Never done anything like this before, have you?'

Jyzer moaned again, eyes closed against the pain.

Tommy shook his head. He was starting to look scared, like he needed his Mammy to take him home.

'Somebody put you up to it? Somebody force you?'

'Naw,' he said defensively. 'We were offered this. Hand-picked. He gied us the information, an' we'd tae gie him forty percent o' the cally efterwards.'

'You been inside before? Recently?'

'Aye. Oot six weeks. Baith ay us.'

'And I take it you weren't inside for armed robbery.'

He shook his head again.

Parlabane nodded. He reached into his pocket and pulled out his compact little mobile phone.

'Whit ye daein'? Put that doon.'

'Just let me call the cops outside, okay? Save us shoutin' through the wall the whole time.'

'Aye awright.'

He dialled the number for Gayfield Square, explained the situation and asked to be patched through to the main man on-site.

'Are you sure you're all right, sir?' the cop in charge asked. 'What's your name? Do you need us to get a message to someone?'

'I'm fine. My name's Jack Parlabane. Yes, *that* Jack Parlabane, and spare me the might-have-knowns. I didn't *try* to get myself into this, it just happened. Now, Tommy here's not quite ready to end this, I don't think. But I was wondering whether you might want to scale down the ARU involvement out there. I've got a feeling you'll be needing them elsewhere fairly imminently.'

'Too late,' the cop informed him. 'Somebody hit the Royal Bank at the west end of George Street about fifteen minutes ago while we were scratching our arses back here. By the time any of our lot got there it was all in the past tense. We've been had.'

'You're not the only ones.'

'What was that?' Tommy asked.

'Bank robbery, Tommy,' he told him. 'A proper one. Carried out less than a mile from here while the police Armed Response Unit were holding their dicks outside a post office. Now who do you think could have been behind that? Same guy gave you "the information", maybe?'

'But… but… we…'

'You were right about being hand-picked, Tommy. And you can both take some satisfaction from the fact that you carried out the plan exactly as intended. Unfortunately, you were intended to fuck up. What were the instructions? Grab the mysterious Insurance Bonds, create a hostage situation, keep the polis occupied, then escape via the magical underground railway? And were you given a specific date and time, perhaps?'

There was confusion in Tommy's eyes, but on the whole resignation was starting to replace defiance. Jyzer gave a last mournful splutter and passed out.

'Don't suppose you want to score a few points with the boys in blue by telling them who set you up so they can get on to his tail?'

'Mair than ma life's worth.'

'Fair enough. But it's still over, Tommy. Jyzer needs medical attention. The wounds might be superficial, but then again they might not. Come on. Put the gun down.'

Tommy looked across at the unconscious Jyzer surrounded by bloodstains on the beige carpet, then at the locked door, then back at his hostage.

'Ach, fuck it,' he rasped angrily, knuckles whitening as he gripped the gun tighter.

Parlabane took an involuntary breath, his eyes locked on Tommy's.

'The cunt's name was McKay,' he said with a sigh. 'Erchie McKay. Met him inside. He got oot last month, same as us.' Tommy put the shotgun down on the floor and slid it across to Parlabane. 'Just make sure they catch the bastart.'

At eight-thirty that evening, the nightly performance of 'Whoops Checkov' was abandoned after a number of powerful stink-bombs were thrown through the door of the auditorium by an unidentified male. It was, the unidentified male admitted to the woman driving his getaway car, childish and puerile, but then so is much of the Fringe.

Mary Scott

Notes

Forget that nonsense about needles and haystalks. Finding a needle in a mountain of dried grass is a piece of cake as long as you have infinite hours and a thousand-strong search party prepared to devote meticulous attention to the task. It's finding a haystalk in a haystack that's difficult. Not just any old haystalk: the one someone stuck into the pile in the hope of concealing it.

Difficult, but not impossible. A botanist could do it: or a finicky, pampered thoroughbred horse who's free to take his pick between the best timothy and the coarser rye in his manger. For the fact is that every living thing (apart from Dolly, the cloned sheep, and her ilk) is different, individual. People especially are.

It's a fact that the managers of institutions too easily forget. Prisons, hospitals, asylums: the inmates are all of a piece to the people who run them. I was struck by this when, a couple of years ago, I inspected convalescent homes on behalf of my father. The people who ran them were competent and respectful – to me. Towards the residents they displayed a patronising, over-familiar, 'there-there' sort of attitude which would be enough to rot the soul of anyone who stayed there. Needless to say, Dad stayed at home: and got better.

To these managers the inmates were, 'Doris who has a problem with her waterworks,' 'Reginald, who doesn't like sharing: the other old gentleman is very nice, though he does suffer with his bowels. Makes wind rather too frequently.' This particular manager whisked me off – past a kitchen smelling of overboiled cabbage – to show me proudly yet another room containing twin beds neatly shrouded in candlewick.

He didn't register that the people who lived in his Home had a personality apiece. That they had a past.

An Hour After Lunch

by Mary Scott

Frank Marchant QC eased his brittle body on the plump, soft surface of the bed. He had to do that every twenty minutes, he had so little flesh on his buttocks that to maintain the same position for longer was intolerable. So was being here. Not, of course, that he had anything against John and Lizzy who ran the place, they seemed to do everything they could for the old biddies. But the fact remained that once someone was put in a Home he was expected, sooner or later, to die. In a way he was put in a Home to die. It was only a matter of time. He fumbled on the bedside table for the familiar, lumpen shape of his watch, then pressed the knob on its side.

'Eleven-forty-three and twenty seconds,' whined an electronic voice. Time to reposition if he wasn't to become uncomfortable again.

The door of his room burst open and Pam rushed in and dumped herself on the end of the bed. She was the best thing about this place, a breath of fresh air. Bright, blonde hair, pink cheeks and – he'd always been a good judge of character, none better – as affectionate, goodhearted and straightforward as they come. It was the highspot of his day to hear her chattering away about the trivia of her busy little life. But today she seemed down in the dumps.

'Boyfriend trouble again?' he guessed.

She nodded. It seemed that Tony had been ticked off by John for being in one of the old people's rooms instead of out in the grounds where he was supposed to work. He was a light-fingered lad, Frank was sure of that; Pam'd be better off without him. Couldn't tell her that, though. Instead he reassured her that if that was all it amounted to there was no real need to worry. And then she was smiling again and helping him to his feet and towards the dining room.

Lunch was a dull confection of limp leaves of lettuce and scrolls of cardboard ham followed by a tasteless slop of a dessert. He'd mentioned the food once to Lizzy, but she'd said that the others liked it bland and Pam'd get him some nice boiled sweets next time she went into town. More likely, he thought that the old folks' taste buds had gone the way of their other senses and they would eat or drink anything that was put in front of them.

John and Lizzy insisted he join the others for the meal and for an hour in the TV room afterwards, said it would do him good to socialise, he needed stimulation. Socialise indeed! What would he have to say to people like these? He looked at them lined up in a row, their faces fixed on the screen. Every half-hour Lizzy would bustle in and stop in front of one of them and ask, 'Want to go to the toilet, dear?' and a watcher would gurgle and nod and be led away.

He couldn't see well enough to determine what the programme was; he thought it was racing by the sound of the commentary and by the fact that Tony had drifted in and was standing rivetted, hands clenched tight at his sides.

But he could certainly see well enough to distinguish between the watchers. Besides which, as his sight had worsened, his perceptive powers – the ability to spot the characteristic gesture which set one individual apart from another, to read mood and feeling from the slump of a shoulder or the persistent tapping of a slippered toe on the floor – which had always of necessity been keen, seemed to have sharpened immeasurably.

But there was nothing on which to exercise them in this place, nothing to keep his mind in trim. Really it would be as well to die sooner rather than later, he thought as he imagined a future in which all his senses faded, in which all contact with the world was closed off while his still-agile brain ached for intellectual challenge. In a way the other people in the room were luckier; they were losing their minds first.

In the meantime he occupied himself with watching the watchers, imagining the impression they would have made on him had they appeared before him in his court. What crimes would they have committed? Like him they had once been professionals – doctors, solicitors, architects, bankers, officers in the RAF – so their offences would not be petty-theft or joyriding in stolen cars. These people would stand before him accused of grand larceny, major fraud, or murder. He considered each of them, noting with meticulous care the tone of voice in the often garbled utterances, the sudden tilt of the head which in the old days would have signalled some shift in emotion, some hint of whether they were telling the truth.

This afternoon he had a full house for his observations. On fine days the Three Furies – Mrs Gray, Mrs Evans and Mrs Topp, they of the ill-fitting cardigans and skirts bulging over incontinence pads – preferred to sit in a row on folding chairs in the garage with the door rolled-up, and wrangle interminably about whose turn it was to hold Mrs Evans's knitted rabbit. In fact, the rabbit belonged to Mrs Topp, he'd seen her toddler grandson drop it into her lap over two months ago, on the family's most recent visit: though none of the Three Furies remembered that. But on cold days, like this one, they stayed indoors, deprived of the rabbit, arguments over which, John and Lizzy felt, might encourage the rest of the residents to take incoherent sides. Beyond them was Mr Topp, seated – by Lizzy – next to the wife who no longer recognised him: though Lizzy insisted she did. Then there was Mr Byfleet in an old, checked shirt and yellow waistcoat: this afternoon he had reached the red-upholstered wing chair by the fire in advance of Mr Baines and claimed it for his own. He looked smug. Mr Baines looked murderous.

A tragedy to reflect that these people who had once been eminent in public life were now reduced to bickering over a stuffed toy or a favourite chair. Frank looked away from their faces, down at the row of scuffed, unpolished shoes, the torn slippers and holed socks and felt a heavy weight of sadness descend, followed abruptly – surprisingly – by a wave of guilt at his own cold, voyeuristic assessment. For somewhere beyond – inside – their so called dementia persisted, he was sure, the emotions – greed, lust, envy, love, jealousy, compassion – which he had been trained all his adult life to recognise. Was it too much to wish, he wondered, that the home could buy an identical chair for Mr Baines and a couple of extra knitted rabbits for Mrs Gray and Mrs Evans? It wasn't as if they weren't all paying enough.

It was time to return, slowly, to his room. After the effort he was glad of the cup of tea which Pam brought. Then another struggle: to reach and use the toilet. Back in bed, he lay stiffly still and let pictures seep into his mind of the home he had left behind. Staffordshire china on the shelves. Flames leaping in the hearth. The lawn stretching out from the french windows in a wide, well-tended sweep. But he had slipped and broken a shepherdess, he had stumbled and burnt himself on the logs which Mrs Lane had laid and lit; and he could no longer make it into the garden he paid old Joe to tend. His daughters said what could he expect at ninety-four? They said he must come here.

He sighed, switched on the bedside lamp and prepared to take his medication. On his first day here, three months ago now, Lizzy had stood over him, ready to dole out the pills. But he had told her, as crisply as his quavering voice permitted, that the district nurse would deliver a pack every week with each day's dose enclosed in a plastic bubble. He was perfectly capable of extracting the things, telling by feel which were large, slippery capsules, which were small, chalky tablets: which the pain killers, which a remedy for his faulty waterworks, which for his heart, which for his liver. He proceeded to demonstrate. He showed her his bottle of expectorant and how he measured the dosage accurately, by feel, in a small, ridged glass. Then he showed her how he used his two kinds of eyedrops, his inhaler, his eardrops and rounded off the performance by producing a pack of Fibrofil ('for the bowel,' he explained) and mixing it with two-parts water. When he'd finished she'd said fine, she could see he was the independent sort and that it was quite all right, in future, for him to handle his medication on his own.

But today, as he started on the usual ritual, surrounded by his paraphernalia of bottles, jars, measuring glasses and bubble packs he thought why? Why was he taking all these remedies when there was nothing wrong with him but old age? Nothing that death wouldn't cure.

In the event it was Mrs Gray who died first. It came as no surprise. In fact it seemed that the army of sons, daughters, grandchildren, nephews and nieces who arrived had been expecting her death for so long they had shopped for it. They were dressed top-to-toe in smart, new outfits. They thronged the home, black finery aswirl, eager faces anticipating the reading of the will. After the flurry of activity subsided, Frank Marchant was pleased to hear that Mrs Gray had thought of the person who had cared about her to the end; she'd left Pam a little legacy.

'Wasn't it nice of her?' Pam demanded, bouncing on the end of his bed. He moved his legs carefully out of range of her enthusiasm. Though, truth to tell, they felt, if anything, less fragile than before. He had anticipated, after the day of his epiphany in the hour after lunch in the TV lounge, that he would have his wish and die sooner rather than later. But now the opposite looked more likely to become the case.

'I can't wait to tell Tony,' Pam chirruped on.

'As long as you remember that the money's meant for you.' He looked out of the window. He could make out a solitary figure, standing stock still. That would be Tony, doing nothing for his wages.

After Mrs Gray's death the arguments in the garage on sunny afternoons reduced in volume, but increased in acrimony. There was a great deal of snatching and pushing and once Mrs Evans was seen to grab Mrs Topp's hair and pull. Then Mrs Evans died too and only Mrs Topp was left, clutching the stuffed toy to her bulbous chest, rocking and keening like a child who could not be consoled. Perhaps he had been wrong, Frank thought, to imagine that she would be happier having the knitted rabbit to herself.

It was only after Mr Topp died, the following week, that alarm bells rang for Dr Carr, the home's GP.

'He's thinking of calling in the police,' Pam reported anxiously to Frank Marchant.

'So he should if there's the slightest cause for alarm. Best thing for all concerned. No call to have suspicion hanging over everyone's head.'

'Tony says they're bound to want to question me. Because every-one who's…' she paused, 'gone, has left me something.'

'I expect he's jealous. You deserve every penny. And, of course, when I go,' he paused and smiled, 'well let's just say you won't be forgotten. But remember it'll be for you to spend on yourself, not to throw away on Tony.'

Sure enough, the next day when Pam came to collect him for lunch, she reported that she had been asked all sorts of questions. She said the police were also going to talk to the families of all the people who had recently passed away – sons, daughters, grandsons, nephews, nieces. Everyone.

In the dining room Frank chewed on flabby macaroni cheese, spooned tinned pears and custard into his mouth. Then, unusually for him, he stayed on in the TV lounge, not remembering to shift every twenty minutes as he watched his fellow residents. Later, the familiar theme of the early evening news drew his attention. It was full of guff about people in the home 'dying like flies', cause of death not revealed by the police: and of politically correct nonsense on the rights of the elderly. It mentioned other instances in which residents of retirement homes had been abused by staff, tricked by their rela-tives. His anger rose. Why should they assume we are victims just because we're old? If there have been murders here, why couldn't one of us have been responsible?

He looked at the row of watchers, he looked at the ill-shod feet tapping on the carpet, and he tried out certain scenarios. He imag-ined that for a fleeting moment the veil which had long since come between Mrs Topp and the real world had lifted and she had found herself – horror! – seated next to the husband who had tormented her through fifty years of married life. He watched, in his mind's eye, Mr Byfleet bear down on Mr Baines with murderous intent, because his favourite chair had been taken. And he watched Mrs Topp fight for the right to hold her knitted rabbit to the end.

That night it was Mr Baines who died.

Next afternoon Frank was again observing with care the interac-tion, such as it was, between his remaining fellow residents when Lizzy ushered in two policemen. She didn't introduce them to the row of watchers, Instead she announced, waving at the row of chairs, 'Most of them have only short-term memory loss. They could tell you anything and everything about their childhoods, but nothing about what happened last week. Their memories of the here-and-now tend to be linked to things which you and I would consider minor: what they had for lunch, which chair they sat in, what programme they watched. That's what's important to them.' She left, promising copies of lunch menus for the past two months.

They were all questioned. With little success. The police didn't even pay them the courtesy of talking to them separately, they had so little expectation they would have anything of value to say. The Inspector snapped off the TV to a ripple of aggrieved consternation all round, while the sergeant snapped on a tape recorder. As far as Frank could gather, the pair of them were trying to establish what Mr Baines did on his last day, who he spoke to and so forth. He could have told them that Mr Baines never spoke to anyone, just glowered at Mr Byfleet when he was pipped by him in the after lunch race for the re-upholstered wing chair by the fire.

'Now,' the Inspector began, speaking slowly and loudly, 'you all knew Mr Baines?'

Most of them shook their heads with dumb cunning as if accused of something they knew they'd done wrong: such as peeing in their pants. Only Mr Byfleet hung his head.

The Inspector tried another tack. 'Yesterday you all had,' he consulted his notes, 'shepherd's pie for lunch, followed by,' he wrinkled his nose in disgust, 'stewed prunes. Now who can tell me what happened after that?' His words were met by an obstinate silence.

Surely, thought Frank, the man could show a little more respect, use a little more tact. He opened his mouth, tried for the deep, authoritative tone of his courtroom years, but managed only a tremulous, old man's voice.

'If you could be more precise officer,' he quavered, 'about the time of day you have in mind, then I am sure they could be more helpful. If you asked them for instance,' he waved a blotched and shaking hand, 'about anything that happened while they were watching *Rikki Lake* or *Love in the Afternoon*. As a matter of fact,' he added, his voice growing a little stronger, 'I might be able to help you in a number of other ways with your investigations.

The Inspector glared at him, dismissing him, incredulous. But he did grudgingly pick up a copy of the *TV Times* from the table and riffle through its pages. '*Neighbours*?' he prompted brusquely. '*Home and Away*? *Pet Rescue*?'

Mrs Topp came to life. 'They had rabbits!' she announced. 'Black and white ones.'

So did the usually silent Mrs Clarke. 'I wanted to watch the other side,' she complained. 'I can't abide animals, especially that dog they bring in every week. We're supposed to stroke it.'

'And what was Mr Baines doing while you were watching *Pet Rescue*?'

'He likes to watch it. He had a dog at home. Lady. But they took her away when he came in here. Best thing for him.'

'And why was that?'

'The hairs. You can never get them off the sofa. The white dogs are the worst.' Mrs Clarke smiled as though she had prevailed in a complex debate on the finer points of case law: and swayed the jury.

'Thank you,' the Inspector shrugged at the sergeant as they left the lounge. 'Frustrating as hell. They're all vital witnesses, but they can't tell us a thing.'

Perhaps they could, thought Frank, smarting from the way he'd – they'd – been treated; but why should they? He'd enjoyed seeing the Inspector trounced; had he imagined it or had there been a conscious – an intelligent – gleam of triumph in Mrs Clarke's cloudy eyes? He raised his own to the french windows and saw Tony leaning, immobile, on – presumably a garden implement on the patio.

Later that afternoon, Tony, minus implement, slouched into the TV lounge but he didn't stop and gaze at the set or clench his fists, he came straight over to the chair where Frank sat, slightly apart from the others.

'Pam says you think I've got my eye on her money.' He loomed, glaring from his vastly superior height. 'You shouldn't be saying that. Not with the place swarming with police.' And he turned on his heel and slouched away again.

Frank was shaken. Not with fear, with anger. He knew what that young man was up to; he knew that several of the residents had missed small valuables recently – he'd heard them mutter and sensed their loss – but were too accustomed to be thought confused to be able to state their case. And he knew Tony was the guilty party. Young people! Tony, the Inspector, the sergeant, Lizzy, Dr Carr, the families of the deceased who came expecting something for nothing – he lumped them together in his mind. They were all of a piece, thought they knew it all. Except Pam. He smiled as he thought of her and decided, yes, he would ask her for her help. The police might regard him with contempt, the TV news might fail to disclose the cause of death; but he knew murders had been committed here; and he knew how and why.

'I plan to make a statement,' he told Pam next morning. She was incredulous, but he insisted. 'More to the point,' he added, 'I want you to help me dress.'

'You are dressed,' she pointed out.

'Not in these clothes.' He swung a dismissive, woollen clad arm at his old slacks and slippers.

It took time and effort. The still neatly pressed but worn and shiny trousers of his ancient, made-to-measure, black suit. Threadbare black silk socks and black shoes which he insisted Pam buff with a cloth. She laced them for him, he'd only make himself dizzy if he bent. A clean white shirt, a thin black tie and, lastly, his suit jacket, far too big for him and smelling of mothballs.

When he was finished and ready, he longed for a moment to return to bed. But Pam read his thoughts, smiled, plumped the pillows and said, 'As soon as you've done you can come straight back and have a rest.'

She was right, of course. For this, he thought proudly, would be his finest hour. In the past he would have had notes to hand, prompts to ensure he made his most telling points in the most telling way, the most telling order. These days he couldn't see to make notes or to read them. He didn't need to. Months of observation of his fellow residents following upon years of failing sight during which he had learned, more and more to rely on his memory had trained him to retain words in his mind in the exact order in which he planned to utter them. Yes, he had it all absolutely off pat.

He imagined the entrance he would make; or no, on second thoughts, they would come to him, that was his prerogative. He paused, asked Pam to help him to the chair on the other side of his room (his part in what was to come was not that of a bedridden weakling), instructed her to take a message to the Inspector and returned to his reverie.

The sergeant would switch on the tape recorder and the Inspector would listen to his deposition. First Frank Marchant QC would set the scene, as he always had, catch their imaginations, steer them the way he wanted. In this case, the scene was a world dominated by inobservant young people who rode roughshod over their elders, believing that the aged were nothing more than rotting hulks, that they felt nothing, saw nothing, *were* nothing. He wanted to be sure that they understood what he had realised on the day when he had looked at that pathetic line-up of ill-shod feet and been attacked by guilt at the patronising assumptions of which he himself had judged himself guilty. He wanted to make it clear to them the depth and strength of feelings which Mr Byfleet and Mrs Topp still retained: even if they were about matters which the younger, ruling world would consider of no import. He would set the scene and then he would move to the specifics.

But he was no more than halfway through his introductory remarks when the Inspector raised his eyebrows at the Sergeant who turned off the tape-recorder. And then they left.

Oh they thanked him politely enough for his co-operation, but they didn't mean a word of it. As the door closed he heard the Inspector say, 'Pity. Apparently he was a High Court judge in his day. Couldn't make head nor tail of all that nonsense about knitted rabbits and elderly gents racing each other to chairs.'

'One thing, sir,' said the Sergeant. 'There might be something in what he said about the odd-job man.'

Frank lay quite still on his counterpane, his brittle legs stretched out like sticks in front of him. His head lay heavy on the pillows which Pam had plumped. The future lay before him like a desert, mile upon mile of daily struggle in and out of bed, to the dining room, to the TV room, to the toilet and back. He could have told them, *would* have told them. He had quite decided, before they arrived, that a prison hospital would offer greater scope for observation than the one in which he was currently confined.

He fumbled at the handle of his bedside cabinet and withdrew from the top shelf behind a pile of big-print books which he could no longer see to read, two spectacle cases. He snapped them open, one after the other and caressed the contents with his fingertips. Capsules in one, tablets in the other; and, at the very back of the cabinet, an orange squash bottle full to the brim with expectorant. At the time his only thought had been that Gloria, the district nurse, would need proof – empty plastic bubbles, empty bottles – that he had taken his medication. He couldn't throw them away or wash them down the plughole; with his sight how could be sure that every trace was gone?

In the days that followed their disposal he had expected to sicken quickly and to die. But no, Dr Carr, like so many young people, had been wrong – GPs, these days, had only to look at someone they classified as 'geriatric' to start prescribing all and sundry panaceas.

Misguided, that's what Dr Carr was. Probably thought anything that softened the edges of a life no longer worth living was a blessing to the patient.

Certainly his remedies had been a blessing to the other old people. Frank had been clever, very clever. He thought of how, day after day, he had waited until they were all seated in the lounge after lunch, their faces fixed on the TV screen, a cup of tea in front of each of them. It would be half an hour before Lizzy put in her first appearance. He eased himself stiffly from his chair, managed, with difficulty, the few steps which brought him to his victim and slipped a lethal dose of one or another of his medications into a cup whilst its owner gazed blankly, uncomprehendingly past him. Then he returned to his chair and watched every single one of the watchers drain their tea to the dregs: with profound satisfaction. After all, *he* wasn't in a position to buy new chairs or stuffed toys; the best he could do was to reduce the competition for them.

Now he fingered his treasures and thought – it would be only kind to put Mrs Topp out of her misery, she wasn't, after all, happy with only a knitted rabbit for company. And after that? Well, perhaps his own time had come.

He shook his head with a depth of decision he hadn't felt in years. Mr Byfleet deserved to go first, life hadn't been the same for him since the last of his post-prandial races with Mr Baines for the red-upholstered wing chair by the fire. In the meantime they'd probably arrest Tony. Wouldn't do him any harm to spend a few days in a cell until they released him for lack of evidence. Might even have the added bonus of bringing Pam to her senses; Tony wasn't a murderer, but he *was* a petty thief. Even the police must have the wit to detect that.

He sighed and eased his frail body on the plump, soft surface of the bed. What now? Complain about the food, that's what. No more pap! A steak – Aberdeen Angus, prime rump – was what he wanted for lunch tomorrow. Of course, it would be a challenge to eat it with his dentures. But when had he ever avoided a challenge? And it would be doing the old folk a favour to order them a decent meal before he put them, one by one, painlessly, to sleep.

John Tilsley

Notes

L ike most fiction, the idea for this story sprang from a real life experience on a cold October night in downtown San Francisco. It was October 18th, 1989. The previous day an earthquake had ripped through the Bay area and crippled the city. The city was at a standstill. Water, electricity, communication and transport were disrupted. Five freeways and San Francisco Airport were closed. I'm walking across town to visit a friend to see if she had come through the devastation unscathed.

Then, like the story, I fall in behind two women on Geary. I see a wallet lying in their path. They miss it. I scoop it up. To tell the truth, I was strapped for cash and on the bones of my arse at the time. I pocketed close to fifty bucks from the wallet, handed the wallet to a night manager in a hotel and called the owner next morning. At least he got his driver's licence and credit cards back, and if he should recognise this incident, get in touch, he can have the fifty back – with interest. That's how the idea for the story began.

I was asked to give my view on the national fiction crime scene. My reading these days is mainly autobiography. Perhaps I don't read fiction because there could be a conflict to my style of writing. But one crime novel I did read and enjoy was *Close Pursuit*, by the Canadian, Carsten Stroud. Fast pace – strong content – highly recommended.

One Way Ticket

by John Tilsley

Concealed in dark shadow, two men lie dog-eared beneath a ragged tarp. Beside the chain-link fence on a used car lot, Jimmy Smithson and Woody Wilson had settled into their new-found security one hour ago. Jimmy had said nobody would find them here, but Woody wasn't so sure; hadn't he heard this same line of bullshit in every goddamn state west of Indiana during their six month trek through Mid-West greenery and the warm sirocco winds of the American south-west?

Woody shifts his weight across the wooden pallet, easing the pain between his shoulder blades and lies motionless for a while listening to Jimmy's even breathing. Tired of his friends facility to sleep easily and the smell of stale sneakers straining at his nostrils, he lifts his head from the makeshift pillow and wafts the tarp for ventilation. Earlier in the day they'd unlaced their sneakers to suck in much needed air, rinsed their socks and soothed their raw feet in the tepid pool of the Golden Gate Park. Before the socks had time to dry, Jimmy became irritable and footloose and they'd trudged off for a look about on Fisherman's Wharf.

It didn't seem to cross Jimmy's mind that they'd barely two bucks between them, and that Pier 39 was all tourists and T-shirt hawkers. Jimmy always had a plan. They'd mooched around the Pier's fairground atmosphere, filled their empty stomachs with discarded half-eaten hot dogs, found a half-empty pack of cigarettes and two-bucks-fifty in loose change. They'd spent two hours on the Pier and things were looking good. On the way back up Hyde Street's gruelling climb, Jimmy knowingly tapped the Camel soft-pack in his shirt breast pocket, lecturing Woody on the finer points of street survival.

They swung down Market Street for another one of Jimmy's sure things. At the end of Market, trimmed lawns around the Civic Center were littered with canvas tents and shanty town lean-to's. They were soon to learn this canvas village belonged to a class of floaters a cut above their station. As they approached the lead tent, a keen eyed bearded face appeared through its flaps. Then, as if by signal, uneasy looking men struck out from the nearby lean-to's. There must have been a dozen of them, mostly middle-aged with the same greying faces and menacing eyes.

At first glance their colourful head bands and long unkempt hair reminded Woody of the neo-hippies they'd shared skag with on Haight Street two days ago. A closer look told Woody these men were unlike the hippies. Their leader wore combat fatigue bottoms, a stained Confederate T-shirt and made it plain as day the two drifters had stumbled unknowingly into Johnny Reb and an army of Vietnam vets. Close to hand, Reb's tooled leather belt held a sheathed bowie knife, his business-like stance and narrow eyes packing a reserved force. Reb deftly flicked the bowie's release and dead-eyed the two intruders to an abrupt halt, then snarled their only course of action was to fuck right back from where they came. Realising their company wasn't desired, they took the hint and retreated quick-time up Market where they'd panhandled outside a porno theatre with little success until sundown. As darkness wrapped its blanket around the city's downtown district, they trudged their way uphill to Sacramento Street to find a suitable site to rest their heads for the night.

Patrolman Sam McNally zips tight his leather jerkin against an impending gale blowing in from the Bay. Stepping from the sheltered confinement of Sutter Street onto the wide windswept avenue of Van Ness, he ducks into a draughty storefront doorway and cusses his luck that he'd drawn the short straw to be walking the beat on a night such as this. Lowering the brim of his cap he snaps at the brass Zippo and lights up.

For a while he watches midnight hour traffic sail up and down the six-lane avenue, thinking how his beat should take him eight blocks north onto Pacific. Should he walk it? Naw, fuck it. He's only out here to chase away street bums sleeping in the same kind of doorways he's taking a smoke right now. They ain't gonna cause any harm, so he'll walk four blocks up Van Ness, cut a right on to Sacramento, call in at the corner café and grab hot coffee and Danish pastries.

An old timer shuffles into view, his string-tied bedroll bunched tight beneath his arm. McNally moves forward to make his presence known, the old timer acknowledges the patrolman with a nod of the head and keeps walking. McNally draws on his cigarette, watching the old man turn into Sutter, thinking one day, with good fortune and God's blessing, he'll draw his pension in comfort, and not be walking the streets like that poor bastard. Who cares about these people? Surely someone misses them? Ah, fuck it, he'll take a rain check on Pacific. The cigarette butt spins and splutters across the sidewalk,

McNally lifts his collar and steps reluctantly into a whistling head wind and makes his way up the avenue.

Taking a table alongside the café window, McNally wipes clear steamy glass with his jacket cuff. The waitress arrives with his regular order, remarks on the inclement weather and places the tray before him. Blending cream into his coffee he peers across the way through glistening rain at the car lot's security lighting. A flicker of light catches his eye. He squints harder for a better look. In the shadows a flame dances from a cigarette lighter.

Woody rolls back and draws deep on their afternoon find. This brand of cigarette is new to Woody's throat and he feels the need to cough, but is frightened of disturbing his quick tempered sleeping partner. Jimmy's last words before he fell asleep were not to light up in case some sharp-eyed cop should happen upon the cigarettes crimson glow. Woody scratches around beneath the pallet, unearths a short length of angle iron and props it between the wooden slats to form a pitched canopy. Woody feels rather snug with his manoeuvre; in one easy action this improvisation will conceal the cigarette, vent its smoke and shelter his head from the coming downpour.

Relaxed in the café's warmth wand savoury aroma, McNally sips slowly at his third refill. He'd given the waitress a knowing wink of the eye as she'd poured. She'd flirted with him for a moment then tantalisingly swung her ample rear between the red and cream check table covers. Normally she'd have pulled up a seat and talked a while, but the café's crowded with dime-rich street bums hanging in out of the cold. With men sobering up before calling a cab to take them home, and young couples anticipating their voyeuristic treat amongst the pastel padded piano bars of Polk Street's gay community. McNally fixes on Mary's tender rump all the way back to the coffee station and shakes his head woefully; how he'd like to be tucked into the warmth of Mary tonight, instead of bracing San Francisco's cold and wind-swept streets.

The cigarette extinguished, Woody took one last look at the dark clouds skimming overhead and reasoned perhaps this spot wasn't so bad after all. Last night they'd slept in a car wreck in the Mission District. Jimmy had taken the back bench while he'd struggled for comfort on the threadbare bucket seats up front. He barely got an hours sleep, tonight though, at long last, Jimmy's come good. He squeezes numbed hands into tight jean pockets and inches clumsily onto his side. His awkward movement dislodges the angle iron, knocking it sideways onto Jimmy. Woody forces his eyes tight and bites his lip. Holy shit! The steel angle rattled against Jimmy's head.

Bolting upright, Jimmy swipes the tarp to one side, rubs the back of his head and rounds on Woody, 'Christ Almighty! What the fuck you playin' at? You tryin' to kill me?'

In the half-light, Woody sees the anger in Jimmy's face, knows his partner can turn meaner than cat's piss in a heart beat and reels out of arms reach. Realising his raised voice may have exposed their position, Jimmy, mumbles obscenities under his breath and rubs at his injury. Moments later he adjusts the oily blanket and rests his head onto his holdall.

'Goddamit, Woody! You got to be the worlds dumbest bastard,' hissed Jimmy, nudging his body into a comfortable position and settling back to sleep.

'Sorry, Jimmy. I was only-', mumbled Woody, cutting short. He knew there'd be no reply. Jimmy wasn't the kind of guy who fucked around with small talk. Jimmy was all business when it came to the verbals, but wasn't it Woody who'd pulled them out of the shit so many times on their past travels. Working godforsaken hours for peanut wages in burger joints and car washes along the highway, while Jimmy sat on his butt all day long and tossed ideas that never mounted to zilch.

Woody lay restless and counted aircraft lights between the sweeping clouds. Sure enough, Jimmy snuggled down and fell into a deep sleep. Ten minutes later a beam of light traversed Woody's vista, confusing his concentration and plane count. Keen eyes followed the flashlight's spot as it broadened and glistened silver like along the chain-link fence. He momentarily froze at the sound of a sure footed stride accompanying the flashlight's radiant arc. Woody figured it had to be a cop or some security jerk. Some fuckin' luck! He slid beneath the cover, hoping his vanishing act would send whoever it was out there in another direction.

It wasn't to be. The heavy tread was now on top of them, the flashlight's brightness burning a hole into the tarp. Jimmy was still in the land of nod, not a care in the world. Woody held his breath, his stomach sunk, he felt alone stretched out on the pallet. There was an almighty crash as leather met timber and Woody knew the game was up. They wouldn't be booked, or run down the station house that's for sure. He knew they'd be hustled along to find some place new, the best spots would be taken this time of night, they'd end up hoofing it for hours.

Jimmy jolted off the wooden frame as the cop's boot smashed into the pallet for the second time. Woody curled into a ball and thought with Jimmy being the smart ass, he would leave the talking to him. Jimmy felt the sticky wet clay beneath his palms and scurried back onto the pallet. His hands came up to shield the flashlight's glare, beside him, Woody was rolled up like a turkey ready for the oven.

'You boys gotta beat it,' commanded the cop.

'We're on our way,' Jimmy croaked, lowering his arm as the flashlight searched out Woody.

'Get the fuck outta here right now, or I'll bust your fuckin' heads. You hearin' me?'

'We're hearin' you, officer', said Jimmy, propping himself upright, rubbing sleep from his heavy eyes.

McNally waved the flashlight between the two as they gathered their meagre belongings. He watched and listened with amusement as they argued amongst themselves and felt kind of sorry he'd had to move them along. If it was up to him, he'd let them stay, but come the morning the owner of the car lot would call the station, be on his back, there'd be unnecessary paper work and maybe a visitation to calm the owner down. Before they moved on, McNally drilled them on staying clear of his beat and pitched the pallet over the fence. Woody was impressed with the officer's show of strength, that pallet must weigh all of sixty-pounds. Woody promised on his dear mother's life the officer had seen the back of them for good.

Jimmy and Woody sauntered to the corner of Polk, then made a downhill right. Downhill was the only option as far as Jimmy was concerned, he was up to the teeth with this city, never before had he encountered a city to ply so much agony on the leg muscles. This place was slowly giving him the shits.

'Where we goin', Jimmy?' said Woody, struggling to keep pace.

'How the fuck should I know, dipstick? You know this goddamn city as well as me. You decide where we go,' Jimmy called over his shoulder.

'Wish we had a return ticket back to normality, Jimmy. I'm just about done with all this movin' to an' fro,' called Woody, stopping to lace his sneakers.

Jimmy checked his stride, hitched his holdall high on his shoulder and turned sharply, 'I didn't promise you I'd set the fuckin' world alight, Woody. Nobody forced you to come along, so get your ass into gear an' let's clear this street. Man! These queer joints give me the fuckin' hump.'

Gaudy red and blue lighting slinks the sidewalk, aiding Woody to thread an eye-hole with the ragged lace. He peers through the piano bars glass door, men lined the bar, huddled together on tall stools, their arms locked around each other. Two guys begin to kiss and caress. The lace is quickly knotted and he smartly steps in line with Jimmy.

'Man alive! You see that, Jimmy? Two guys, kissin' and cuddlin'. Jesus! That can't be right. What you say?'

Jimmy was non-committal, he'd expressed his views on shirtlifters a thousand times since they'd arrived in the city five days ago. The second day on arrival, they'd been moseying around the Mission District and stumbled by chance into the Castro: San Francisco's notorious gay community. Woody couldn't believe his eyes, one square mile of nothing but, and figured if you were that way inclined, you'd never have to leave its confines to be serviced by a fellow faggot for any manner of commercial assistance. The neighbourhood was completely self contained, and Woody wandered its streets in disbelief. At one point, Jimmy became so concerned about his partner's inquisitiveness that he worried his friend was on the turn.

'Unfuckin' believable', said Woody, as Jimmy steered him out of the district down 18th Street.

Steady drizzle kept them tight to store fronts and brickwork as they gathered pace down Polk. At the intersection with Geary, they made a left and broke into positive stride and busy-eyed alley ways for a suitable spot to curl up for the remainder of the night. Woody hoped they were out of the cop's beat sector. Jimmy said he didn't give a monkey's fuck. The upshot was: if they didn't get under cover real quick, they'd freeze their luckless balls off before sunup. Woody knew this was gross exaggeration but played along with Jimmy, pointing enthusiastically up several darkened alleyways. Jimmy made quick appraisal and dismissed Woody's thoughts out of hand.

Half a block in front of them, two Negro women step around the corner of Leavensworth. Jimmy looks behind him and sees they are the only people on this stretch of the block then indicates for Woody to slow down to keep a respectable distance. The men hear the women's laughter, watch them sidestep puddles of water and gather in their shared umbrella as it catches a sudden gust of wind. Without warning, Jimmy stops dead in his tracks, tugging urgently at Woody's sleeve, pointing in front of the women to a bulky leather wallet lying discarded in the middle of the sidewalk. The men hold their breath as the women inch closer to it, Jimmy's grip tightens on Woody's arm, the wallet spins from the heel of one of the women and teeters at the kerbstone's edge. She looks down then back fleetingly at the men standing statue like and nudges her friend to quicken their step.

The men remain motionless, relishing the thought of their good fortune, and wait for the women to make distance.

'Sweet fuckin' Jesus! I think we just lucked in,' hissed Jimmy, scouting up and down the street with quick-silver eyes. Not a soul in sight, Jimmy dashes forward. Woody's heart begins to pound as he watches Jimmy scoop the rain-soaked wallet and stuff it deep into his side-jean pocket.

Woody remained still and dumb struck, surprised that Jimmy hadn't thumbed the wallet to purge its contents.

'What we got?' Woody calls out.

Jimmy shrugs his shoulders, crosses the street and waves Woody on.

'We ain't lookin' on the street, you dumb motherfuck. Supposin' some cop should turn the corner?' shoots Jimmy, from the corner of his mouth. 'Worse still, the fuckin' owner.'

'Yeah, but supposin'…' cuts in Woody, feeling he's about to lose his piece of the action. Jimmy might try counting what's inside the wallet out of eye-sight and pull a stroke on him.

'Supposin' nothin', just leave it,' said Jimmy, stabbing at his chest. 'Tell you what we gonna do. We gonna hit that all-night diner two blocks down the road.'

Woody paused to harness his property around his aching shoulders, closed his eyes and dreamed rib of beef and creamed potatoes, hot coffee and blueberry pie. That wallet must smell mighty rich for Jimmy to be so confident.

'What'd I tell yer, Woody? I just knew we'd come good. What'd I say back there in the park today? Give it time an' this old city would bless us plenty. That right, Woody? Didn't I say?' quipped Jimmy.

Woody shook his head and steadied his sneakers on the steep pavement, turned into Ellis and spotted the diner one block below, its neon freaking colour against murky brickwork. A smile came over his face. He felt elated; this time they could have scored big-time.

The diner serves as a regular drop in for the city's graveyard-shift. Security guards, taxi-drivers and patrolmen take up the window booths. Further back towards the restrooms, red vinyl booths are occupied by a mismatch of young and old. Age is of no consequence, the old, they slump at their tables, the young look about them with vacant eyes. Jimmy takes a table between the clock-punchers and the dead-beats, signalling Woody to a seat.

'Well, come on then! Take a look, goddamit,' said Woody, anxiously, as a waitress makes her way towards them. 'What the fuck we gonna order? All we got is nickel and dimes.'

Jimmy looks about him cautiously and discretely opens the wallet under the table. Woody sees Jimmy's eyes light up, his mouth twitching nervously.

'Bingo! We hit the motherfucker, Woody. I'll check this baby out in the restroom. Here's a twenty, you order the works.'

Woody palms the bill, then looks sharply at his partner, 'C'mon, Jimmy. You ain't gonna stitch me, are you?'

'Hey! What the fuck you take me for? This is our ticket home. No more sleepless nights, bro, we'll be ridin' all the way back to Indiana on the first Greyhound headin' east tomorrow morning,' said Jimmy, taking off for the john.

Woody tenderly stroked the twenty-dollar bill as the waitress sidled alongside and placed a menu in front of him. He knew she'd seen the twenty. Normally she'd be expecting a coffee order and a long stay from guys like this. Woody smiled up at her, it had been a long time since anyone had paid any kind of attention to him. He felt pleased with himself, tomorrow they'll be homeward bound with tall stories for his sidekicks down at the Silver Dollar Saloon. But there's a nagging doubt at the back of his mind; what's Jimmy up to in the john?

Not knowing how much is in the wallet, Woody edged on the side of caution and ordered omelettes and hash browns for starters. Jimmy appeared in the restroom doorway, the expression on his face told Woody they'd scored big time.

'Give it up, Jimmy,' said Woody, leaning into Jimmy's ear, 'what we got?'

'We bust the fuckin' bank, partner. Wait on this. Eight hundred and sixty bucks in hard cash,' whispered Jimmy, waiting on Woody's reaction. 'Plus a stack of credit cards a mile high.'

Woody whistled long and low, then rocked back in the booth, 'Holy shit! You sure? Let's have a look.'

'Where you comin' from? Stop being so fuckin' dumb. We'll divi up when we book into a hotel, OK?'

'Hotel?' replied Woody, with surprise.

'Sure as hell, you don't think we're gonna be sleepin' rough with this bundle high on the hip, do ya?'

The omelettes were polished off and they scan the menu for further treats. During their time in the diner customers have come and gone. In the beginning, Jimmy constantly eye-balled the doorway in case the owner of the wallet walked in. But he knew there'd be no chance of that. He'd bet his life the guy dropped it getting into a cab, and wouldn't miss it till he came to square his fare. All the same, he was on edge, and it made matters worse when the door opened and in rolled the same cop that had moved them from their perch on Sacramento.

'We gotta be movin' it. Look what the cat dragged in,' said Jimmy, side-glancing the entrance.

Woody looks across and splutters into his coffee, 'Shit! What we gonna do?'

At that very moment the waitress arrived with their order of rib steak and fries. Both men look up at the waitress, down at the steak, then across to McNally.

'He's comin' over. Leave the talkin' to me,' gasped Jimmy.

'How ya doin'?' said McNally, glancing down at the steaks, shaking his head. 'Thirty minutes ago I bust your butts off a wood pile. Now you're eatin' a rich man's meal. What you been up to, boys?'

'We ain't done nothin'. Truth of the matter is, my ol' man just wired three-hundred through Western Union for the ride home tomorrow,' said Jimmy, looking into the cop's eyes for signs of disbelief with his tale. 'That's the story, officer.'

Woody fumbled at the steak with his fork, spilling fries from his plate: what if the cop should ask Jimmy to turn out his pockets?

'That so,' said McNally, shrugging his shoulder. 'If I should take a call that something's gone down on my beat tonight, I'll chase you down before you make the fuckin' bus terminal. You got that?'

'Loud and clear,' piped in Woody.

'Good,' said McNally, making to move over to his buddies. 'So your tellin' me I ain't gonna be seein' you around no more?'

'Sure thing, officer,' confirmed Jimmy.

'Yeah, sure, thirty-minutes ago, you swore on your dear mother's life that I wouldn't see you again,' said McNally, looking down at Woody. 'Well, let's see what the mornin' brings, hey, boys?'

McNally acknowledges his fellow officers that were by the window, then walks to the rest-room.

The boys have suddenly lost their appetite.

'Let's go,' said Jimmy, sliding a two-buck tip alongside the unfinished steak. At least no way are they gonna call us cheap bastards, he thought, urging Woody from his seat.

They found a low-rent hotel within a block and shouldered judgmental appraisement from a night-manager who appeared in no better shape than they were.

While Woody fed the cigarette machine, Jimmy peeled off two twenties like it was just routine. In the room, Jimmy flipped a coin and Woody hit tails for first shot in the bathtub. Woody splashed and whistled 'Dixie', Jimmy stretched out on a single cot and fanned out the wallet's contents.

They sure got lucky, those two old gals sure missed out on a sitter, thought Jimmy running a finger over the American Express Gold. There's over a dozen of them. He'd like to make them work, but once they'd crossed the first State Line, they wouldn't be worth diddly. The two telephone cards would fetch fifty a-piece on the street, that's for certain. He studies the photo on the driver's licence. The guy looks a regular looking nine-to-five, middle aged and heavy. This guy must be real pissed he mislaid his wallet. By the collection of gold credit cards, Jimmy reasons losing the dough ain't gonna hurt him. But all the bullshit; calling banks, the telephone company, the Driver's Licence Bureau. Cancelling this and that, would tie the guy up for the best part of a day. Hey, maybe this guy, Lou Salvucci, would come good with three-hundred bucks on a safe return of his wallet?

Jimmy would have to make contact before the rightful owner starts ringing around. Inside the wallet pocket, he finds Salvucci's business card with home and business numbers.

Woody came out of the bathroom squeaky-clean and full of beans. Jimmy ran his plan by Woody. Woody said he'd go with the flow so long as he got a new pair of sneakers out of the deal, 'I'm leavin' it to you, partner. You're doin' pretty good so far,' he said.

Salvucci's phone was engaged the first time around. Five minutes later, Jimmy got the dialling tone.

'That you, Mr Salvucci? Yeah, I know it's late, but I got somethin' of interest to you.'

'Better be good, pal,' came back a harsh voice that commanded respect.

'I found your wallet on Geary... Yeah, it's right here in front of me... Cash? There ain't no cash, mister, just a string of credit cards... No, I told you, there ain't no money. Tell you the truth, I seen a couple of niggers pitch it in the gutter. So, I'm just doin' the right thing, lettin' you know I got it.'

The line went quiet for a moment. Jimmy heard muffled voices, then Salvucci came back on line.

'OK, so tell me where you're at, an' I'll pick it up.'

Jimmy sent a wry smile down the line.

'Here's the deal. It's gonna cost you three-hundred—'

'Three-hundred!' shot back Salvucci.

'That's right, or it goes in the Bay. I couldn't give a fuck either way. Three-hundred's shit to what it's gonna cost you in calls and paperwork. You and I know that. So what's it to be?'

The line went silent again. He throws Woody a wink of the eye, he's got the guy by the balls.

'OK, you got the three. You sound out of town. Listen – I gotta be someplace up state at noon, so we'll make a meet on Leavensworth and Geary at eight sharp. At least we both know where that's at, right?'

'Right on, mister. See you in the mornin',' said Jimmy, placing the receiver, punching the air.

'You believe that, Woody? The dumb bastard fell for it. Think on this, bro',' said Jimmy, falling back on the cot. 'We got us some extra spendin' money.'

Woody lay awake for an hour or so, he wasn't too sure about the next move. He'd heard the cross talk, and reckoned this guy wasn't the soft touch Jimmy had made him out to be. Still, what the hell. Jimmy's on a roll, this time tomorrow they'd be homeward bound with enough money to enjoy every goddamn lay in station this side of Lafayette, Indiana.

Jimmy and Woody didn't need their early morning call. They were up and about, their bags left in care of the night manager - for a small fee. They said they'd be back in twenty minutes.

'You sure we're doin' the right thing? What's an extra three? We've enough money for a one way ticket,' said Woody, keeping pace with Jimmy.

'We're takin' it all the way, man. How many times have we dreamt of a chance like this? I tell ya – you'll see,' cracked Jimmy, impatiently, as they neared their rendezvous.

On the corner of Geary, Woody sparked a Marlboro and asked a passer-by the correct time. Five minutes had passed since the eight o'clock deadline. Woody said to forget the deal, collect their bags and hit the Greyhound station. At that moment of hesitation, Jimmy spotted a sleek terra-rosa coloured Mercedes coasting in their direction.

'Betcha life this is our man,' said Jimmy, peering at the sedan's dark tinted windshield.

Jimmy was right, he knew he'd show, and stepped to the edge of the sidewalk as the sedan glided to a smooth halt. The autos rear-side-window slowly inched half way down, 'Mr Salvucci?'

The passenger nodded. Jimmy waved Woody over.

'You boys got somethin' for me?'

'Yeah,' said Jimmy, nonchalantly, placing his hand on the opened window, 'you got the three-hundred?'

Woody looked about him nervously, there's no one else on the block, he moved to Jimmy's side for comfort.

'Hand it over,' came the husky voice. Jimmy then realised the money wasn't so important. This Salvucci was no nine-to-fiver, he looked and talked like someone with Mafioso street cred.

As the wallet left Jimmy's shaking hand, Salvucci beckoned them closer. They watched him place the wallet inside his jacket, then drop down to his side pocket. Their eyes fix for a half expected reward – a blur of hand speed – a second later they're staring into the business end of a menacing stainless Magnum.44.

'Thanks boys,' said Salvucci, coolly.

McNally's shift had ended a couple of hours back. He'd sat in the canteen and penned his log-sheet, waiting for the clock to tick before heading across town to make a Savings and Loan deposit. Taking a short cut down O'Farrell for the Business District, he noticed an assembly of squad cars on the corner of Geary. He checked his watch. Fifteen minutes to go before the bank opened. He'll take a look, it's on his patch and perhaps it's concerning someone local to the neighbourhood.

Skirting yellow cordon tape, McNally searches out the crime scene officer.

'What's gone down, Bill? I ain't seen so many uniforms since St Patrick's,' said McNally, looking down at an old sneaker protruding out of the blood-soaked sheet covering the two bodies.

'Two kids, Sam. Both took one to the head – close range. For sure they didn't feel a thing,' said the captain, ruefully.

'Jesus! Any ID?'

'Naw, but they were carryin' plenty of dough. They must have pissed somebody off. Go on, take a look, you may know their faces – what's left of 'em,' said the captain, pulling back the sheet.

'I don't believe it,' said McNally, leaning forward for a closer look. 'I only moved these boys along last night. Said they wouldn't see me again.'

'Well, they ain't seein' ya, believe me,' said the captain, sarcastically, dropping the sheet.

'They were off to buy a one way ticket home,' said McNally, turning and lighting a cigarette.

Poor bastards, he thought, heading off for the hustle and bustle of downtown. Hey, who cares about them anyway?

Lauren Henderson

Notes

This story was written in tribute to the Scala cinema in King's
Cross, beloved by me especially for its Saturday all-nighters:
lesbian vampires, tongue-in-cheek gore fests and Arnold
Schwarzenegger triple bills, the only place I've ever heard straight
men yelling at Arnold to get his kit off. I used to live first in Camden
and then in King's Cross and still remember the walk home at four or
five on Sunday morning, blinking and bleary eyed and feeling that
life had nothing more to offer than this exhausted happiness.

The Scala has now been shut down. I heard that the pool-hall next
door had expanded into it, but don't know for sure. It leads the list of
other cinemas in the area which have closed down, to stand with
their frontages boarded up, ugly and rotting, a waste and a crime. So
this story is not only an homage to the Scala, but a curse on greedy
developers who close down cinemas and then don't even do
anything with the site. May these people rot in hell, strapped into a
cinema seat for all eternity and forced to watch endless re-runs of
films by Peter Greenaway, Hal Hartley and Robert Altman, inter-
spersed with made-for-TV, based-on-a-true-story films featuring
actresses from *Charlie's Angels.* I can imagine no worse fate.

Last Night at the Scala

by Lauren Henderson

The film was ending. I had seen it so many times that I could have closed my eyes and painted the final image from memory: the pastel sunset, the balcony, the woman in white standing there as the camera pulled back and left her alone, fixing her forever in that moment of infinite, hopelessly glamorous solitude. The titles began to roll and I shifted in my seat, wanting to be gone, to talk to no-one, to take Susan Sarandon's face with all its weary resigned beauty away with me to study. Not that I particularly aspired to become a bisexual, nearly-immortal vampire, my basement stacked with coffins of desiccated, rotting, undead lovers, though I doubt I would have declined the fate if she or Catherine Deneuve had offered it to me. Rather, I was fascinated by their quality of self-possession, the balance those women trod so elegantly between their detachment from the world and the needs which tied them to it. I had always taken it as a paradigm of existence.

There was a short break between *The Hunger* and the film which followed. The lights were raised and seat-backs thudded up in a series of padded slaps as people headed off for a last pit-stop to the toilets and then the bar, fuelling up for a bout of energy which would keep them awake during the final film. Others had given up the struggle and were hunched over in their seats, eyes closed, necks slumped at strained angles, coats bundled around them, dozing.

It was past one in the morning: we had been in this cinema for over four hours. Suddenly I was tired, not wanting chocolate or coffee or anything else to keep me going. The bout of anomie that had washed over me these last few weeks, marooning me in my own preoccupations, seemed to have peaked at this moment, centring itself on the image of Susan Sarandon, alone on her balcony, gazing out over the city. I felt as if there were a glass wall between me and the world which I had neither the energy nor the will to break down.

The impulse to slip out, mumbling an excuse, before any of the zombies I was with could do more than mumble their goodbyes, was too strong for me. But Judith was between me and the aisle, and as I stood up she said at once:

'Are you off, Sam?'

'Mmn. The prospect of hanging around for the Ingrid Pitt double-bill doesn't exactly raise my adrenalin levels – Hammer House's rather a let-down after *The Hunger* and *Daughters of Darkness*.'

'You're too fussy, Sammy,' Tom said, rooting around for another can of beer in his carrier. 'One lesbian vampire's much like another, all things considered.'

'Didn't know you'd had enough to get blasé about them, Tom.'

I pulled on my coat. So much for my hopes of a smooth escape; Judith was on her feet, winding her scarf around her neck.

'I'll walk back with you,' she said. 'You've got to pass my place to get to your van, don't you?'

I wasn't feeling churlish enough to deny it. There could be no further sign needed that I was not quite myself.

It was chilly on the staircase leading down to the huge antechamber of the cinema. In the far corner, tucked into a tiled niche, was a small bar with a few people hanging around it, lost in their own eyes, flotsam of the night that had washed up here: near-motionless tableaux, perfect subjects for a 1990s Edward Hopper. Behind the bar leant a girl whose dead-black hair, skunk-striped with white Mallen streaks, fell plumb-straight over her face, concealing it almost completely. Propped against it was a boy whose bones were hung about with chains and leather in lieu of flesh; he chinked and rustled every time he raised the cigarette to his mouth. His eyes were ringed with black liner, his eyebrow and lip studded with silver. I had noticed him earlier tonight, seen that he kept, instinctively, trying to slide the cigarette to the right side of his mouth and being blocked by the heavy stud pulling down his lip. It would take him a while for his body to remember what he had done to it.

There was a single table in the room, a small plywood affair pushed against the near wall, dwarfed in the vast cold echoing room. Over it lay a boy, passed out, one hand still clutching a polystyrene beaker of tea. His dreadlocks poured down over the side of the table, honey and caramel strung with paler threads, so heavy and rich it seemed that the thin brown stalk of his neck would bend and break under the pull of their weight. Two girls squatted against the wall beside him, sipping at cups of coffee, staring straight ahead with empty eyes at the murals which, though faded now, still rioted over the purple walls, floor to ceiling.

The Scala was a Gothic version of the Sistine Chapel; Italian heroin addicts came to Kings Cross to hang out and see the sights. The new Europe, founded on cultural exchange. This hall had always seemed to me a kind of ballroom, as if the ghosts of the dead junkies and winos and prostitutes of the Cross gathered here on the nights that the cinema was dark, to dance the minuet and saraband, filling the huge echoing room with their shadows. Palestrina, the music, a lone faint harpsichord. And then Tom Waits as they faded away again.

It was no colder outside than it had been in that room. If I had been alone I would have headed to the fast food stand on the promontory opposite the station and bought a bag of hot greasy chips, dripping with fat and vinegar, to eat on my walk back to the van. I wasn't hungry, though the thought of the chips made my stomach rumble in reflex; but they were the perfect counterpoint to the King's Cross backstreets by night, their salty warmth a visceral comfort, filling one up against the dark lonely alleyways.

However, feeling anti-social, I avoided prolonging time spent in Judith's company. We turned instead towards Rosebery Avenue, past the barred and bolted Thameslink station, past the bus stop whose shattered glass puddled around a body so bundled in scraps of blanket and plastic bags that I had to look twice to see that there was someone there at all. Down the hill from the Angel swept a cold wind, stirring the drink cans and bus tickets on the pavement, lifting them briefly and discarding them at once, moving on restlessly down towards St Pancras.

I shivered and pulled my leather coat closer around me. Judith, unfashionably sensible, had upholstered herself so thoroughly in woolly hat, scarf, gloves and a big fake fur duffle coat that the only part of her the wind could touch was her square, out thrust chin. She looked like Paddington Bear, minus the Wellington boots, her short, stocky body toddling along purposefully by my side.

'I'm glad I didn't stay,' she said after a while.

'You didn't feel like the Hammer Horror either?'

'Oh, it wasn't that. No, I'm a bit worried about Melissa. That's why I thought I'd walk back with you, just to make sure she's OK.'

'Won't she be fast asleep by now?'

'She often stays up really late. Usually she wants to talk, and I do try, but I have to get up so early in the morning…'

Judith was a gardener at the huge nurseries near Little Venice. I knew her through Tom, who worked there occasionally whenever his poetry wasn't bringing in enough to maintain his Guinness habit. I had always suspected her of having a hankering after Melissa, her flatmate; Judith reminded me of the middle-aged spinsters in tweeds who pop up in Agatha Christie novels, living in a cottage, breeding bull terriers and doting on their more femme companion. Melissa I hardly knew but firmly disliked, having never held with the school of thought that says you should know someone well before pronouncing judgement upon them. She was the kind of girl, simultaneously sulky, shy and arrogant, whom men found irresistibly attractive and women detested; all she had to do at parties was slump into the corner of a sofa, pouting, legs sprawled, looking profoundly bored, to draw a stream of suitors. The only thing one could say in her favour was that she was a brunette.

'… she stays up waiting for Van, her boyfriend, you know he DJs at this club up in Islington, so she's always hoping he'll drop by afterwards.'

'And does he?' We crossed the zebra, its orange lights flashing at nothing, our voices, even muted, ringing in the silence.

'Sometimes. Though never when he says he will. J – the landlord goes crazy, though, if he does. J makes a fuss if we even watch the TV after eleven, let alone play music or ring the doorbell. Apropos of nothing, Judith added viciously: 'I don't like Van anyway. He's unreliable, he's not what she needs.'

'Oh, there's no harm in him. And he's nice to look at.' Judith made a humphing noise and picked up speed.

'Melissa needs someone much more stable,' she said crossly. 'She's far too sensitive to be messed about. She can't take it. God knows she's made that clear already. She – oh, good.' We had turned up Whiston Street. 'Her light's off. She must be asleep.'

'Or with Van,' I suggested meanly.

'No, his bike's not there. Would you come in for a second? There's a book I promised Tom and forgot to bring tonight. You're seeing him tomorrow, aren't you?'

'Yes—' I said unwillingly.

Judith was already unlocking the door, and now she held it open. Entering was my second mistake that night.

She didn't turn on the corridor light, again for fear of disturbing the landlord. We tiptoed through the dark into the sitting room, and Judith lit two old-fashioned lamps, set on spherical brass bases, whose strangely puckered and dappled shades always made me think of tanned human skin. The room was Victorian Gothic, dark red walls, heavy armchairs, cluttered with occasional tables draped in lace.

Judith went straight upstairs to get the book. I heard her footsteps criss-crossing the hall overhead. Alone in the room, the red walls grew strangely oppressive, the oval pools of light cast by the lamps spreading down the sides of the tables, strange shadows encroaching beneath them. A great gold-corniced mirror hung on the far wall, its surface blotched with age, tilted to catch most of the room in its frame. I found myself crossing the room to the picture windows, pressing my face to the glass, looking into the darkened garden as if to remind myself of the existence of the outside world; the room was so heavy and still that even the air could have been hanging there for decades. Out of the corner of my eye the walls were closing in on me.

Though it seemed an endless space of time, it could only have been a few minutes later that I heard Judith running down the stairs, the noise she was making indicating that something was very wrong. She burst into the room, shaking, her eyes red, her mouth working convulsively, and when she did finally manage to speak all she could do was repeat Melissa's name again and again, louder and louder, till it became a keen, a wailing cry of grief, which was still rising as I ran up the stairs and into the one room which had its lights on.

The bath was full, and some of the water had slopped over the edge, staining the white bathmat pink. It was the first thing I saw. I walked slowly around the tub till I was looking down at Melissa, floating in liquid the colour of raspberry tea, her face tilted back, more serene than I had ever seen it simply by virtue of being wiped clean, any expression washed away. A few strands of her hair clung to her face and I found myself wanting to lift them off, smooth them back. Instead, for form's sake, I felt for her pulse, and took my fingers away almost at once, finding nothing. Her arms hung in the water, wrists down; I turned one over. The cut was clean and deep: one confident incision, no tentative scratches to help her summon her courage. But there was a kind of pale cross-hatching below it…

'Oh Jesus Christ, oh God,' someone wailed from the corridor behind me. It was J, the landlord, and instinctively I blocked him in the doorway, moving him back.

'I heard the noise,' he said faintly, 'and I thought—'

As if my hearing had been switched back on, I realised that Judith was still screaming, loud enough to make the walls echo with Melissa's name. I felt half-dazed; for a few moments, alone with Melissa's body, it had been strangely peaceful…

'We should call the police—' J was stammering. He looked terrified.

'Come downstairs,' I said, shepherding him gently away from the doorway. He was right: we should ring the police. Though it was probable that one of the neighbours, woken in the dead of night by Judith's frantic screams, would already have done that for us.

*

'It was that boyfriend of hers,' J repeated as the door finally closed on the last of the police. Melissa's body had been manoeuvred down the narrow staircase some time ago; poor Melissa, who had lived on coffee and cigarettes to keep the weight off her substantial bones, would have hated nothing more than to be a heavy burden on a stretcher, lumped downstairs with much puffing and panting. Her wrappings had dripped on the pale carpet. I had noticed J noticing them; for a moment I could have sworn that he was going to get some carpet-cleaner, and was only prevented by how it would look in the eyes of the rather-too-sympathetic policewoman who had interviewed us. Commiseration in her voice, but a mouth like a steel trap. If they had found the razor, her mouth might have softened a little. As it was…

I went into the kitchen and put the kettle on, wanting a hot drink to wake me for the drive home. No point making one for Judith, who was upstairs, having passed into a daze of shock, answering the questions put to her in a dull monotone just as frightening as the hysteria had been; I had dosed her with one of Melissa's sleeping pills and told her to go to bed.

J followed me into the kitchen, by now as attached to me as Dopey to Snow White. Though of normal height he managed, by dint of perpetual hunching and strange grimaces, to look like a gnome. The baseball cap he wore to cover his bald patch was in place, even at this hour of the morning. Technically, he should only enter this part of the house by invitation; he lived in the basement, where he spent most of his time reproducing Mills and Boon covers in acrylic paint, the colours even more lurid than in the originals. As far as I knew he had never sold a single picture, which he took as proof of his extreme originality, and lived meagrely, his only income provided by his tenants.

There was a third lodger, but he was in Hong Kong, and thus safely out of the loop. Otherwise he too would doubtless have been questioned, as Judith and I had been, on whether he could have absentmindedly picked the razor up and put it somewhere, or moved it with his foot, or indeed altered anything in the bathroom…

'It was the boyfriend, I'm sure of that,' J said again as the water started boiling. 'They were always fighting. Crying, screaming – once she hung out of the window, shouting at him to come back inside – begging, really. Must have been one in the morning at least. Meanwhile he's revving up that bike of his so the whole street shakes and shouting back at her to leave him alone. I had to have a word with her the next day.'

'About the noise?'

'Not just the noise.' J's lips were pursed. 'The way they both slammed the front door, it was rocking on its hinges. And the sash window in her room. I told her if it happened again I'd charge her for repairs.'

Go off and clean the carpet, I wanted to say. I won't tell anyone. Instead, I said baldly, wanting to see his reaction:

'You think Van killed her.'

To my surprise, J didn't flinch from the word. Instead, he crossed his arms, pumping up his chest like a bodybuilder, and nodded slowly.

'Well, she didn't top herself, did she? Not without something to do it with.'

'Sensitively phrased, J. Tell me why Van would have killed her. Coffee or tea?'

'Tea, please. She would never have left him alone. You should have heard the way she carried on. I can't think what Melissa saw in him – she could have had anyone she wanted. As long as that friend of hers let her.'

'Do you mean Judith?' I passed him a mug of tea.

'She was jealous of anyone Melissa went out with. That was clear enough.'

I didn't dispute this. 'But don't you think that killing someone verges rather on the extreme as a method of giving them the push?'

'She was obsessed with him, she'd have made his life hell if he tried to leave her,' J said darkly. 'She'd wait up for him every night, pacing and pacing up here. I'd hear her feet going back and forth above my head. And then when he went she'd sob and try to make him stay longer. The floor's very thin, you know,' he added hastily. 'I have to ask them not to play music or watch the TV after eleven.'

Something he had just said clicked into place, but a very long way away, down a tunnel shrouded in mist. Stirring my coffee, I tried to focus on it, but the effort only made the clouds roll in more. I would have to leave it for a while.

'I wanted to paint her, actually,' J was saying. His expression held more than a hint of the salacious. 'Put her face on some of the covers I use. She was behind with the rent, you know. Months in arrears. I thought maybe she would pose for me to make it up. She'd have agreed in the end. I wanted to try a new series, something a little different. I expect I could try it from a photograph, but it's not the same.'

The thought of Melissa immortalised, even if only in J's concrete-walled basement, as a sequence of pouting damsels averting their gaze demurely from the smouldering swains who held them in a firm manly grip, was fairly nauseating, even before I remembered seeing her as a modern Ophelia floating in her own diluted blood. J seemed to read my thoughts, and wiped his face clean of anything but the proper respect for the dead.

'I'll never forget the sight of her, lying there like that,' he said, blowing prosaically on his tea. 'That poor girl, she looked so young. It doesn't bear thinking about, does it?'

I paused a moment in the act of lacing my coffee with a decent dash of the absent flatmate's brandy. From where he had been standing in the hallway, he could not have seen Melissa's body in the bath. Either J was dramatising, which was perfectly possible, or he had already seen her body before Judith and I returned from the cinema.

I stirred my coffee slowly, watching him. He seemed unaware that he had said anything at all significant.

For a minute or so I had been noticing an odd clattering sound outside, almost like hail, and was just about to look out of the window to investigate its source when the doorbell rang. The box was in the hall, close to the kitchen door, and vibrated as crazily as if a swarm of bumblebees were trapped inside it. J jumped, the spoon shaking in his mug, spilling tea to the floor, suddenly panic-stricken. The mug looked so unsteady in his hands that I took it from him and put it on the counter. I left him attempting to tear off a length of kitchen roll with jerky, impatient gestures. He was as edgy as a chainsaw.

Van stood on the step outside. The light was full on his face, which was perplexed, his eyes squinting in concentration as he stared at me.

'Who's that?' he said. I realised that, with the light behind me, he was trying to work out my identity from my silhouette.

'Come in,' I said, holding open the door.

'Oh, hi, Sam,' he said, recognising my voice. His own sounded strained, as if he were making an effort for lightness and failing. 'What's going on? How come you're here. You guys having a party?'

'No.' I closed the door. 'Look, come into the living room.'

As we passed the kitchen door J straightened up, a wadge of paper towel in his hand, outrage written on every feature.

'What's *he* doing here at this time of night? It's practically morning! Do you even *know* what the time is?' he said furiously, waving the mess of kitchen roll at Van in a way that was supposed to be threatening.

'Hey man, let's keep things cool, OK?' Van said rather guiltily. 'I know this is a bit out of line, but it won't happen again.' He ran a hand through his crop of dark wiry curls. 'I just wanted to see Mel – we had a fight earlier and I wanted to make sure she's all right.'

'All right? *All right?*'

'Van, just come in here a moment, will you?' I said, wanting to head this confrontation off at the pass. But J was doing that thing again where he crossed his arms across his chest, flexing up his pectorals to full effect, his body swelling up like a pouter pigeon.

'She's very much not all right!' he said, and then, as if realising the inadequacy of this statement: 'She's dead! Satisfied now? Well, are you?'

'I don't think that's very fucking funny, man,' Van said angrily. 'I don't know what kind of sick mind you've got, but—'

'Van, will you come through here a moment!' I yelled, wondering simultaneously why I didn't just leave the two of them to get on with locking horns – or rolls of paper towel; they could choose their own weapons. But something J had said was still nagging away at me, and I wouldn't sleep till I had tracked down the reference.

Van turned to face me. He was wearing a puffa jacket and snow-boarding trousers made of equally synthetic material which slithered and rustled at every move he made. His brows were drawn low over his eyes, his full lips thrust out in an angry pout. The unrepentant animal in me acknowledged once again how good-looking he was.

'Is it true? Sam? Is it true, what this wanker's saying?'

J opened his mouth to object and, as Van swung round to fix him with a glare, closed it again so smartly I almost heard his lips smack together. I jerked my head at Van to follow me into the living room, and knew he was obeying by the swish of his trousers in my wake.

'The fuck is going on, Sam,' he said, but his voice was weak now. 'She's dead? Mel's dead?'

I nodded.

'They've taken her away already, Van. There was nothing to be done.'

'Oh Christ—'

'You saw her earlier this evening?'

In shock, he answered without even thinking about it. 'That's right. I dropped round before my spot started, about midnight. She was OK then. Well, not OK, but—' He tailed off, unwilling to say 'alive'. 'I told her I probably wouldn't be back later, and she threw a real wobbly. I couldn't really handle it, I wasn't in the mood, y'know? So I told her that if that's the way she felt she'd be better off without me – I thought we should call it a day. She started screaming, I pushed off, slammed the door, y'know, the usual thing. Pretty stupid, really.'

'Did you mean it about breaking up with her?'

Van wriggled in his chair as if uncomfortable. 'Well, I did at the time, y'know? Then I got home about half-an-hour ago and there was this really strange message from her on the machine. Crying and saying that she'd had enough, I'd never see her again and she hoped I'd be satisfied. She didn't sound good, I'm telling you. Well, I was feeling up – it went really well tonight, I had lots of energy – and I just got on the bike and came over to see if she was OK. Threw some stones up at her window to see if I could wake her up.'

He looked up at me. 'OK, we fight a lot, I know. But we have our good times. If she could only loosen up a bit, not make such a fuss about every little thing… OK, sometimes I don't show up when I say I'm going to, but you know how it is, something's going down and I don't make it round here…'

His eyes were dark and pleading, his hands clasped in his lap. 'She really is dead, isn't she?'

I nodded.

'How did it happen? She do it herself?'

'It looks that way,' I said slowly.

'Oh Jesus…' He buried his head in his hands. 'Oh Jesus… You know, there was this old scar on her wrist. I thought she'd tried it before, but she told me it was a ganglion, like a kind of lump they'd had to cut out. But maybe after all…'

It couldn't help occurring to me that someone who had seen that scar and didn't know what had caused it might well have thought that it would corroborate what would seem like a second, more successful attempt of Melissa's to take her own life. Van was still talking:

'I knew when I heard that message that something was wrong, but I never thought…'

'You didn't wipe it, did you?' I asked. 'Her message, I mean.'

'Yeah, I always do. Otherwise they all pile up—' His head came up, his hair ruffled. 'Why d'you ask? What's that got to do with anything?'

I shrugged. 'The police might have wanted to hear it.'

'The Bill? What've they got to do with anything?'

'Well, as suicides go, it's not as straightforward as it could be. Melissa seems to have got into the bath and slit her wrists.' There was no way of saying that more delicately, even if I used longer words. 'Only there's no razor that anyone can find. Which is pretty strange: if she did it herself, it would be there, and if someone else did it, why on earth did they take the razor away? Hard to think that it could have identified them. We're nearly at the millennium. Not many people nowadays use ivory handled safety razors made in limited runs for exclusive barbers' emporiums.'

Van blinked. 'Take your word for it.'

'And there wasn't a note either.'

'She'd have left a note,' Van said with unexpected decision.

'Why do you say that?'

'Don't get me wrong, OK? I really cared about her. It's just… well, Mel would have wanted to tell everyone why she was doing it, y'know? Get as much sympathy as she could. She wasn't backward about coming forward about that kind of thing. Blackened my name across half north London, the way she made me out to her mates.'

'Congratulations, you win this week's Sam Jones Trophy for best use of political incorrectness in a casual comment.'

'Hey.' Van grinned at me, his teeth white against the dark plum of his mouth. 'If I can't call a spade a spade, what's the point?'

But he sobered up at once, his smile dropping from his face as abruptly as if it had been switched off.

'I can't get my head round this,' he said. 'Mel – but if she didn't do it—' He twisted in the armchair. 'Judith thinks it was me, doesn't she?' He read the answer in my face. 'I bet she told the coppers that, and all. She's never liked me. Shit, I'm in trouble, aren't I? That miserable old sod downstairs'll have said I came round earlier, and we had a fight – but she was alive when I left! She was screaming upstairs loud enough to wake the dead!'

He stopped in horror, listening to his words, their echoes fading away into the shadows. It was thick with surfaces to catch sound and absorb it, this room, cluttered with furniture, insulated as if to shut off the world outside. How heavily the walls were lined with crimson paint: they looked as if one coat had been applied on top of another for the last fifty years, no-one bothering to strip it down and start again. The windows were covered with faded brocade curtains, too long for them, falling in awkward clusters to the floor; the armchairs with their cracking leather were half-disguised with too many cushions and throws, the carpet concealed in its turn by a series of overlapping rugs.

Judith had told me that the house had belonged to J's mother, and he wanted nothing altered in what had been her sitting room. Perhaps he had her body embalmed downstairs and brought it up, when no-one was around, to sit her in her favourite armchair. Perhaps Melissa had come downstairs and caught him at it, and he had stunned her, taken her upstairs, put her in the bath, lacking a shower stall, and cut her wrists… Somehow, the *Psycho* reference seemed not implausible. J invited those kind of comparisons.

Dragging myself back to reality, I said slowly:

'But J says he didn't hear Melissa at all after you left.'

'What?' Van grasped the implication of this quickly enough. 'That fucking liar! He's putting me on the spot,'

'Which is where you should be!'

We both swung round to face the doorway. J stood there, two high spots of red on his cheeks. His words had had more than a trace of Dutch courage, or rather French; I should have put the brandy back in the kitchen cupboard.

'If anyone's responsible for her death, you are!' J continued, though without crossing the threshold into the room. Apparently the brandy would only propel him so far and no further.

Van was on his feet. 'You fucking liar!' he exploded, staring J down. 'You know bloody well Mel was alive when I left here! I don't know what sort of game you're playing—' His jaw dropped. 'You did it, didn't you! You killed her! And you're trying to pin it on me.'

He lunged towards the doorway. J scuttled back in a clumsy retreat, not fast enough to avoid the onslaught. By the time I had gained the hallway Van had pinned J against the balustrade to the basement stairwell, one hand gathering the neck of J's sweater into a ruff just under his Adam's apple, which was jumping as frantically as a rat in a bag. The red spots on J's cheeks had spread over his face in a series of unaesthetic blotches which in the Middle Ages would have got him stoned out of any village which was plague-free and prided itself on staying that way. I was just about to pull Van off when he said contemptuously, letting go of his grip:

'Nah, you wouldn't have done it. You haven't got the bottle.'

But looking at J's eyes, narrowing in fury as he skittered away from Van, readjusting his sweater with little jabs and pulls, I wasn't so sure.

'You know what I think, Sam?' Van continued. 'I think it was Judith. She was always queer for Mel, though she'd never have admitted it. All that frustration, it's got to go somewhere, doesn't it?'

J was triggered into a babble of agreement. His words tumbled over themselves so fast they blurred at the edges:

'Such a strange moody girl... she'd give Melissa such a hard time when she was upset enough already – Melissa would be begging her to leave her alone, and Judith would be following her from room to room, telling her what she should be doing, never letting up...'

This had not just been gleaned in the evenings where J sat listening to the girls overhead in the living room; he must have lurked on his staircase. It had better eavesdropping potential than his concrete basement.

'Judith was with us at the cinema tonight,' I pointed out. Sam Jones, voice of reason: competitive rates, will travel. 'She couldn't have killed Melissa. By the time we got back she'd been dead for a while.'

J rounded on me at once, eyes flashing.

'She could have come back in the intermission! It's just round the corner!'

'Come on, J, the breaks don't last more than ten minutes at the outside. There's no way she could have done... everything, and got back in time for the next film. We'd have noticed if she were gone for long.'

'Then she slipped out during the film!' J said, no whit daunted. 'Where was she sitting?'

'On the end of the row, but I was next to her. I'd know if she'd left.'

Surely, in thrall as I was to that double bill, I must have been aware if Judith had disappeared for the half-an-hour she would have needed. But there was just enough lack of hundred-per-cent conviction in my voice to make J pounce on this triumphantly.

'Look, it's nearly seven-thirty,' I said wearily, cutting through his explication of Judith's means and motives. Exhaustion, or over-speculation, had hit me full in the back, and it was all I could do to fight it. 'Van, you'd better get in touch with the coppers first thing in the morning. I'll give you their number.'

I walked him out to his bike and watched him roar away down the hill. Dawn had broken through in slow motion, no rosy fingers, just a lightening of the grey that hung over London like a pall. The mist was thick and damp, clinging to me like wet clothes. I walked slowly up the incline, towards my van. At the top of Whiston Street I reached one of the large, beautiful, leafy squares, linked by tree-lined roads as wide as avenues, which ran from here to the Angel, hidden away like a secret behind the ugly, lorry-ridden thoroughfare of Pentonville Road. Even the air seemed fresher here, just a couple of streets away from all that concentrated pollution, filtered through green foliage. I stood for a moment, looking at the square, enclosed in a low iron fence, rich with fog-shrouded trees; and then, on a sudden impulse, I found myself walking round it, to the gate, bracing one foot on the crossbar and vaulting over.

Once inside, a sense of peace settled around me, as if I were floating in my own private cloud of London fog. It made me wish I were a resident of the square with my own key to the gate, a symbol that I owned a little part of this place. It had the effect of a secret garden. The benches were wet with damp, the leaves heavy with mist; I could see only a few feet ahead of me. Beyond were just the misty outlines of trees and a few, very few, golden squares hanging high in the houses beyond, the lit windows of people who started their day much too early. Footsteps echoed down the street and I slipped back behind a tree, watching a back wrapped in a long raincoat, its shoulders hunched forward, progress down the hill and out of sight. In the distance, over the station, I could see my first faint nebulous glimpse of where the sun must be, a whiter glow, low in the grey sky, as much as we would see of it today.

I yawned and reached into my pocket for the bar of chocolate I hadn't finished in the cinema. Munching sleepily, leaning on the railing, I looked down Whiston Street, feeling like the blessed damozel in heaven, so content to be on her own that she was very much disinclined to pull anyone else over the bar to spoil her happy solitude. All the disenchantment, the malaise, that had smothered me for weeks was gone, purged, in the release of my escape from the tensions in that house. Things had turned and reformed and snapped into perspective.

Sartre had hit it on the nose: hell was other people, a claustrophobia that crowded J's house as tightly with people as with things, people whose personalities were colliding, sucking out the space from each other as if they were trying to vacuum up each others' souls. No wonder the air felt stale; it had been through each occupant more times than I could count, filtered through the clogged-up dust and emotional debris J and Judith, and Melissa, till so recently, dragged around with them.

I finished my chocolate and shoved the wrapper back in my pocket. From long experience of my endurance capabilities, I gave myself another half-an-hour till I flaked out completely. It should be enough. Leaning on the railing, thoughts swirling in my head, the points which had been puzzling me earlier had fallen into place; now all I needed was to talk to Judith to be sure.

I expected it to be J who would answer the doorbell, near psychotic by now with this last disturbance; but it was Judith, wrapped in a lumpy candlewick dressing-gown, eyes swollen with sleepiness and past tears, who stood in the doorway, blinking at me. Her hair was parted in the centre and pulled into a little stubby plait behind each ear. The effect was so old-fashioned that all she needed was a lamp held high in her hand to complete it.

Beyond her I could see daylight filtering through the chinks in the curtains. I did what I had been wanting to do all night; I went into the sitting room, crossed to the windows and dragged the curtains back, jerking at the rusty rings to make them obey me. Then I unfastened the catches and wrenched the windows open, chink by chink, until there was a gap of about a foot at the top of each one.

'Sam, what are you doing?' Judith wailed. 'It's freezing out there…' I was already bending down to turn up the radiators. She switched over like a train on parallel tracks. 'He'll have a heart attack, he's really strict with us about the heating…'

But her voice had started to fade as soon as she referred to an 'us' which no longer existed; the last few words had followed only by reflex. I stood up and turned to face her.

'Sit down, Judith. We have to talk.'

She plopped into an armchair, her eyes never leaving me. 'You sound so… so…'

'I think I know what happened to Melissa. I'm going to tell you and I want you to correct me if there's anything you don't agree with.'

She nodded, rubbing her eyes with the back of a hand.

'Right. After Van left, I think J came up to see Melissa. He knew you were out, he heard her crying and maybe thought he'd catch her in a vulnerable moment. She was months behind with the rent, according to him, and he wanted to suggest that she pose for him as a way of making it up. I was pretty surprised when he told me that; as far as I know his only income is the rent you lot pay him. It would be a major sacrifice for him to give up several months' worth. Which indicates to me that he had quite a hefty crush on Melissa. Anyone who didn't would have thrown her out instead. I don't know what went on when he came upstairs – I can't envisage his actually making a pass at Melissa, but who knows? It seems more likely that she took what he was saying as badly as she could, pulled any sad little subtext out into the open and threw it in his face. I imagine J scuttled downstairs in pathetic disarray, leaving Melissa in chaos; she didn't feel secure in her own house any longer, because J now had a hold over her, even though she'd told him to get lost. She rang Van, but he wasn't there, and that was the last straw. She felt completely abandoned and let down by everyone. So she left a message telling him he would never see her again, ran a bath, got in and cut her wrists.'

I perched on a table, watching Judith. The sun was up by now, and the light in the room was clear and pale and true.

'It was always a mad idea that someone might have killed her. They'd have had to stun her first, and that might well have shown up at the autopsy; stun her, but not kill her, because she'd have to have been alive when they cut her wrists, or that would have shown up too. Neither Van nor J had a motive remotely strong enough for that kind of bother. Whereas Melissa already had a history Of suicide attempts... It wasn't a ganglion, that scar on her wrist, was it, Judith? She'd tried it before. You knew she had.'

'But the razor,' Judith said faintly. 'Whatever she used... it wasn't there.'

'You took it away, didn't you? Melissa, with typical consideration, had left the bathroom door open for you to find her when you got back. You walked in and saw her and the first thing you thought was to try to put the blame on the two people who, as you saw it, had driven her to kill herself... When I was waiting for you I heard you crossing the hallway upstairs; you went from your room to the bathroom a couple of times before you came downstairs. I only realised it later on; J kept talking about hearing you two overhead going back and forth, and it rang a bell with me, finally. As soon as you saw Melissa dead you should have come pounding downstairs. But you had a couple of things to do before that.'

'I read the note first,' Judith said, her voice a mere whisper. 'It was in my room, on my bed. I couldn't believe it – I thought she was all right now, but it was true – they'd upset her so much between them she couldn't think straight any more – I wanted them to suffer like she had. So I took the razor and hid it. I've got the note here.' She pulled a crumpled envelope out of the pocket of her dressing-gown. 'It doesn't matter any more, does it? What matters is that she's dead... she's dead...' She was in tears again, but this time the sobs were slow, painfully slow, as if only now Melissa's death were sinking into her conscious mind. Before she had been buoyed up by revenge, her emotions turned up to their fullest extent; now she was truly starting to grieve.

I rang the policewoman who had taken our statements earlier and waited with Judith till she and her colleague arrived. She asked me to hang on and I said I would, but as soon as I closed the sitting-room door on the three of them I was down the hall and easing the front door open quietly, shutting it behind me as smooth as glass. My half hour was more than up. It was time for me to go home.

Outside the mist had turned to drizzle and any colour that wasn't grey looked wrong. It was that sort of day. Not that I was going to see much of it. I was going to sleep at least till the evening, wake up, eat abundantly while watching some trashy television, and then go back to bed again. And I hoped I would dream about Susan Sarandon and Catherine Deneuve rather than Judith and Melissa. Despite my recurrent existential crises, I am, at heart, an optimist.

Phil Lovesey

Notes

It's about time.
Of all the things I have to be grateful for, my regular bowel comes high up on the list. Every morning, ten o clock precisely, the rumbling begins, with the sphincter loosening precision of an atomic clock.

The advantages of this all too rare biological miracle are obvious – I work for an hour, then retire to the khazi with a short story of some description, meaning I get to flick through at least one most mornings – 250 a year. Disadvantages? Equally obvious – try being caught at Tesco's behind some crumbling fool trying to pay for six quid's worth of groceries with some unheard of Albanian credit card at 9.58am…

But I digress. One morning, could have been any number of mornings, as I resumed my place at the PC, flushing cistern still audible as background, it occurred to me that the short stories I liked the best often coincided with the time taken to read them – fifteen/twenty minutes, trousers by my ankles, answerphone switched on, front doorbell ignored for the duration.

Which set me thinking about writing in 'real-time'- choosing an episode to accompany the reader throughout the tale – initially as an academic exercise. I opted for strangulation, setting the action in a suburban bathroom, tribute to the original throne of inspiration behind the story (my bog).

The setting, the pub, the street names, are all real, all just a few minutes from my front door. God knows why, but I love Chelmsford, though this affair is hopelessly one-sided, the town itself completely indifferent to my presence. Part genetic ditch, part post-Thatcher boom town, this ever-expanding pedestrianised shopping centre housing 192,000 fascinating souls at it's edges has wound itself tightly into my imagination, as I set out to ponder what lies behind the commercial facade of such a 'respectable' enclave.

Come and see the place, seek me out, buy me a few beers, I'll tell you stuff about Chelmsford you wouldn't believe. Like the one time when… hang on, it's 9.59… I've got to go for a sh…

Stranglehold

by Phil Lovesey

Ever wondered just how long it actually takes to strangle another human being? The effort required, muscular and mental?

I shouldn't think so. I hadn't – until I was three sweating, bewildering minutes into the ghastly task.

No, let me correct that, I had sort of wondered, idle fantasies, but when it actually came to getting to grips, so to speak, with the dread business, let's just say I was ill-prepared for the struggle.

Christ, how the bitch clung to life!

I'd naively speculated that the whole episode would be over within half a minute at most, just like the movies, eyes closing gracefully as her throat yielded to the heavy pressure of my gloved finger-tips. If only it had.

It took over seventeen minutes to kill her.

Seventeen horror-filled minutes, my pulsing temples counting each dry-throated second. All one thousand and twenty-odd of them.

It's about as long as the average reader will take to digest this sorry little story of mine.

So how long have you spent so far, about forty-five seconds? That's when I first began to panic, about a minute into it, fast realising there was to be no Hollywood ending to this one.

How she struggled to live! Superhuman stuff, horribly unexpected from an amateur like myself. And all the time, I had to be so damned careful, avoiding blow after blow as she struggled in my tiring grasp.

Then we fell, onto the bathroom floor, jamming ourselves under the sink. The irony of our last dance – me panting on top, her moaning underneath, as I never dared to meet her loveless, bulging eyes.

Die damn you! Fucking die!

I'd known Terry as long as I'd lived in Chelmsford. A lot of people know Terry. Everybody in The Compasses knows Terry. Why? Because Terry's makes himself out as a private detective, and knows most of the dirt on it's customers, and surrounding community. Private dick – bollocks Terry was simply a hired snoop, sliding into other people's misery and mistakes, feeding from their lapses, broadcasting their shame. Parasite.

And so he'd saunter up to the bar, smiling broadly with assurance that his most recently unearthed piece of tittle-tattle would be enough to prise several drinks from an eager audience. Worse still, shame on me, though I'd pretend to be absorbed in the evening papers, my ears would strain to catch the latest local gossip drawing 'No fuckin' way', 'Jesus wept, Tel,' and 'Christ almighty, you sure?' from his paying audience. Better than the soaps – my weekly fix of overheard slander.

I used to be content to do that, then – just sit and listen, an audio voyeur. And maybe the mystics amongst you would say that karmically I had it coming, universal pay-back. Maybe – who knows? I like to think that it needed to happen – for me.

Then came that night. My beginning.

Terry sees me and approaches confidentially, all camel hair coat and close-cropped silver hair, an old hand at the cheepy-chirpy-cockney routine. He sits at my side, and I look up from the sports section in feigned surprise. I'd already seen him coming, of course, was well aware of the other's interest in Terry's movements.

Piss off, Terry! Can't you see I'm trying to look anonymous? Get back to the bar and start dishing the dirt, (just loud enough for me to hear).

'Evening. Mike, isn't it?'

I nod.

'Your missus. Out on Thursday nights?'

I nod again, grateful his gravelled voice is no more than a whisper, and the ghouls at the bar have returned to their own idle chatter. 'Evening classes,' I confirm, very man-to-man. 'Indian cookery.'

'Got the touch for it, has she?'

'Getting there,' I reply cautiously. What the hell does he want with me? 'Put it this way, I don't have to put the bog-roll in the freezer anymore.'

He nodded slowly, an admirer's cigarette dangling between tightly pursed lips. There was a sci-fi series on the television a few years back. Aliens had come amongst us, artificial skin masking their true lizard-like form. I wondered if the producers had arrived at the concept after a brief encounter with Terry.

The words slipped from behind his yellowed teeth. 'That's what she calls it, is it? Evening classes?'

He knew more. Had something. I stared blankly back.

He obliged, 'Look, Mike, can't say I know you real proper. Just as a face, like.'

I put down the paper, found out, blushing slightly.

'Got a little something for you.'

Was he about to break an unwritten law? Was Terry going to buy me a drink? No such luck.

'Got a call the other day. Work.' He tapped the side of his weasely nose confidentially. 'Woman up The Avenues wants me to check on her old man. Standard stuff. She reckons he's playing hide-the-sausage with a bit on the side, wants me to confirm or deny.'

My blank stare continued under the torrent of his bad acting. I'd heard tell Terry was actually born in Suffolk somewhere, but to listen to the hateful prick, you'd think he'd spent the last thirty years in isolation watching Sweeney re-runs.

He cheekily chirped on. 'Anyway, turns out this geezer spends Monday to Friday in his own office at the local council.' Another nose tap, this time followed by a wink. 'Connected, you know?'

'Right,' I heard myself reply. What the fuck was he on about? But it was coming, I felt that. The punchline.

'So I've unpacked the Pentax and banged off a few ten-by-eight black and whites for her. Hard-core. Her old fella up to his apricots with the third party, so to speak. Now she's got a few photo's to ensure a healthy divorce settlement.' A chuckle. 'News of the fucking Screws be jumping over themselves to run 'em, believe me.'

He'd taken some photographs. So what? He was too close. Too intimate. I wanted to overhear all this, not get it, face to face. Piss off, Terry, people are starting to stare again. Two men hunched over a corner table, speaking in whispers – what the bloody hell would they take us for?

'It's a sad old world,' I say, attempting to look casual and knowing. Why, I'm not quite sure. I'm forty-seven for Christ's sake, been married over twenty-five years, bought up two kids – yet for some debilitating reason I still felt like a little kid next to people like Terry. It's like, and I can see this now, I somehow needed their acceptance, wanted to be in their gang. Yet the moment they'd gone, I'd be completely relieved. Anna would call me spineless, chastise me constantly for 'not standing up for yourself' whenever I'd just spent an uneasy evening agreeing with every word anyone said.

Spineless? Bit OTT, surely? I just didn't want any trouble, that's all. Make all your enemies your friends, and you have no enemies. (But I never dared tell Anna that.)

Terry gradually unravels the plot. 'Point is this, Mike.' He extinguishes the cigarette at this point. Tradition dictates I instantly offer and light him another. 'Ta. Kind of affects you.'

I knew it, just fucking knew it. Anna.

"Fraid it's your missus, Mike.'

I stare blankly back.

'Been following them for about a week, now. Got the pics here if you don't believe me.'

'Anna?'

'And him. Turns out they must have met at that evening class. They're both enrolled in it.' He blew a plume of filthy yellow smoke straight over my shoulder, eyes never leaving mine. 'I'm sorry, mate, but they don't go there no more. They're off up the common in his company passion wagon. And as for the Indian she brings you back – they call in at a take-away on the way home.'

Still with me? How long has it taken you to get this far? Four, five, maybe six minutes? Just think of me now, well into my first strangling – still doing it! Christ, how much longer? She's moaning now, but just as I think she's finished a leg kicks out, an arm tries to reach my eyes.

Sweat pours from her head, making gripping her neck like struggling with an oily fish. She can move more than I can, but with less strength. Suddenly I realise that I too have been holding my own breath, strangling myself in my own fear. I let out a great gasp as my body presses down onto hers. I'm so grateful for the precious lungful of life-giving air I'm making such a dreadful job of denying her.

She groans horribly. Saliva begins to pour from her mouth. My grip slips again. I have cramp in my left leg.

Please, please, please! Just die!

It takes just a few minutes to walk from The Compasses back to the house, but on that night my mind must have travelled a million miles. Thoughts, ideas, scenarios popped into my shattered brain uncontrollably.

And the pictures. I'd never forget the pictures. Terry had been kind enough to let me see them in his car. There was no mistake, even under the weak yellow maplight, I saw Anna arm in arm with her... her what? Lover, I'd had to admit after several more photographs. I won't detail them, save to say Terry's got a remarkable camera, diligence and a great deal of natural talent for his work.

Turned out he'd seen the collapse of my marriage as another business opportunity. He wasn't making much money on this particular job, and wanted to 'cut me in' on a double divorce deal. For five hundred, he'd let me have a copy of the shots, then I could do what I wanted with them. And he was full of ideas – plaster them all over town, was one, let Chelmsford know what a 'fucking old trollop' I'd married. Revenge, he kept on at me, a dish best served cold.

Truth was, I heard myself distantly agreeing to this ludicrous offer, thanking him for his information.

Spineless. Anna was right.

Why stop here, just another minute or so into the strangling? To tell you how it was, truth stranger than fiction. By now the cramp was so bad I had to stand up and hop around the bathroom, massaging my left leg with my aching hand. She started to move, slowly, agonisingly, her bruised throat emitting the most vile noise. Shocked and frightened, I set to again.

Very un-Hollywood.

Next day, Friday, I left the office at lunch for the Avenues, a series of tree-lined roads home to large semi-detached properties our parents, school teachers and college lecturers are all keen we eventually aspire to.

As I walked the quiet pavements my thoughts turned to the previous night, my chat with Terry. Anna was already home, as always. It was our arrangement, ever since last September. She wanted to learn something different, meet a new crowd, I simply wanted my night out at the Compasses. She'd toyed with car mechanics, before settling on Indian cookery – an attempt, I now realise, to add some much needed spice to her life.

But that's by-the-by, sour grapes, maybe. The table was layed, and true to Terry's word, out came the take-away bought on the way back from her tryst. I sat in stoic silence digesting the exotic fare but tasting nothing, watching my wife, seeing her flushed fleshy tones in nothing but black and white, and wondering why I hadn't made the connection sooner. She too, ate in silence, then went straight to bed, exhausted maybe from her evening's labours in the company car.

And why, at that point, didn't I confront her with the stomach-churning truth? You've guessed it, the old lack-of-backbone problem. I cleared away the debris and washed up, glad I hadn't been treated to her version of events, suspecting in reality that I was as much to blame for her meanderings as she.

I ring the doorbell of the address I caught and memorised in the half-light in Terry's car. Amazing how much of this has gone on in cars, tin boxes moving from one place to another, hiding secrets and betrayals in their leather upholstered interiors.

A tired blonde answers. 'Yes?'

'I think we need to talk,' I reply, throat drying.

Nine, maybe ten minutes in now, and I re-discover my motivation for the scene. Had this been Hollywood, this would've been the chunk which would've made it to the big screen, your local Odeon. Rage consumed me, hate pushed me on.

I viciously dragged her from the hidey-hole under the sink, ignoring the rasping breath and ploughed on with renewed vigour. This was hard work, but this was the right way. No messing. I closed my eyes and saw my wife's dying face staring into my own. But this was better, suddenly so much better than any imagined sex.

There was blood now, running freely from the nose, a sure sign the body was contemplating surrender. My grip was sure, ignoring her thrashing as I sat astride and rode her all the way to Hades.

Suddenly she stopped, went limp in my iron grasp. A single bead of my sweat dropped onto her face. Quickly I wiped it away.

Was she dead? At last?

Pity – I was just beginning to enjoy it.

I sat awkwardly on a white leather sofa, a shaking cup and saucer in my hand. 'You knew?'

'Suspected,' Mrs Karen Simmons replied brightly, languishing in a single armchair. 'Of course, I needed proof. I needed Terry. He obliged, as always.'

I tried to age her, arriving at early forties struggling to convey mid-thirties. A game effort, she obviously worked out, the sort of woman my mother warned me against. Hard. 'You encouraged your husband to have an affair?'

'Made it easy for him, I suppose. And with his money, man of his position…well I knew he'd need a little extra persuasion to agree to the kind of deal I wanted. I'm sorry it's you, your wife. Then again, it was always going to be someone.'

She'd ensured it was, played Mr Peter Simmons like a sucker since the day she chose him from a clutch of lonely hopefuls starring in a dating agency video tape. She made no bones about telling me, either, gave me the full low down. How she'd tried, teased and physically blackmailed the poor man into marriage three years ago.

She smiled. 'Men are fools. Lonely men are easy fools. Once I had the gold on my finger I simply shut up shop. He had to go elsewhere. Terry gets me the proof and the court date, I get the house and a nice little bonus.'

Things were becoming frighteningly clear. 'You've done this before, you and Terry?'

'Twice in the last ten years. We go back a bit, Terry and I.'

I swallowed hard to absorb the shock. 'He wants me,' I faltered. 'He wants me to…'

'Pay him for the pictures,' she replied. 'I know. It's worked before. He always does that. It's his way of earning some extra cash out of the deal.' She smiled purposefully. 'I tend to pay him in kind, if you know what I mean.'

Even with my head spinning, I knew full well, could picture the whole sordid arrangement with the greatest of ease. Indeed I shocked myself with it. God, I was naive. Then.

She must have noticed. 'Don't be too hard on your wife,' she added. 'Pete's a smooth guy. A soon to be penniless smooth guy, but a ladykiller, nonetheless.'

I sat gasping for breath on the side of the bath, shaking with excess adrenalin pumping through my exhausted body. Thank God! Thank God that's over!

Then, quite suddenly, just like some low-budget horror-film where the slain, bloodied psycho makes one final lunge for the traumatised heroine – she moaned.

She moaned and twitched.

She moaned, twitched and coughed.

Thirteen minutes and she was still alive!

This was turning into more fun than I'd imagined.

Ladykiller. Ladykiller. Ladykiller. All the way back to the office the word kept rushing round my mind. Is that what Anna wanted? A ladykiller? Was it such an attractive alternative to a spineless husband?

I worked without purpose for the rest of the afternoon, adding nothing to the company's profits, too absorbed in my own dilemma, replaying every argument, every lean patch in our marriage, wondering how it might have been different if I'd been a killer of ladies. It was obviously what she preferred.

And maybe, just maybe, a small dark glowing fraction of my soul might prefer it too. Redemption through terrible retribution. Her death shaking loose a black phoenix from the chrysalis of suburban conformity, re-spining me. The only way, my friends, the only solution. And suddenly I wanted it so very badly.

I began planning how to show the cheating bitch just how much of a ladykiller I could be. A clever cunning ladykiller, doing the deed above suspicion, beyond the law. A real smooth operator.

Anna was in for something of a surprise. It'd take her breath away.

For much of the next week I became Terry, noticing with growing unease just how much I enjoyed spying for a living. Not that I ever intended to make a career out of it.

This was personal, you understand, I was directly involved – duped by Anna, and about to be taken by Terry himself. I met him one more time, the following Thursday, one week on from our first sordid encounter. We sat in his car once more, as he repeated the offer. What the fuck did he think of me? That I was stupid enough to bite on the deal? That really pissed me off. But as his accomplice had told me, it had worked before. Others had paid his price. In retrospect I can't blame him for thinking I'd be another mug. I sure as hell acted like one.

I said I needed more time, then committed a trivial inconvenient crime. My first real crime.

Why on earth would I want to get divorced, anyway? There was another possibility, altogether more gruesome, but a good deal less costly. I invested in a camera instead, and a lame flu excuse which gave me a precious few days grace from my desk.

And I watched them, all of them. Peter Simmons on the golf course, stroking the ball proficiently into the clear blue sky on Saturday afternoons; my wife and he ordering Chicken Dhansak and a vegetable curry on Thursday evenings, giggling in the aftermath of their deception, oblivious to my fuming presence close by.

And Terry. Yes, you've guessed by now, Terry had his own squalid suburban secret, played out behind closed curtains with Karen Simmons less than half an hour after she'd waved her unsuspecting husband off to the wide honest fairways and his afternoon's sport.

But most of all Anna. All week I watched her, observing every inch for the first time in years. Part of me felt in awe of her cool duplicity, part felt desperate to confront her with a hundred angry questions I never wanted her to answer. Begrudgingly, at first, I had to admit she possessed a rare attractiveness in an older woman. A new found thing, an obvious sign I had missed, a carnal pointer to the real spice she'd sought and found. It was as if he was sculpting a new Anna from the wreckage of my routine disinterest. She was reborn by his simple nocturnal automotive adoration. Excitement had banished the wrinkles, brightened the eyes. Anna had literally grown in his forbidden confidence.

I seethed, sickened and wept, knowing our familiarity forbade me from taking his role. After the long wilderness years of our marriage I couldn't change her without changing myself. And why should I? I was perfectly happy with our mediocre lot.

Why wasn't she?

No amount of thinking helped me avoid the painfully obvious answers.

I had my own photographs by now, my own file of proof. I didn't need anything else, save the confidence to kill. After much thought I opted for simple strangulation. Ought to be easy, shouldn't it? Looks fairly straightforward on the television.

Certain distressing things happen to a body when it dies. Private, personal things I shan't detail. The final twitches and spasms were hers, I felt rather embarrassed to share them. But grateful it was happening at last.

Seventeen minutes and she was clearly, very nearly dead.

So why couldn't I relax the grip on her neck? The seconds ticked by in my throbbing temples – seventeen minutes and six, seven, eight…

It took the police just three days to pin it on Terry.

Naturally they were very interested in what I had to say, taking me down to the station to 'help them with their inquiries' less than two hours after I'd showered and changed. Maybe it was because I was rather economical with the truth, or simply that their experienced crime-drenched eyes suspected I was too spineless for the task, that they seemed to dismiss me from their list of possible murderers. It takes real guts, you now realise, to strangle someone.

In an interesting aside, the chief investigating officer told me so, dredging his own pool of knowledge on a subject so often misunderstood by the layman such as myself.

'Can take up to twenty minutes, by hand like that,' he cheerfully informed me.

I told them what I knew about Terry, the scam with Karen Simmons, now in it's third cycle, their 'arrangement' for payment of his services; my refusal to buy in on the deal. I reluctantly showed them my photographs of his movements, saying that although I'd never done anything like this before, I was merely taking precautions. They nodded and understood, agreeing they'd have probably done the same. I also told them, that, if anything, the person I'd most likely want dead was my wife. They nodded respectfully, bored by my illicit confession, anxious to trace the real culprit.

No doubt you are hungry for the physical mechanics of that Saturday afternoon, events leading up to the bathroom. I'd thought, long and hard, you see, about the real villain of the piece. I hated my wife for what she'd done, but couldn't separate my own lethargic complicity from her adultery. The old lack of vertebrae problem. She'd given me enough warning and no matter how much I agonised over it, I couldn't find it in me to kill her. Or divorce, either. Her affair was surely a turning point, a chance for me to provide the spice she had so furtively searched for. No, Anna wasn't to blame.

Karen Simmons, however, was another matter. Hers was a life of material acquisition by emotional deception. The duper of men. She had to die. And Terry had to take the rap for it. Terry – the oracle of filth, unveiler of secrets, parasite of other's misjudgment.

So after I'd seen Peter Simmons leave unknowingly for the bright green links which would prove his flawless alibi, I set to work. Access was easy, she was surprised but let me in none the less. I had about thirty minutes before Terry arrived, boozed up, duplicate key slipping in his sweating palm.

The rest you know, save the incidental stuff, Terry's driving gloves I'd lifted from his car the second time I'd seen him to discuss his proposition. My first real crime vital to the success of the second.

I've heard Terry is going to plead not guilty at the trial, but the odds and the circumstantial evidence seemed stacked against him. Unfortunately for him, the chances of finding twelve good local men and women to sit in silent judgement who are entirely free of his professional reptilian voyeurism are astonishingly slim. He'll go down. And of course, in prison he may well meet a few of his former 'clients', too. I'm quite delighted by this violent prospect.

And Anna and I? Who knows? But we hug a lot more than we used to, and cuddle too. And sometimes, although I resist the temptation, my fingers wander to the innocent swell of her throat. I am changed, reborn after an agonising seventeen minute labour from Karen Simmons' last shallow breaths.

Anna knows nothing, suspects nothing. We both go to evening classes now, motor mechanics. Sometimes we'll stop in for a curry on the way home, and I'll catch her blush slightly out of the corner of my eye. But she's happy, much happier than before.

She'd better be. After all, she sleeps with a real ladykiller now.

Mike Ripley

Notes

I always wanted to write a story entitled *There Are Worse Crimes Than Murder, Geoffrey* because it was something I once said to a Geoffrey in the heat of a drunken debate about crime fiction.

It is heresy in some quarters, but I really do not believe that crime fiction *has* to be about murder. There are lots of crimes happening every day to the majority of the population, though most will not figure on the crime statistics. We are all criminals and all victims.

My novels tend to focus on loyalty, betrayal, dishonesty and bending the rules just for the hell of it. To be honest, I couldn't write a *whodunnit?* If my life depended upon it. My books are of the *how the hell does he get out of this?* school, or even *the how the hell did he get* into *this?*

And, let's face it, if you are trying to write comedy, it is a lot easier if you don't have to make a joke about a corpse.

Normally, I think of a crime and try and make a joke out of it. With *MacEvoy's Revenge*, I have started with the joke and composed a series of events to go with it. Are they crimes? Is there a moral? Is it funny?

A word of warning. This joke was told to me by a London taxi driver. Do not try this at home, children. They are professionals.

MacEvoy's Revenge

by Mike Ripley

'**C**roydon? This time of night? Ooooh…' the cab driver sucked in air like a drowning man. 'That'll be thirty quid, guv.'
'But I've only got seventeen,' said MacEvoy.

It had been a bad night.

It had been a disastrous night.

Wipe out; a slaughter; they had seen him coming and taken him to the cleaners without passing GO and certainly not collecting £200. The Gods of Chance had not only deserted him, they had left the answerphone on and were refusing to pick up.

He had lost the lot; well, everything except the seventeen pounds in change he had reclaimed from the various pockets of his dinner-suit and, in the case of four pound coins, a tip he had left for a waitress who had been too slow to collect it.

Not that he had been drinking anything stronger than tonic water. He never drank when he was working – gambling – except perhaps a large scotch and water to end the evening, to celebrate his cashing in of chips, the counting of his winnings, the end of a hard night's work, while he calculated his percentage spread.

That was The System and the only system which counted. Number patterns, card counting, Red only spreads; they were systems for the social gambler, the amateur. MacEvoy was a professional. He gambled for a living and he played the only system which mattered: the fifteen percent rule.

Fifteen percent of his allocated evening stake after four hours and he would quit. Fifteen percent down and he would also quit. His end-of-year target was to be fifteen percent up on the previous year. That was enough. Don't be greedy.

Of course it never worked, or at least not perfectly. The best he had done in five years was to be eight percent up. But that was enough for him, even though it had not been for Mary.

Mary was the problem; that's why he had lost so badly, breaking his own golden rule.

For a week now she hadn't let up, giving MacEvoy grievous bodily harm of the earholes, going on and on, nagging, threatening, even taking a swing at him one morning – not with anything as clichéd as a rolling pin or as serious as a bottle of milk, but with a rolled up copy of the *Racing Post*. And then in frustration, she had shredded it to pieces before his eyes before he'd had time to read it.

That was when the rot had set in. Not a sniff since, not a horse better than fourth, not a single number up on five Lottery cards, a spate of away wins which tore up the form on the pools coupon. Even the fruit machine down the pub had eaten twenty pounds without spitting once and then a spotty oik had jackpotted with a single 20p coin he'd got in change from a pint of lager.

And all because she had found his accounts book.

'Sorry, guv, it's thirty quid to Croydon this time of night.'
'Aw, come on, mate, I've had a nightmare. They've fleeced me in there. I've lost a packet. I'm talking third mortgage here, mate, give us a break.'
'Not my fault, guv. Thirty quid.'

For years he had recorded his progress in the little red accounts books which had suddenly proved so popular now that self-assessment of income tax had come in. At the end of each year he had drawn a double line in red ink and worked out how close he had come to his fifteen percent ahead target.

How Mary had found the book, hidden in plain view on a shelf of airport thrillers he knew she despised and ignored, he wasn't quite sure. But find it she had and appalled she had been.

Not, as he would have expected, at the recent poor showing of his system: the fact that he was nowhere near fifteen percent ahead. What Mary had gone spare over – totally ballistic – was the turnover.

'You gambled over twenty thousand pounds, you shit!' she had yelled at him.

So he had, but he hadn't *lost* twenty thousand. You win, you lose, you play the spread. Didn't she understand anything?

'So how far can you take me for seventeen?'
'Brixton? Somewhere like that?'
The cab driver stared straight ahead, refusing to make eye contact.
'Give me a break, man, it's three o'clock in the morning and I'm desolate.'
'Sorry, guv. Like I told you, this time of night…'

Yes, yes, but she'd *known* he was a gambler when she'd married him five years before.

She had accepted the fact that he worked the casinos three nights a week, ringing the changes around nine venues, never too regular a visitor or too big a winner to become a nuisance. Never drunk, always polite, the star of a million feet of security video tape.

So maybe she hadn't realised about the afternoons in the betting shops and the pubs, following his own circuit of pubs where new fruit machines had been installed – his theory being that pay-outs were more generous in the first few days of a new machine to encourage the punters.

What did she think he did all day whilst she was at work?

Had he ever complained when she'd worked late or even gone on sales trips abroad with her boss, the absobloodylutely perfect Paul Parrish?

Other husbands would have put their foot down, or at the least been suspicious. But MacEvoy had trusted Mary because he knew human nature. He had studied it for years across a green baize table. He had out-bluffed the best card players and dealers in London, but he had also retained control of himself. He knew when to quit, that was his great strength. In the study of human nature he had graduated with honours in himself.

'That's yer lot,' said the cabby, reaching for the meter. 'Seventeen quid exactly.'

In the back of the cab MacEvoy stared out at the shiny wet streets.

'Where are we?'

'Upper Norwood. That's it, guv.'

MacEvoy leaned into the glass partition and pleaded into the driver's ear.

'Oh go on, mate, take us the rest of the way. I've been hung out to dry tonight. Nothing's gone right. I've lost a packet, the wife's not talking to me...'

'Yeah, yeah. Seventeen quid, squire. I told you. Croydon, this time of night, was thirty quid.'

MacEvoy sighed and handed over the coins which had weighed down his pockets and become slippery with sweat as he had counted and recounted them on the journey.

He got out of the cab and turned up the collar of his dinner jacket against the rain.

'I just hope somebody smiles on you when you're down on your luck,' he said.

But the cabby didn't look at him, just swung the wheel and turned in the road and disappeared into the night.

MacEvoy walked home.

MacEvoy came awake just before noon. He was on the sofa covered by the spare duvet which normally lived in the cupboard under the stairs for just such an occasion. After the first year of marriage he had camped downstairs rather than disturb Mary when he returned from a shift at the casino in the small hours.

She would have gone to work hours ago. Gone to work as personal assistant to Mr Paul Perfect Parrish at his perfectly successful management consultancy in the City.

A man less in control would have worried about his wife's devotion to her work. But MacEvoy had looked at the situation and weighed the odds. Parrish was old enough to be Mary's father and had two broken marriages and four kids behind him. Too much emotional baggage there for Mary, despite the trappings of wealth and security: the Jaguar Sovereign, the holidays abroad, the big house in Dulwich.

Why was he even thinking such things now?

The spat with Mary would pass. He would cook something for her for when she came home tonight, before he went to work himself.

In the kitchen, he flipped on the kettle and opened the fridge door.

Inside was a carton of orange juice and about half a bottle of milk Neither were cool, let alone chilled, and there was nothing else.

It must be on the blink, thought MacEvoy. Mary had moved things out until the repairmen came.

The doorbell chimed.

'Come about the fridge, mister,' said the youth at the door. He had a two-wheel trolley with him and in the road was parked a white Electricity Board van with the back door open.

'That was quick,' said MacEvoy, moving aside so the youth could wheel the trolley into the hall. 'Through there.'

'That's handy,' said the electricity man, 'she's defrosted it. You'd be surprised how many don't. Leave 'em in a right state, some of 'em.'

MacEvoy grunted in agreement and busied himself making a cup of instant as the youth pulled the fridge on to the lip of his trolley and heaved it away from the wall.

'She's unplugged it too. Dead thoughtful. She said there'd be no trouble. There usually is.'

MacEvoy looked at him.

'What are you doing?'

'Repossessing, mister. Sorry you couldn't keep up with the payments.'

*

MacEvoy found the note and was reading it when the men came for the flat-screen television and the VCR. There were two of them and they were big and expecting the worst. People might let their fridges go without a murmur, but taking the television amounted to a declaration of war.

They had no trouble with MacEvoy. He just sat on the sofa reading a single sheet of typed paper he had found in the centre of Mary's bed.

```
Brian,
I have put up with a lot these last few years but
what has hurt most is that you just don't seem to
notice me any more. Have you even noticed I have
gone? Will you be surprised to hear that I am going
away with Paul? You were never one to hold a
grudge. Revenge doesn't play any percentages you
used to say. I'm cutting my losses, so should you.
                                          Mary.
```

The man carrying the video recorder nodded to him as he left, but MacEvoy remained inert, clutching Mary's note as if trying to focus in an eye test.

The man with the video let himself out but didn't bother to close the door.

The men coming for the washing machine had just arrived.

*

She was so *sure*. That was what got to MacEvoy.

She was sure he would do nothing, just accept it. Sure he wouldn't waste time and energy on revenge. Sure that he wouldn't do anything stupid. Being sure of that meant she could leave with a clear conscience and sleep easy in Paul Parrish's bed.

Her very certainty that he would just go with the flow of things, that was what hurt.

Don't talk certainties to a gambler, Mary.

MacEvoy taking revenge would be totally out of character. There was, as Mary had said, no profit in it, no system, no sense. That would show her. He would have his revenge on all of them.

It had started with her finding his account book and him trying to explain how sensible his system was, never overreaching, just playing for a decent spread. Their fight over that had seen her turn to Paul Parrish and his luck desert him. He had lost over eight grand the night before, more than he had ever lost at one sitting before.

She had broken his concentration and the casino had taken advantage of that, leaving him short of even the taxi fare home. And the cab driver putting him out like that, making him walk home and leaving him so exhausted he had slept like a log, not hearing a thing as Mary must had packed and loaded her car and left him.

They were all to blame.

MacEvoy knew where Paul Parrish lived, had even been there once with Mary to a party, but he checked the address in the phone book just to be sure.

Then he took the Yellow Pages and let his fingers do the walking through the alphabet until he reached Waste Disposal, and reached for the phone.

Upstairs, he took a clean white shirt from the wardrobe in what had been *their* bedroom. As he did so, he pulled open the wardrobe door on Mary's side and saw a rail full of dresses, slips and blouses.

With the kitchen scissors MacEvoy slit every dress lengthwise, bunched the material of the blouses and cut holes front and back and slashed inverted v-shapes into two silk slips. He left all the clothes on their hangers so that at first sight there was nothing amiss.

Satisfied, he turned to Mary's dressing-table and gathered up an armful of cosmetics, creams and lotions, unscrewing caps and removing bottle stops as he moved to the bathroom.

He was pouring the second bottle of perfume into the toilet bowl when he saw the note cellotaped to the mirror.

```
Chuck all the cosmetics down the loo and give any
clothes of mine to the Oxfam shop. There's nothing
here I want anymore.
```

She hadn't even bothered to sign this one.

'Oh, bugger,' said MacEvoy.

By the time his minicab arrived, he was ready. Over his dinner-suit he wore a crumpled raincoat, the right hand pocket weighed down with an ancient one-inch diameter spanner.

He had found the spanner in the tool box under the stairs and it had given him his third plan. He had opened the tool box to retrieve his emergency stash of £300, enough cash to see him through until he could get to one of his various Building Society accounts in the morning.

He checked his watch and found there was just time, if the cab got a clear run, for a brief diversion.

The minicab driver shrugged his shoulders and nodded. If the punter wanted to go via Dulwich, fair enough. It was his money, but he had no idea where Duffy Street was.

MacEvoy did, though, and he directed the cab to it and told him to slow down as they approached a detached Victorian villa set back from the road.

The minicab had to slow down anyway, to pull around the police car and a Ford Galaxy parked outside the entrance to the drive.

Blocking the drive, MacEvoy saw, was a huge metal skip, one of the biggest, he knew, you could hire and which could take over nine cubic yards of building rubble. Standing in its shadow were two uniformed policemen, hats pushed back, barely able to keep their faces straight. Arguing with them was a young Indian couple, the woman quite strikingly beautiful, a child holding her hand and a baby balanced on her hip.

Above her head, framing the scene, was an estate agent's pole and board. The words FOR SALE had been covered with a strip banner saying SOLD.

MacEvoy sank back into his seat.

'Oh, shit.'

She was still in there; the minicab had made it. That was definitely Mary's blue Escort in the small private car park shared by Parrish Management Services Ltd.

MacEvoy knew there were security cameras on the car park and knew that Mary could come out of work and round the corner any moment. He had no intention of confronting her yet.

He unbuttoned his raincoat and pushed the heavy spanner through the lining of his pocket so the jaws showed through. If anyone saw him, he was a man in a dinner-suit walking with his hands in his pockets.

He walked across the car park, angling towards the Escort. As his coat brushed the headlight, he stiffened his arm and through his pocket felt the spanner dig into the paintwork. He dragged it the length of the car and only when clear did he risk a look back.

Parallel scratch lines one inch apart ran the length of the car.

MacEvoy smiled to himself and then jumped as two girls – early twenties, short skirts, chatting to each other – almost collided with him.

'Sorry,' he muttered and moved out of their way.

They hardly noticed him, breaking step but not conversation to avoid him.

'It's really good to be independent, though,' one was saying to the other. 'And it was such a bargain! I couldn't believe what Mary said she wanted for it last week. I mean, I know she's got the Range Rover now, but… Jesus Bleedin' Christ! Look at that! Some bastard…'

MacEvoy hurried around the corner, looking for a bin in which to drop the spanner.

'Oh, fuck,' he said under his breath.

By nine o'clock, MacEvoy was drunk in a pub off Grosvenor Square. He hadn't eaten all day, he hadn't washed or shaved either. He must look a sight in his dinner jacket and greasy raincoat. He could tell from the way the other customers avoided him that he was beginning to smell.

Perfect.

He was ready for Plan Four.

There are few reliable ways of taking revenge on a casino. In fact,

MacEvoy knew, there are only two: break the bank or, failing that, annoy the hell out of their best customer.

By midnight, MacEvoy had his mark.

He had flashed his membership card at Security and the dinner-suit had done the rest. He had bought five £50 chips and spent an hour clicking them in his hand, resisting the temptation to play, just circulating through the rooms watching, occasionally nodding at a blackjack dealer or a croupier he recognised.

He broke the habit of a lifetime and took large scotch and waters from the hostesses. He chain-smoked cigarettes, letting the ash fall down the front of his shirt. He gobbled any snacks and savouries going. Not enough to sober him up, just enough to leave a patina of crumbs on the lapels of his jacket.

By the time he spotted his victim, his swaying was not an act.

The mark was a young Italian, obviously rich and with an entourage of two blondes who giggled and wiggled in all the right places.

MacEvoy watched the Italian lose over a thousand at blackjack before boredom set in. One of the blondes pointed towards the roulette table, as they always did.

MacEvoy made his move so that it would seem as if it was pure coincidence that he and the Italian would sit next to each other. A bump of the chairs, the apology, the leaning in, breathing whisky fumes, lighting a cigarette under his nose.

The realisation that one of the Italian's bimbos might want to sit in. The slapping of the knee, indicating, 'Sit here'. The cold snub.

The Italian bet columns and fours, the blondes went red and black alternately. MacEvoy feinted as if to place a chip then seemed to think the better of it.

MacEvoy ordered more free drinks, demanded champagne for the blondes. The Italian cut him dead.

MacEvoy flicked cigarette ash on to the Italian's dinner jacket, apologising profusely as he brushed it worse. The Italian gave the croupier a killer look. The croupier asked if MacEvoy was going to place a bet. MacEvoy slapped the Italian on the shoulder and said something stupid about letting his new friend warm the wheel.

The Italian lost steadily, the blondes won alternatively, but moved out of reach when one of them felt MacEvoy's hand on her thigh.

The Italian was getting testy, the croupier was asking louder if MacEvoy wanted to play.

In the mirror above the wheel MacEvoy saw two of the casino's security men advancing towards him. They couldn't – wouldn't touch him if he was playing; that was a house rule, gambling etiquette, custom and practice through the ages.

MacEvoy flipped a chip on to the table. The croupier said no more bets and the ball clicked and bounced over the wheel.

MacEvoy leaned into the Italian's face and slurred: 'How much for one of the girls, then? Just for an hour, outside, up against the wall?'

The Italian recoiled from MacEvoy's stagnant breath and either he had not understood or he thought he had misheard, but either way, he had had enough and he snarled and swore quietly and made to stand up.

'Eighteen,' said the croupier. 'Winner.'

MacEvoy snapped his face back to the table and registered his chip full square on number 18. Single-number bet. A crazy way to gamble. Odds of 35- (or 36- depending on the house) to-one.

The croupier piled £50 chips and pushed them across the table.

MacEvoy forgot the Italian and snapped his fingers for a hostess, ordering a large orange juice with plenty of ice.

He squared himself up to the table and began to examine the table as if seeing it for the first time.

To hell with Plan Four, he thought. Mary had been right. There was no percentage in revenge.

*

It was 2am when he quit and he was £17,000 up on the night. No-one had seen such a run for years. MacEvoy had not been able to put a chip or a card wrong. The casino management had even loaned him an electric razor and use of the executive washroom when he had taken a break to freshen-up. The Italian had gone, but the two blondes had remained. MacEvoy had given them a £100 chip each. It seemed only fair.

MacEvoy cashed in his winnings and stuffed bundles of notes into every pocket. Security asked if he wanted to bank it but he declined.

The doorman asked if he wanted a cab, but MacEvoy said no, tipped him just the same, and walked towards the rank of black Austin cabs sharing a pitch outside with the hotel next door.

Sober now, and high on the adrenalin of winning, MacEvoy had spotted, third in the rank, the cabbie who had dropped him in Norwood twenty-four hours before.

Plan Five came together in his head as he walked towards the first cab in the rank and the cabbie lowered his window.

'Can you do me Croydon, please?' asked MacEvoy.

'Croydon, guv? This time of night?' The cabbie tried to look concerned. 'That'll be thirty quid.'

MacEvoy kept his hands in his pockets, convinced that bundles of cash were about to fall from him like leaves in Autumn.

'But I've only got seventeen,' he said lamely.

'Sorry, guv, thirty quid, like I said.'

MacEvoy leaned in towards the open window and lowered his voice.

'Take me to Croydon and I'll give you a blow job when we get there.'

The cabby's voice contorted into fury.

'Fuck off out of it, you pervert!'

'OK, OK, keep your hair on.'

MacEvoy backed off, took his hands out of his pockets and showed the palms; classic appeasement gesture.

He approached the second cab in the rank, flashing a glance to see if the first cabby was going to get out and make an issue of it.

The second cabby had his window down as MacEvoy approached.

'Yes, guv?'

'I want to go to Croydon,' said MacEvoy, all innocence, no trouble.

The second cabby pursed his lips.

'Croydon? This time of night? That's a thirty quid job, guv.'

'But I've only got seventeen,' said MacEvoy meekly.

'Tough shit, mate. Thirty quid this time of night.'

MacEvoy leaned in to the window and whispered.

'Look, I'll give you the seventeen and do you a blow job on the way, OK?'

The cabby narrowed his eyes, sized up MacEvoy and hissed: 'Piss off, sicko. Don't even breathe on my fucking cab.'

The window slid up and MacEvoy turned, a look of desperation on his face, towards the third cab.

The driver did not recognise him from the night before. MacEvoy had gambled on that, but it was a safe, percentage, bet.

'Can you do me Croydon?' he asked.

'This time of night, guv?' said the cabby. 'That'll be thirty quid.'

'That will be perfectly all right,' said MacEvoy, reaching for the door handle.

And as the cab pulled out of the rank to pass by the first two cabs, MacEvoy lowered the window in the passenger door and leaned out so that his head and smiling face were framed by it.

He put his fists to his cheeks and stuck his thumbs up in the universal sign of the winner, grinning wildly into the horrified faces of the first two cabbies.

Ken Bruen

Notes

Mother's *Ruin* came about as a result of a chance remark. I heard a lady say: 'Boys love their mother.'
I thought, 'Oh yeah?'
And, 'What, if…?' Thus the story began.
This is a tremendous time to be a crime writer. The Americans,

> *Elmore Leonard*
> *James Crumley*
> *James Sallis*
> *James Lee Burke*
> *Lawrence Block*

Moved crime writing into a new area of acceptance
daring
And
wondrous experimentation.
Now we're taking them on.
Here we have

> *Jeremy Cameron*
> *John Harvey*
> *Bill James*
> *Maxim Jakubowski*
> *Stella Duffy*
> *Mike Ripley*
> *Gerry Byrne*

Turning the format on it's head
And mugging the genre into the '90s.

The Do-Not Press are gunning their way into the very front ranks of cutting edge fiction.

With my novels, I like to blend a major literary figure with the villains of south-east London and let them rip.

Thus *Rilke on Black, Her Last Call to Louis McNeice*.

Rock 'n' Rolling in a whole new London mode. MTV. The

dialogue of south London, sharpen it with literary reference and serve *noir* as it's painted.

Twenty years down the pike, they'll say:

'Wow, wasn't that when British crime went ballsy if not outright ballistic?'

Like that.

Mother's Ruin

by Ken Bruen

Stephen rose on December first with a resolution to seriously alter his life. He'd return to literature and read one quality book a week. He spoke aloud, 'Well, OK, a month – let's not go totally ape-shit… and I'll only drink on weekends. I'll join a computer-dating agency and not worry about my hair.'

He made scrambled eggs, large tea and began to read a book by Louis de Berniéres. This he selected because of its dedication:

To all those who are persecuted
for daring to think for themselves.

Between bites of egg, he said, 'Sounds a winner!'

Stephen was relishing a character in the book who had elevated masochism to such a level, that he learned to smoke in his sleep.

The phone rang. Stephen was still in throes of amusement as he said breezily, 'Hello?'

'Stephen Beck?'

'None other.'

'This is Nurse O'Brien. I'm afraid there's been an incident here at the hospital.'

'A what…? Good Lord, is it Martin, is he all right…? hello…'

She could be heard taking a deep breath.

'I don't really think I should go into it over the phone. Could you come to the hospital?'

'For God's sake, is he dead, did he hang himself? Do I bring sweets or condolences? Tell me.'

'No, he's not dead. Please come. I must go…'

And she rang off.

The thought of his little girl zoomed into his head and he called her name like a lamentation: 'Suzy… little Suzy.'

He could feel the warmth of her tiny hand and looked down. Looked down, half in dread that he might see her tiny fingers. What he saw was the fork with a dilapidated shot of scrambled egg still clinging. He flung it across the room and said, 'I always hated fuckin' eggs.' The phone rang.

Snapping it, he shouted, 'Hello.'

'Stephen, no need to shout, it's BB.'

'For Jaysus-sake, Mother. What?'

'Got out of the wrong side of bed, did we?'

'Was there something you wanted, Mother?'

'I've had some news about Nina.'

'Nina…! What have you got to do with her?'

'I can't go into it on the phone.'

'Jeez-louise, you don't know a Nurse O'Brien, do you?'

'What…? When can you come over?'

'Tonight, Martin's in some kind of trouble.'

'*Plu-eeze*, Stephen, don't mention that boy to me, he's a heart-scald. I sent him a Get Well card and he never replied, the little pup.'

'Get Well card! Mother, it's not the friggin measles, he's in a mental hospital. Look, I'll see you tonight.'

And he banged the phone down. Give her a sore ear for a bit.

Then he remembered the Walkman for Martin. *Ker-ist*, he thought, I'd better stop off at the market. He rang a minicab number and told them he'd be outside the Oval tube station.

The station was thronged with winos and panhandlers. A guy was roaring at the height of his lungs: 'Buy the *Big Issue*… Buy…'

It seemed to Stephen it must be like a bad night in Beirut. The cab came. A Pakistani driver whose geography was as bad as his English, got hopelessly confused by the roundabout at the Elephant and Castle, and twice ended up heading back to the Oval.

Stephen said: 'Yo, buddy… let's pack this in. I'll walk. I'd like to get to the market before next Sunday. How much?'

'Fifteen pounds, friend.'

Stephen gave him four pound coins, and said, 'Leave it out, Buddy, OK… I'm a Londoner and not a fuckin' tourist, OK… just don't start. You might consider a new career with British Rail.'

His mood further deteriorated as he saw the crowds on East Street. Time was burning in his head. Rodney, the market perennial, came out of the caff.

'Steve, what's the story?'

'Rodney, am I glad to see you or what? I have to get hold of a Walkman… for Martin, he's… well, you know, he's away.

'No worries, son, give me five minutes.'

Back he came, with the latest Japanese model.

'Yo Stevie, this is state of the art. It does everything, in fact… treat it right and it will even walk the dog for yah.'

'Smashing… what's the damage?'

'Tell you what, I might be able to put a bit of work your way, and there might be a drink innit for the both of us. Take this as a sub. All right.'

'Yeah, wonderful.'

'So give us a bell towards the end of the week.'

A wino bumped into Stephen and he nearly dropped the Walkman.

'Sorry Sir… so sorry.'

Stephen noticed the man had a full head of hair. Tangles, dirty, but definitely luxuriant… He realised he'd never seen a bald wino. Had he discovered a cure, albeit a rough one. 'Lose everything, but save your hair.'

He spotted a 12 bus and managed to leap on to the platform. Anxiety or speculation as to Martin's condition hadn't had time to torment him. Rushing into the hospital, he asked at reception for Nurse O'Brien. A teenager, a girl with spiked blond hair, was waiting in admissions. She had her head in her hands and was moaning quietly. A small bag with an Adidas logo was beside her Doc Martens, the scuffed laced-up boots were tapping rapidly.

Nurse O'Brien appeared.

'Doctor O'Connor will see you now, Mr Beck.'

'Mister, what happened to Stephen?'

'Really, Mr Beck, I thought it would be more important to know what's happened to Martin.'

Thus reprimanded, Stephen was led into an office. The doctor was behind a desk, reading a file. One chair, hard-backed, in front. This was the doctor who had ordered Stephen from a chair on his last visit. He didn't look up.

Stephen said, 'Will I just park it anywhere?'

Doctor O'Connor looked up… he had half-framed glasses which he straightened and peered through.

'Ah, the brother.'

Stephen thought, 'Uh uh.'

'Your brother…' He picked up the file, checked something with his finger, snapped the file shut, and continued, 'your brother, Martin, got hold of two forks from the refectory, and somehow used them to…'

He hesitated. Stephen knew he was supposed to say something here, but all he could think of was the Les Dawson line, 'Poor? you want to talk poverty? Till I was sixteen, I thought cutlery was jewellery.'

He didn't say it, just waited.

The doctor said, 'He used these to puncture his eardrums… Rather seriously I'm afraid.'

'Jesus Christ… what?'

'He's under sedation now, of course, but it would appear that the severity of the action will mean he's going to be permanently deaf.'

The room spun. Stephen could see the doctor, his mouth forming words, but for an instant, he too, was deaf. In that moment, something died in him. He felt a huge kick of pain. Dazed, he felt reality return.

'Mr Beck… Mr Beck, are you all right?' The doctor was standing over him, shaking his shoulders.

'Get your hands off me.'

'Mr Beck, I realise it's a bit of a shock, but practicalities must be discussed.'

'So, let's discuss them.'

'Well, we can't really keep Martin here, the risk of further incidents…'

'Private… get him in a private place.'

'There are excellent facilities, but a bit costly.'

'Do it then, I'm good for it.'

Stephen stood up. The Doctor extended his hand, 'I'll be in touch.'

Outside, at reception, Stephen saw the teenager still waiting. He said, 'Here, have a Walkman.'

She took the machine and looked at it closely.

'Where's the batteries?'

'In it.'

'Got any tapes?'

Stephen didn't answer, and headed for the exit. Nurse O'Brien came running, catching him at the door.

'Mr Beck, where are you rushing off to?'

'Fuck off.'

Outside, he thought, Martin's got himself a permanent Walkman. The sounds of the world were now forever blocked out. A nightmarish thought then hit: What if the sounds in his head, in his new silence, were worse than the world's…what then? Stephen clenched his fists and swore quietly, he swore he'd function on a harder level for pure maintenance… his and Martin's.

There were no through trains to Morden, he got off at Kennington. The lift was out of order. The spiral staircase is the steepest climb in London. Rumours are that Chris Bonnington trained for Everest there. Totally knackered, Stephen emerged to a deserted station, save for one lone Santa who blocked his path.

Gasping, Stephen asked, 'Bit early for it… isn't it?'

'Penny for the guy?'

The smell of drink was ferocious.

'Afraid you've got your festivals mixed fellah.'

Santa swung at him. Stephen side stepped, then moved in and kicked him in the balls. Santa dropped to his knees and Stephen leaned in close.

'They told us… Martin and me… as kids like, that Santa had no cobblers. Another myth gone… eh? But here's something for the guy.' And he head-butted him.

A couple looked in… decided not to take the tube. The man muttered, 'Muggin' Santa now.'

He went home, lay on his bed and waited for the time to arrive when he had to visit his mother. He waited and grieved.

He couldn't – and indeed, never had – grieved more for a lover lost than he did for Martin. If he couldn't ever speak to him, then it was as if he were dead to him. When Father Jim's mother had died, he'd quoted a poem of James Joyce. Stephen couldn't remember all of it but he could hear the solemn, measured tones of Jim as he said the lines. Now Stephen repeated what he could remember, and repeated them softly, over and over…

'She weeps over Rahoon
Rain on Rahoon
falls softly, softly falling
where my dead lover lies
sad is his voice that calls me
sadly calling
at grey moonrise.'

He knew he'd spend the rest of his life calling to Martin, he knew, too, that his voice would never reach him.

Then the anger began to seep to his heart, and he felt if he could hug that cold rage, he could function and continue. Thus he began to mutter, 'Someone's to blame, it's got to be some fucker's fault, and by Christ, some bastard will pay. The tab will be paid.'

*

It was evening when he stirred. Amazement hit him as he realised he hadn't gone on the piss. A change indeed had fastened to him, part hate, part madness, he knew, and said, 'Whatever gets you through.'

He thought of his Mother and of his upbringing. She had never neglected them as regards food, clothing and the essentials. But she had wielded a subtle campaign of belittlement and undermining. It wasn't a coldness within her, more of an insidious spite. Father Jim had said: 'It's not
Forgive them
for they know not what they do,
Because, alas, They do know.'

He'd gone on to say: 'You can search for all the motivation in the world and make every allowance but every now and then, a person appears who's just a nasty piece of work.'

'Amen to that,' said Stephen.

Stan, her 'companion' was a constant visitor to the house. Like a shadow, you knew he was there but you didn't notice him. A gruff man from Yorkshire, he had elevated the concept of unobtrusiveness to a fine art. Stan's face looked like someone had flung a pan of grease into it. Not only had it stuck, it had set. Stephen reckoned there was a factory up there that produced Stans. They were solid and silent and said things like: 'I'm a no-frills man, I tell it as it is lad, Yorkshire-pud-and-two-veg, that's yer staple, can't go wrong then lad.'

If you misplaced your current Stan model, they'd slip you a new Stan by return, and you'd never tell the difference.

In the years when Stephen cared, he'd once asked him, 'Don't you ever get excited, Stan? I mean, are you ever *really starving*, could you really wallop in a few cold ones…?'

Stan had said, 'Moderation in all things, lad.' Yes, yeah.

Stephen had searched through literature to find the meaning… if not of life, then perhaps… of Stan. In Henry James, he'd read:

'I never read a good English novel without drawing a long breath of relief that we are not part and parcel of that dark, dense, British social fabric.'

Ironically, Henry James had said to his brother: 'I revolt from their dreary deathly want of intellectual grace, moral spontaneity.'

Stephen made coffee. A mug of black, strong instant. He put in two sugars and racked his mind as to what might give coherence to his thoughts. Anything, rather than the thought that he'd never say anything to Martin again.

Jim had introduced him to Schopenhauer and he searched the bookcase for him. Behind his Ruth Rendells, yeah… still there.

He took a large gulp of coffee… felt it burn his tongue, and exclaimed, 'Jaysus, that's sweet… I'm giving up sugar but not today.'

He read aloud in the hope that volume would bring clarification: *Suicide was thought of as one of the options open. It wasn't. It was the end of all options.*

Stephen was nodding his head and gulping coffee. 'Yeah, OK… Schopy… I'm with you so far…'

Suicide may be regarded as an experiment. A question which man puts to nature trying to force her to an answer. It is a clumsy experiment to make, for it involves the destruction of the very consciousness which puts the question and awaits the answer. While we live, there is always the possibility, the certainty of change.

He read the last lines louder, several times. Then he made more coffee, powdered heaped spoons of sugar, said, 'Mother gives the lie to them lines.'

He was about to put the book down when a few lines caught his eye. 'Hello? I don't remember this bit.'

When a man has reached a condition in which he believed that a thing must happen, when he does not wish it. And that which he wishes to happen can never be. This is really the state called desperation.

'Now you're fuckin talking,' he roared, drained the coffee and got washed and dressed.

He caught the Northern Line to Clapham, the Morden train.

The carriage was empty save for one old black man who appeared to have silver tips on his shoes. As soon as the doors closed, he got up and began to tap dance… tap, tap,tap, tap.

It grated on Stephen's caffeined nerves. At Stockwell the man sat and as soon as the train moved, up he got …tap, tap, tap, tap.

Stephen shouted, 'Hey… Hey, cut that out!'

…Tap, tap, tap, tap.

And the man said, without looking at Stephen, 'What's it to do with you man? Ain't hurting you… why I should heed wotcha say, man.'

Stephen stood. …Tap, tap, tap, tap.

'Cos if you don't, I'll fuckin tap dance all over yer head.'

The man sat.

An uneasy silence followed.

When Stephen got off at Clapham South, he looked back at the carriage. The man was dancing and he had his middle finger rigid in the air. Stephen suppressed a grim smile.

Stephen felt the cold December night pinch at his cheeks. He turned at the Rose and Crown after Clapham Common. The pub seemed full of pre-Christmas warmth. 'Come in,' it beckoned.

He moved on to his Mother's house. She had an intercom recently installed. He ignored that and went down a quiet street at the back of her building and looked up. Her small balcony threw light invitingly.

'As if a person of welcome lived there,' he said.

A quick flick of the back door, and he was in.

She threw open the door. 'What kept you?'

This evening she was sporting what the mail-order ads call a 'soft velour leisure suit' in dashing pink. Her hair was jet black with a flash of silver. Cigarette smoke caressed her.

'Christ, Mother, you're in the pink.'

He moved to open the doors to the balcony, as the smell of nicotine was ferocious. A tray of drink was perched on a small table.

'I will, thank you Mother,' and he poured a large gin. Mrs Beck faced him.

'Your ex-wife is in Khartoum, and Suzy…' he perked up as she mentioned his daughter's name. 'And Suzy is in the care of a man named André in Paris.'

'What… Good God, how do you know that?'

'I hired a private detective, a friend of Stan's… it's my Christmas present to you.'

'What, you're giving me a detective… sure beats socks and after-shave.'

'Really, Stephen, don't be facetious… I should think you'd thank your Mama. All my boys are so unfeeling.'

'Two, Mother, you have two. Did you get a detective for Martin, he'd like one.'

'*Plu-eeze* don't mention that boy, there's no talking to him.'

'Ain't that the truth, no never, no more.'

Mrs Beck moved to pour a drink. Créme de Menthe – she was visibly angry.

'Don't you care that that… whore has left the child with some whore-master in Paris?'

'Don't call her that!'

'Oh I'm sorry Steve-o, how shall I put it… your wife is "a care worker" working with the deprived of Sudan. She's staying at a place called… the Acropole Hotel. What are you going to do?'

Stephen drained the gin and walked out to the balcony. He didn't know.

'I dunno.'

Mrs Beck marched up behind him and said, 'When she was in the hospital, I took one look at the baby and knew you weren't the father. She had the nerve to call me a… a walking disease… me!'

Stephen felt as if a knife was slow twisting in his stomach. An urge to throw up was near over-powering.

'Do you hear me, Stephen… do you hear what I said? She foisted some man's bastard on you.'

Stephen turned, his left hand grabbed the top of her suit, the right gripped her hip. He moved one step, two, like the old waltz, then hoist…

hold…

…said, 'Fuck you BB.'

…and flung her over the balcony.

She never cried out. A sound like a sack of spuds hitting the ground reached him. He stepped back into the room. Took his glass, rinsed, dried and put it on the tray. He uncapped the gin and créme de Menthe and poured it down the toilet. As he did, he saw a packet on the bath. It read 'Midnight Black Hair Colour.'

The Créme de Menthe bottle he left on the floor, the gin he stood on the balcony edge, looked at his watch.

8.10pm.

Stan would come at 9pm on the dot and use his key. Stephen let himself out and didn't meet anybody. By 8.40, he was getting off the train at the Oval… he headed for The Cricketers.

*

The barman had a name tag, Jeff. Long, thin and bald. He spotted Stephen instantly as the unacknowledged fellowship of baldness dictates. Tighter than Masons. Stephen took a vacant stool and said:

'Yo Jeff, a large gin and Créme de Menthe.'

'Not in the same glass, I trust.'

'Good old London town, everyone's a comedian, a touch of "dancing on the Titanic", eh? No… the Créme de Menthe is for my old mum, a pre-dinner aperitif.'

'Her birthday, is it?'

'Yeah… she's going over the top tonight. Give us a shout when she comes in… can't miss her, she's got jet black hair with a silver streak!'

'Bit of a girl, is she, then?'

'Oh, she's a one, all right, have something yourself.' Jeff set the glasses on the bar. Stephen took a hefty belt… and muttered, 'Mother's ruin.'

The green liquor stood sentry as Stephen loaded down a chain of gins. He 'n' Jeff were getting as matey as magpies and as drunk as farts. Stephen was thinking of Oscar Wilde.

'We always kill the thing we love.'

And reckoned he'd never felt a day's love for her… ever… When Jeff roared, 'Stevie… hey, Steve, yer old Mum's at the door!'

Heart pounding, Stephen turned. A slap on the back from a jubilant Jeff.

'Just kidding, buddy! Gotcha, yeah?'

Carol Anne Davis

Notes

I formed the background to this story when I worked as a Development Officer in an area of multiple deprivation. I use the word *worked* advisedly as I was so terrified of the natives that I rarely left my desk! I'd grown up in a violent working class home – but this place was a whole new ball game. A place where a woman would go out on a bender for weeks leaving the nine stray cats and dogs she'd rescued from the streets without food or water in her flat. She returned to find that the larger animals had started to kill and eat the smallest ones but simply re-locked the death house and went round to a friends...

I aimed the story at a fiction anthology which was offering up to five thousand pounds. The anthology folded the day I sent off my entry. I then fine-tuned it for the Library of Avalon Short Story Competition where it happily won first prize.

It's a crime story in that various criminal acts are depicted – but I hope that it will equally appeal to readers of realistic dark fiction. I loathe forcing a story into a tautly-defined genre so that it can sit on a specific bookshop shelf. Larger publishers have done this to the extent that some very good writing doesn't get taken on – and that's a crime against common sense, the exchange of ideas and art.

The Ghosts of Bees

by Carol Anne Davis

Paul's first day as a social worker was meant to be Ben his predecessor's last. Unfortunately the man had left early. 'Got a standby flight, I gather,' the Co-ordinator said. She led him to Ben's old desk then pointed to a stack of cardboard files and a page-a-day diary, 'He left you these.'

He'd left ten mildly disabled widows, twelve single mums, eight solo dads and a family of low IQ who'd been known to start bonfires in their council bedrooms. Paul read Ben's notes from first neat word to last scrawled phrase. It would have been nice to talk to the man, of course, to have soaked up more background information, but Paul figured that he'd soon win his clients' confidence, become a valued listening ear.

He listened to the oldest of his widowed clients first. She insisted on making strong black tea and almost unstoppable conversation. Paul felt something in his chest expand and lighten. He was already replacing Ben! When he finally edged to the door the old lady pressed a dry cake into his hand. 'For your tea break.' He ground the sweetened flour between his teeth as he drove on to meet his next elderly case. The first women had just wanted him to arrange for a home help and phone the hospital to change her outpatients appointment. The second one needed help with filling in some DSS forms and wanted her pilot light re-lit.

His third client, Theresa Maglone, wasn't in when he called round at first – but her children responded to the bell like Pavlovian puppies. Footsteps clip-clopped closer and a tiny hand appeared through the flapless rectangle in the door. Paul hunkered down in his chainstore jeans: he'd decided not to wear designer ones in case the clients didn't identify. 'Can you get your Mummy for me?' he said.

'Ginger,' cried the toddler whose hand was still sticking through the box. Ginger was a herb. Was it also his name, or a nickname? 'Hello, Ginger,' Paul said. He made reassuring baby talk until two or more voices coalesced into whimpers. The next door opened and a woman in a housecoat came out with plastic tubes of cola in her arms. She stiffened and grimaced when she saw him. 'Hi, I was just looking for Miss Maglone,' Paul said.

'She'll be back any minute,' the woman replied. Another cry came from behind the letterbox: 'Ginger! Ginger!'

The woman cast a panicky glance at him then started to return to her flat. Paul strode over. 'I'm here for Theresa, OK? I've taken over from Ben,' he said amicably. 'But I need to know – are the kids by themselves?'

The woman tried to out-stare him for a while. Paul gazed back awkwardly, scanning features which could be forty-five years to sixty. 'No, their great-granny's with them,' she said at last.

'Theresa's gran?' Paul dug through his memory for the details of this case, 'But isn't she bedridden?'

'Aye, but... well, I see that the bairns are OK.'

'You have a key?' He realised that he'd started to sound like The Inquisition.

'Uh huh.' The woman's stare was that of a liar, too intense. Her fingers tattooed over the cola. 'Ah'll need tae go now. Ah've left a chip pan on. An this ginger's hurting ma hands.'

'Ginger?' Paul stared more closely at the vibrant orange brew: he'd have called them unfrozen ice pops. He saw that the woman's knuckles were twisted and red.

'Juice,' she patiently explained. She raised pink-lidded eyes and pursed her lips, 'I'm from Glasgow, and ginger's the Glasgow word for juice.'

Paul let her go. He was driving away when he realised that she'd originally been leaving her flat with the liquid sweetness. She must have been planning to put it through the letterbox for Theresa Maglone's crying kids.

Paul knew that parenthood was tough. Even the best mothers needed a break. He'd been on placements and seen their exhaustion. He'd read the books and watched the video too. When he next went round to Theresa's he had details of a local creche and free baby-sitting service. He had the address of a new local co-operative which was offering low cost food.

The outside door was standing open this time. He rang twice then called, 'Miss Maglone?' The rounded tone from a TV or radio drifted out to meet him. Slowly Paul followed the sound. Mustiness clogged his nostrils as he neared a partially-open second brown door without a handle. There was no carpet in the hall.

He found her sitting in the living room in front of a black and white TV. 'Who the hell are you?' she asked, looking at him over her shoulder.

'I'm Paul – I've taken over from Ben Treedham.' Paul walked round to stand in front of her and held out his hand.

Theresa ignored it. 'I've telt them before. I don't need no social workers!' She shoved back the glossless straight fair hair which reached almost to her breasts.

Paul smiled his forgiving smile. He knew Social Work had gotten involved after a Health Visitor complained that the children were being neglected. The report had come in after Theresa returned home with baby number four. She hadn't hit them, though, Paul reminded himself, or let a boyfriend do so. She just hadn't done enough.

'I can see these two are fine!' he said, squatting down beside what was probably the four year old and the three year old. Both kids stared at him then turned their gaze back to the television. Richard and Judy had a chef on who was showing how to make a marbled chocolate cake. 'And your other children?' he asked.

'With their Nan.' She glared at him with blue eyes that were carefully mascara-ringed, then jerked a thumb back at the other room.

'I'll just pop in and say hello to her while I'm here.'

Paul gazed at the twenty-three year old's mutinous face for another few seconds. He was only twenty-eight himself but he was sure that she thought he was a young Conservative, aloof and staid. And he wasn't, he wasn't! He'd driven a bus then helped run a bar for years, taking night classes till he worked his way into University and postgraduate life.

Nan looked closer to death. He found her sleeping in a head-boardless bed. A naked child he knew to be eighteen months was stretched out at her feet clutching an ends-sucked blue wool blanket. The eight month old baby was tucked in beside her, long eyelashes cast down. It wasn't a housing scheme version of *The Waltons* but nothing seemed seriously amiss. He just had to connect with this woman, show her that she had a support network. Paul walked into the living room again and started to ask the four year old his name.

He became aware of a low humming sound and traced the sound to a bumble bee trapped inside the glass. 'Oh, you've got a bee in there,' Paul said affably. He turned back to her, feeling strangely tense with hopefulness. Maybe she'd ask him to let the insect out.

'Bloody laburnum tree out there – get hundreds o' them in,' Theresa said, not taking her gaze from the small screen.

'I could open the sash and let it out for you…'

'Nah, it'll die eventually,' Theresa said.

Bees had such short busy lives. Paul's gut seared with currents of anger. He forced them back. She was just tired out.

'Well, see you next week,' he murmured, backing from the room. He'd done his job: she was only earmarked for observation. Still he hated what he observed over the next few weeks.

After eight such weeks he tried to sound one of his older colleagues out. 'That Theresa Maglone – did Ben find her… *challenging?*' He'd almost said *difficult,* but remembered his positive thinking books.

'Which one's she?' Gerard asked. Paul had to remind himself that the whole world wasn't equally involved in helping the woman.

'You know, the one I've been telling you about. Twenty three, on her own with four kiddies. She's out half the time I call leaving them with their bedridden great gran.'

'Just twenty-three? Christ! She could be dropping them for years.' Gerard rolled his eyes and put two fingers up to the barmaid to indicate another two pints of bitter, 'No, can't say Ben went into much detail. All he talked about was that poor bloody horse at the end!'

'A horse?' Paul had been bitten on the thigh by one of the solo dad's pitbull's the week before. He'd called the police when the creature snapped at the motherless son, and the solo dad had threatened to shove Paul's head up his own arsehole. The police had taken the dog away, but Paul was more worried about facing the solo dad. 'What horse?' he asked again, drinking deeply of his second pint of bitter. On those warm nights the beer went down extra fast.

'That family with the borderline intellect, the one who almost burnt the place down – their downstairs neighbour phoned us cause this clipclopping sound had gone on all night above her.'

'Surely they hadn't…?' Paul felt the unwanted grin spread up his face.

'Yep. Ben went round. Found they'd nicked this mare from that field by the old burn. Wasn't house-trained, of course!'

'They were going to sell it?'

'Were they heck as like!' Gerard wiped moisture from his lip, 'How was it the man put it? 'We seen on the telly that they eat 'em in Germany so we thought we'd have a go.' Ben asked why they hadn't done so and the guy said that they'd applied to the social's hardship fund for a butcher's carving knife!'

'You're not sending me up?' Paul realised that he was vulnerable as a new recruit, but after two months on the job he already felt like he'd been doing it forever.

'Scouts' honour!' Gerard laughed, making a Scout sign then turning it into another pint-request.

'There might have been something in Ben's notes about helping a client give a statement to the police,' Paul said vaguely.

'Followed by the words, "Have taken retirement and gone to Bangkok",' Gerard said.

'Ben was over sixty, then?' Paul queried. Suddenly it seemed important to build up a picture of the man, to understand him.

'Nah, only fifty-five – but no dependents. Reckon he'll end up staying out there and running a bar.'

Paul mentally did his sums. If he worked here until he was Ben's age he'd have spent almost thirty years in social work. He might have Theresa's grown children for his clients by then! The prospect made him clasp more tightly at his glass, but his fingers kept slipping against the ungiving smoothness. He'd have to try harder to make her trust him, to help.

'So Ben quit because his clients stole a horse?' he mused, 'That seems quite funny.'

Gerard shrugged: 'He just got so tired of people nicking bushes, fences, roof slates, cats and puppies – the horse was the final straw.'

He, Paul, would never break under a final straw. As he walked unsteadily home from the pub (the barman having confiscated his and Gerard's car keys), Paul told himself that he'd stabilise Theresa Maglone and stop her neglecting her kiddies. His references from university all said that he was the resolute type.

That week he wrote Ben his predecessor a note. The Co-ordinator frowned when he asked her to pass it on. 'I just want details of what he's tried already,' he explained.

'It'll be in his files, Paul.'

'They're… elliptical.' He knew that Ben hadn't detailed the full story of the horse. Maybe he hadn't told of various strategies he'd used with Theresa? 'I need to be more of a support to one particular client,' he continued, 'I don't want to go over ground that Ben has covered before.'

'Well, his mother will have an address. I can send it to her but he's under no obligation to reply to you.'

His head still hot from the previous night's beer-drinking, Paul pressed the thick white envelope into her hand.

'Thought it was just a note?'

'Well, I had quite a lot of questions.'

Like had he ever seen the woman hug or hold her children? Did she ever take them out of that airless flat?

When he visited the following week the baby was lying on her stomach vomiting on the settee. The four year old said, 'Hup, hup, hup!' in dull-eyed imitation. Theresa came walking out of the kitchen holding a plastic cup.

'Oh *you're* here,' she said flatly.

He stared back: 'The front door was open.'

'Aye, not for you.'

'Has she got a bug?' He knelt down and picked up the child, cradling her in his arms so that he could inspect her.

Immediately Theresa crossed the room and took the child from him: 'She's fine.'

'I was passing the shops…' He set down the weekly bagged gift of bananas, orange juice and milk and the three oldest children threw themselves in its direction.

'Dinnae eat too much. Rab'll mebbe bring us chips in later,' Theresa said.

She sat down on the floor in front of the TV. Paul knew that she wouldn't speak again unless spoken to. He checked on Nan and held a glass of water to her thin dry lips. The woman smelt of almonds and lemon talc: she said that the cancer nurse had been in to give her a bed bath. 'They were on at me to go in again, son, tae the hospice. But I cannae leave the bairns.'

'They're Theresa's responsibility, Mrs Reid.'

The woman looked as if she'd never been cared for. His chest went heavy, as it often did these days, and his throat felt tight.

Back in the living room he watched yet another bee throw itself against the pane. Paul walked closer, closer. The child who he now thought of as Ginger toddled forward, reaching for the buzzing orb. Paul realised that he was holding his breath: knew he feared this woman, feared her hatred. But he had to act. Quickly he opened the window and watched the insect zoom off into the September sunshine. That night he slept soundly for the first time in weeks.

By November the bees had gone, but when he visited the now-chill flat he still heard them, sensed them. Sometimes their rage at being trapped even followed him home. He'd walk up to his windows and inspect each corner of the glass, convinced that one of the creatures remained there. He couldn't just keep sitting and thinking. He had to act.

'Paul, your reports are… well, you haven't seen the Boag family or Mr Lewisan for over a month,' the Co-ordinator said. The Boag's were all adults: they had each other. Still, there was a question over whether they should be in supported accommodation rather than in their council flat. Ben's records had shown that they hated talking to outsiders, had pleaded to be left in peace.

Left in peace to steal and cook a horse, Paul thought as he parked in the concrete square outside their block of flats. The wind stung him as he left his Ford Fiesta. He dug his hands into his pockets and found a bath bun there. Good old Mrs Neece had given him a bun each week for his tea break: now he kept them for Theresa Maglone's reaching kids.

Forget the kids! Well, no, don't forget – just take a balanced approach, the Co-ordinator had murmured. She'd looked pale and watchful. Was she sleeping and eating as badly as he? Still musing, Paul walked the stairs to the Boag's front door. It was open as usual. He took three steps forwards and his body plunged down, down, down. White heat radiated around his waist, and suddenly he was stationary. Paul whimpered, mouth filling with acid for a moment, then stared around.

Only one out of every three floorboards in the hall remained. His legs had crashed through a considerable gap: only the width of his waist had stopped him from plummeting through completely. He tried to move his shoulders and arms, but they were shaking too much to obey.

There were creaking noises in the living room, then Mr Boag came waddling through. His huge feet easily straddled the remaining bare boards. His equally immense wife joined him and together they hauled Paul out and set him on the landing and shook their unwashed heads. 'We just needed firewood, like. We never thought...' Mrs Boag mumbled as the paramedics helped him into the ambulance. 'Will ye be OK?'

'Take some time off,' urged the Co-ordinator when he hobbled in next afternoon on his strange new crutches. But he had to think of the kids...

He went straight there. 'Christ, it's Jake the Peg!' Theresa said. The three year old toddled up to him and hugged his bruised right calf and Paul felt tears of joy and pain well up at the loving contact. He fished out the sandwiches he'd brought them from the hospital canteen. 'That shut you up?' Theresa muttered as they crammed bread into their now-smiling mouths, 'They've been bleatin' for food all day.' She seemed to realise what she'd said and added, 'For sweets, like, which widnae be good for their teeth.'

'I'll just say hello to your gran.' He had to lean sideways against the wall to open the door with his staved right hand. It was so hard to move when you were on crutches. You were reliant on others all the time. He hobbled into the room – and saw the empty bed, now stripped of its blankets. He limped back into the living room and muttered, 'Where...?'

'She died on Monday,' Theresa said.

Paul cleared his throat: 'Someone should have told me.' Now the weans would have no one to hug when their mother went drinking. He picked up the baby and found that she was wet through.

Back at the office he phoned the Health Visitor who agreed that the kids were failing to thrive, that they were going to hold a conference. He went back to Theresa's after he was supposed to be off-duty, but she didn't answer the door. For two weeks he went around again and again, but she and the children seemed to be staying with one of her many boyfriends. He left notes, phoned colleagues. 'She's just one neglect charge against her,' the officials said. 'It's not a clear cut case.'

Finally he hid behind the dustbins. Eventually a man with a black wool hat and a bum bag with a fist on it appeared. Paul recognised him and breathed faster, harder. He ran up and stood beside the man just as Theresa opened the door.

'Will you fuck off? We're all right without you,' she said to Paul. He'd seen the empties in her flat before but this was the first time that she'd looked incapable. She turned to the boyfriend: 'You back for good, or what?'

He shrugged and stared sullenly at the wall. The four year old boy appeared behind her. He'd be turning five soon. How on earth would he get on at school when he hardly ever spoke? He stretched out his grubby hands and stared at Paul. 'I forgot!' Paul muttered, appalled at his own behaviour. He'd been so preoccupied with getting hold of Theresa that he hadn't remembered to buy milk and fruit for the kids or even groceries for himself. The child stared some more then went into the bathroom. Paul followed on autopilot, searching in his pockets for a toffee or stick of gum. He'd taken to chewing sweets in the past few months to relax his jaw muscles. He pushed the partially ajar door fully open – then gagged.

The child was squatting in the bath, his jeans at his feet. The bath was covered with blobs of drying faeces. Paul looked into the toilet bowl to see that it was filled up with bits of the advertising newspaper that was distributed free to every home. He found Theresa arguing softly with her boyfriend in the lounge. 'Why didn't you report that your toilet was blocked?' They must have been using the bath as a loo for weeks now. 'You know the council would fix it for free.'

'You gonna gie me the ten pence to make the call, pal?'

Hot spirals of wrath rushed through him. 'They have an office by the nursery. You could have walked!'

'Aye, an if I left that lot,' she pointed to the TV-watching kids, 'You'd have been on my back in a minute.'

Something gave in Paul's increasingly-concave belly: 'You leave them often enough to go out for a drink!'

He drank a lot himself on the day that the kids were taken away. Everyone in the department assured him that they were going to the best foster home. He put a knife in his pocket before going to see Theresa. She had a well of hate and a large boyfriend, might dart at him with her dirty nails and teeth.

Instead he found her holding up a compact mirror and putting lipstick on. 'I had to bring you these,' he said, setting down the appropriate documentation.

'You hivnae heard the last o' this,' she muttered sourly. 'Ah'll get them back.'

'But you don't pay any attention to them!' He was talking as himself, not as a textbook now. 'You don't feed them or clean them or play with them. Why not let them stay with someone who loves them instead?'

She shrugged, a gesture he had come to know and loathe with a vengeance: 'So? They've my kids.'

He was on his way home when he remembered something that Gerard had said. Paul slammed on the brakes so hard that a Fiat Uno ran into him. When they'd exchanged words and insurance numbers he drove on to the library, but they didn't have what he required. 'How about an inter-library loan, then?' He realised that he was almost sobbing. All he could see was the weeks of mixed faeces in the bath, hear last summer's bees.

'We can get you this one, though it'll take five days,' the librarian said staring at him fixedly, 'But you can try the specialist bookshop at the foot of the brae.'

Paul drove there in his car with its smashed tail lights and bought every relevant book. Back home he drank as he read, turning the dry pages then lifting the slippery bottle. When he'd finished he wrote to Ben care of Ben's mother, explaining the situation. Ben had fled, but he, Paul was the obstinate one who would stay.

He had to sit outside Theresa's flat for four hours until she came home that night. He had to urinate twice on the landing. He watched the stream of yellow waste leave him and felt a surge of loss as the whisky ebbed away. His hands hurt from holding on to the tools as he practiced strong imaginary sessions. His eyes hurt through all the hours spent reading, forcing himself to stay awake.

At last he saw a thin female figure weaving its way towards Theresa's door. She was wearing only a short denim dress, though it had been snowing. 'Baz?' she said as she neared him, then, 'Oh fuck, it's you.'

'Brought you something!' he said. He could hear his own voice as if from a great distance. He held up the second bottle of scotch.

A low cunning entered her eyes. 'Feelin lucky, are ye?' She smoothed the blueness down over her small breasts, and he felt a heave of revulsion as he pictured yet another mouth blindly seeking comfort, tiny hands pushing hungrily through the door.

He'd thought that the drink would act as an anaesthetic, but it still seemed to hurt. She screamed and kicked for a while, then her eyes glazed over and she stopped moving. There was more blood than the books had suggested would be lost during a sterilisation, as his knife and forceps probed sightlessly for her fallopian tubes.

Someone must have called the police for when he next looked up there were two of them standing over him. 'Gerard warned that she could have loads more kids,' he said numbly.

A white-faced officer picked up Theresa's wrist and said, 'Jesus!' He let her arm go after a moment and shook his head.

At the trial Paul waited for Ben to appear. He thought that the man would explain that Paul had stood up for the babies and hadn't run from his responsibilities. But all that he heard were the words, 'Not Responsible' and the murmuring ghosts of bees.

Iain Sinclair

Notes

*N*o *More Yoga of the Night Club* is posthumous. It's an alternate world fable: thunder-flashes in the extinguished consciousness of gangland's most over mythologised stiff. The story belongs to the victim. I have always felt that Jack 'The Hat' McVitie was the most interesting character involved in the spiral of madness that proved as fatal for murderer as murderee. He was a wild card, scruffy, out of control; a pill popping, saloon bar motormouth. He seemed, all through the story, to be willing his own death. Without him, there would be no tragi-comic dimension: an act of hysterical butchery as the sordid conclusion to a peevish squabble.

Jack's fame owes so much to his premature baldness. He could never have gone into politics. He was doomed to racket around east London until he could provoke the hit that would elevate him into the pulp histories. That's where the accounts – all ghosted – begin to overlap. Old lags, busking for the media, contradict each other. The Lambrianou brothers, with their Mediterranean capacity for feud, can't even agree on the geography of the ride the body took in the fatal two-tone Zodiac. Freddie Foreman, a much heavier citizen, still shudders with the horror of having to collect such a clapped out vehicle, a stiffening corpse propped in the back seat in a roll of carpet, to chauffeur it to his lock-up in Streatham. The horror! What if one of the other faces should clock him in such a naff motor.

Dead voices compete, each one frantic to have the last word. But the principal characters have become rancid cartoons, virtual realities. They float over the territory like streams of noxious gas, light from a sulphur moon. They exist, and will always exist, in the chatter of lurid confessions, justifications, bent memories. They pose, in their knife-sharp suits, at the fringes of bribed celebrity. It needs a James Ellroy to take hold of them, to shape a narrative from the brutal farce of their paranoid monologues. To illuminate this nocturnal city of neon and booze, on that borderland where sentimentality and loudly proclaimed fellowship is always looking for an excuse to deliver a sharp slap, the punctuation of extreme violence.

No More Yoga of the Night Club is the title of a song by Jah Wobble that haunts me. Wobble, like Derek Raymond, paid his dues as a minicab-driver, shunting old villains across the river. Most of the stories begin there. A ghostly whisper from the back seat.

No More Yoga of the Night Club

by Iain Sinclair

He was supposed to pick up the Bubble on Queensbridge Road, over the hump, down by the Acorn, then go directly to the gaff of a man named Norton and waste him. Norton, not the Bubble. Only the Colonel, he didn't say, 'waste'. He wouldn't show hisself up. He said, 'It's on Norton tonight. There's a oncer in it, Jack. You'll be doing yourself a favour, son.'

But that was never Jack's forte, doing hisself favours. Not his style. Jack was well-known for it, being a cast iron irritant. A poker in the fundament. Jack didn't so much get up your nose, he potholed your hooter, crampons, icepick and steel-capped Doc Martens. Contrariness, that's what he specialised in. And he wasn't all mouth. Jack was the perfect antidote to bullshit. He was far worse than he knew. Blow off your kneecaps, tear out your Adam's apple, stomp your kidneys, but he'd never hold it against you. Clock you at the bar, your glass half full, he'd help you drain it. Jack had no time for barbers, tailors, all that patriotic cobblers about Churchill and Lawrence of poxy Arabia. 'Bunch of poofs, Tone. Towelhead slags.' Spot a dewy-eyed Alsatian asleep on the doorstep and Jack would give it a good kicking. Pussy cats turned inside out when he passed them on the stairs. He walked in his own force field, reverse magnetism. He hated with good heart, lived on speed and fags still wet from some other geezer's carious cakehole. I never once caught him going without, never saw him buy his own, putting his hand in his pocket. The city, Jack considered, owed him a living. He had as much right as any man to gob on the cobblestones. Leave your wad lying around in your trousers and Jack would share it. He was like that, a legend among his own. He emptied pubs quicker than Barbara Cartland getting her kit off, quicker than karaoke night with the Donoghue brothers from Silvertown. You could chart his progress between Haggerston and Newington Green, up Green Lanes to Finsbury Park, like a tidal wave, a tornado, leaving boozers with their doors off, furniture in the air, blood, smoke, and plaster snowstorms.

Jack was a chaos punter, everything was *now*. Time was no hindrance. Jack felt it, he did it. Look at those other lizards, the stern mugs in the nightclub group shots: fated. Printed with death. Inked over with a sense of their own importance. Destiny, for those berks, was getting rat-arsed with Judy Garland, bunging a couple of grand into Johnnie Ray's bottom drawer. History was engraved in the measurement of Ronnie Kray's inside leg. They stuttered the temporal flow. Tried to dam the stream. Wait. Pause. Let this single moment be the one and all. See the cut of that collar, see the handshake with Sonny Liston. See us share the frame with George Raft. Posers. Window dressers. Jack wasn't going to doff his hat for David Bailey. Jack liked to drink without witnesses, liked to stay off the map, a pub with a couple of entrances, across the precinct from a betting shop. Jack patronised establishments that carried big slates and no chalk. The first sign of an elevated stage, a bit of greenery, a sepia memento of old London, and he was on his toes. He was convivial, but didn't care for society. The Bubble was as handy as anyone for keeping the drinks coming. If he wanted Jack to make up the numbers for a bit of business, that was all right too. Jack was never what you could call socially promiscuous. He didn't speak of Tone as a mate. He did what he had to do, he rubbed along. He'd go over the pavement with a shooter, or take a run up the motorway to Birmingham to put the frighteners on some bent motor trader. He was easy, but he wasn't short of temperament. Given the provocation, he'd reduce any premises to rubble. A Paki had lipped him once, back of Scriven Street, when he questioned the mark up on a packet of gaspers. Jack torched the gaff. Down Hackney Road they still talked about the time when Jack, dissatisfied by the bite of the vinegar, lobbed a moggy into the fish fryer. All the faces acknowledged, he had a very particular sense of humour.

But Jack had his principles too. He'd never sit down to drink. And that's where he got hisself into bother. The Carpenters Arms ran to rules of etiquette as tight as a Mason's lodge, a gathering of samurai. In the normal run of things, Jack kept well clear. But that night, as chance would have it, Tone had the wheels. Tone was picking up change introducing a pair of brothers from west London to the Twins. A fucking genealogist of the inner city. He was putting them straight, adjusting his mirror so they could correct any stray hair, flakes of skull-snow on the padded shoulders. The boys wanted to piss first, against the church railings, so they wouldn't have to show theirselves up when they got indoors. Jack, he didn't like this. He was all for following them out and sticking their Brylcreem'd heads through the bars, getting their slacks down for a good striping. 'Cunts,' Jack said. 'Making cunts of theirselves for a pair of fat poofs.' Jack held that on a good night out, you never, *never*, micturated. 'Go to the khazi when you've had a skinful and you lay yourself open. They'll come at you five-handed and you're fucked, son.' Jack was a master of the Zen art of water retention. He sweated the alcohol out. That was his theory: muffler, leather waistcoat, cardy, sports jacket, tweed overcoat, trilby in the close confinement of the tap-room, he sweated buckets. He was always rubbing his eyes, mopping his greasy brow with a trailing cuff. The look of the man was an affront to the sartorial standards the Twins always strove to uphold. Ron, in the early days, was Reg's mirror. Reg – hair, shoulders, whistle – was the spit of Edmund Purdom.

Jack never was one to gauge the temperature of an event. His entrance, knocking Ron's favourite dwarf off of his stool, elbowing drinkers, setting a grubby suede shoe on the rail and asking one of the henchmen to sniff it for dog shit, was a disaster. The Colonel liked to have space around him, the length of a cutlass, a bayonet's worth of privatised air. You kept clear, unless you was invited to link arms with Ronnie Fraser or Victor Spinetti, squeeze mits with Terry Spinks, give your backing to Babs Windsor for a photograph. They had more pictures plastered on the wall than the National Gallery. Ranks of bottles on the table. Celebrities paying their respects. Another era entirely. Know-nothings talk about the class system breaking down, old Etonian chancers sharing a half with dysfunctional psychopaths, blisters on their knuckles. Taffeta crooners talking horseflesh with bent peers. Gangsters trading rent boys with unfrocked cabinet ministers. All bollocks! Caste was as rigidly enforced as at Versailles. Louis XIV was a fucking laissez faire amateur compared to the Colonel. Even the Colonel's monkey wiped his arse with crested two-ply tissue.

The Colonel's stretch of the bar, teak polished like a coffin, was inviolate. No other word for it. One of his lads ducking in from time to time to keep the menthol-tip aglow, or to slide another gin into reach, that was all the movement he tolerated. And here's Jack, hat perched on his ears indoors, like a potato-basher. Like he's just come in from the cowshed, his corduroys held up with creosoted twine. 'Arright, Colonel? Have one with me. Tone, get a proper drink in for Ron. Some fucking peasant's given the poor sod a poof's glass. Drink that and he'll smear his lipstick. Fetch him a whiskey, Tone. And make mine a double.'

The Colonel never moves. He don't turn round, nothing. All the rabbit stops. The big freeze. Eyeballs on stalks, like their heads was being squeezed in a vice. The Colonel's neck. A vein the size of your thumb, see it pumping. Jack is totally unaware of the mayhem, the potential mayhem, he has initiated. If Jack had more teeth he'd be whistling. Shirt-tails out like a dosser, he starts scratching his bollocks. There's a sound like dice rattling in a plastic beaker. It's the brothers from west London, their knees knocking. All they wanted was the photograph, something to frame in the Portakabin, the visible proof of their connections. Now they were webbed up in a treason trial. Tongues like old rope. Mouths burnt with the scorch of it, time running backwards. What they saw, all of them in that room, was the finish. The blood and cartilage on the carpet. Tone with a red can soaking the furniture with petrol. The house going off like a fire bomb. Jack gazing up at them out of wet concrete. His hat blowing away across the Swanscombe Marshes, under the bridge. They saw theirselves, names, ages, petty deceptions, spread across the tabloids. In their bowels they knew the vertigo of foreknowledge. Jack, oblivious, chucked back his Irish.

The route Jack's body took was like a fucking mantra: Evering Road, Lower Clapton Road, Narrow Way, Mare Street, Cambridge Heath Road, Commercial Road, East India Dock Road and through the tunnel, under the river. Get shot of this over-articulate corpse. Leave it to Freddie Foreman. Tone had sweated his jacket. You could ring the Bubble out. He was memorising the geography of an event which had not yet happened, which might never happen. He was back here, greyer, hidden behind designer bins, giving it the old sincerity in an empty boozer. He was here in the morning, for fuck's sake! Telling the story. Narrow Way. The words stuck in his throat. He looked down at his own hand and he couldn't get it into focus. It was a ghost hand. It was like his fucking hand had died and the rest of him still attached to it. His hand was moving through so many positions in one instant of time. A white fern. The X-ray of a funeral glove.

'It's on Norton tonight. You'll be doing yourself a favour, Jack. Use Tone's motor.' And the Colonel peeled off a couple of notes from a roll. He might be royalty, he might not like spoiling the hang of a suit, but he wasn't soft in the head. Not where readies were concerned. He carried his own wad. Like a hard paper cock pressing against his ice heart.

Jack didn't touch the notes. He put his glass down on top of them, let them lie like a Gulbenkian tip, a backhander. Nodded at the guvnor. 'Do us a triple, Stan.' Ron would never have tolerated a brass behind the bar, too much rabbit. Working women were nothing but fucking trouble. But Jack was in no hurry. Norton? Never heard of the cunt.

*

Now they're on the road. It's daylight. Another day, the same day.

They're looking for a geezer neither of them know. Norton? Sounds like a solicitor, half a bent brief. They're supposed to kill him, but the Bubble reckons that's taking the Colonel too literal. Ron don't know his own mind when he's had a skinful. A good slap'll do it. Shove his poxy hands in the door, crack a few knuckles. A dig. A poke. Use the tyre lever. Kill him for a oncer? Leave it out. What's he done anyhow? Fuck knows. Jack nodding off, needs something to keep him on the job. The Bubble smokes a bit of grass, that's the size of it, he's no junkie. Jack'll do anything. Jack's game. Known for it. The early sunlight, a stranger to the man in the hat, flirts with his stitches. Warmth coming through the curved screen polishes the razor scars on Jack's boat. Jack's always gone private, handled his own medicals. A kitchen scissors and a pair of the old woman's tweezers. Like digging maggots out of wet toffee. Terrible to watch, if you walked in on it unexpected, but Jack was impervious to pain. Anaesthetised by letting a little blood into his alcohol. Tone watched him take the tip off his finger, trying to carve a loaf. Not a word, not a fucking twitch of the lip. The morning's radiance heated the plastic threads in his cheek, brought him back to where he was.

Where *was* he? This wasn't fit ground for a white man. This was the fucking jungle. You'd need Tonto to take you round, a darkie who could read rhino shit. They tried Kinder Street but it wasn't there. Some cunt had nicked the lot, every bleeding stone of it. Sly Street weren't even a tin sign. Rubble and corrugated iron blowing in the wind. Jack wouldn't climb out of the motor. He spun the wheels, reversed sharpish out of a dead end. In his own mind, he did. In the film of it. He could feel the wheel in one hand and the lovely cool metal of a shooter in the other. London settled on its proper axis. He *thought* the Jag into where it was, Paki town. Bits that ain't on the map. Jack floated inside the motor, down streets he'd never seen in his life. Air was water. So was the Colonel. A bag of water in mohair casing. A bag of gin and water. A bag of piss. Eau de Cologne and pure sewage. There's a river in Detroit, one of the boys who came over told Tone, that's all industrial crap, from the car factories, toxic shit. Your foot'd fall off if you tried to paddle. But they pour blue dye into this river every day. And it comes out like the Venice of your dreams. That's the Colonel, that's Ron. Dyed shit. Green skin and pockets stuffed with deceased carnations.

But, truth to tell, Jack wasn't driving. He wasn't in charge. He was there all right, In the driver's seat, the Englishman's position, right hand side for right-minded citizen. Jack the democrat, English as roast beef. Jack the storybook adventurer, working through the karma of his Jock surname. Jack keeping up standards among a bunch of wops, dagos, pikies. Jack on the tenter grounds. Jack with the whiff of the river in his nostrils. He wound down the window, none of that electric bollocks, a decent old motor that would never go out of fashion. A hearse. A scarlet hearse. A motor that had travelled through time. A sixties jam jar still active, revisiting the streets of shame. A revenant wagon. A transporter of dead men. A limbo shuttle.

What if, Jack thought, we was a future nightmare? What if the things we done couldn't be shifted? Knocked out of the book. What if we was the aliens some stupid bastard saw? The old motor like a disk of red light? Still cruising for human meat, still on active service. Moving without touching the pedals. This was an export Jag, exported inwards, straight out of the packing case. Straight out of Tilbury. A snide Jag with upholstery that would never know heat in the desert on the road to Palm Springs. That would never feel the imprint of bare-arsed Californian crumpet. The Bubble was the chauffeur. The motor was in the charge of a left-footer, hung with a voodoo of plastic saints, pierced hearts, prayer beads that glowed like droplets of transcendent blood. Tone drove, took the dictation of Jack's diseased psyche.

*

He could see it all with his eyes shut. The air was sweet. His nose pricked, he sneezed He was stretched out in a meadow. Out of it completely. Hung over without the headache. Breath like violets. He blew into his cupped hand, sniffed it. He couldn't get comfortable. He rolled and twisted. His mouth felt as if he'd been gargling with granite chips. He tried to spit. Had he pissed hisself? Only blood. A nick, a scratch. Lifted his hands to shade the splintering sun. Which end of the day? A new beginning. Roofs and church towers and flashes from distant glass pyramids. Was this London? Not that he recognised. A ribbon of blue townscape on the far side of the water. A meadow. He liked that word. A field in the city. In close proximity. A field that they hadn't noticed. Jack lifted. Jack went with the gentle zephyr that ruffled the grove of trees. He fancied shade, a log to rest his back. He'd sit there, watching the insects in the old dry wood.

Jack let the bleached grass run back into the dust on the windscreen. Let the meadow bleed into the wasteground they were bumping across, dogs guarding a wrapped tower block. Jack's hand found the reassurance of metal. In the meadow was a metal disk. Jack traced the letters with his fingers: *Broads 70c Silent Knight*. A plate that had dropped from nowhere into this field. A manhole cover. A lid securing the drop into who knows what depths. The rush of black water. Had Jack pissed hisself? Being, at one time, in two places? He shook out a couple of pills, took a flat bottle from his pocket, washed them down with the fiery dregs. Chucked the bottle from the window.

In the meadow, exposed in all that hot space, Jack heard the sound of breaking glass, glass shattering on London stone. A pair of pillowcase hags shuffled along, eyes on the ground, determined not to see what was happening in front of them. Don't get involved with heretic business. Stay inside your bin bags. They stared straight through Jack and the motor. The Bubble's head was on fire. He was going through the Piccadillys like they was about to be rationed. Like he could see something in the smoke, the genie at the bottom of the bottle. Like he knew what would happen if Jack caught him. Jack would nick the fucking packet. Remember the night he'd gone with Jack to the turnout at Highbury Corner? 'Wanna come along,' Jack said, 'and make one with me?'

*

An old slapper, who in her prime had gigged at the Palladium, was throwing her annual comeback. The gaff, a Paddy toilet, was packed. Nothing to do with her, though some of the chaps thought it would be a laugh to watch her croak. But her feller, a TV ponce, a safari suit who was about to dump the cow, take a better offer for his services, done a deal with the micks, to cop for the bar bill. And the micks let in a mob of their own, hair licked with sugar water, bum-freezer church suits, hobnail boots. All the flakes in the borough, all the riff-raff out of Chapel Street, all the potato bashers down from Archway, are up for it. Jack was a prince on this turf. He swaggered in through the swing doors like John Wayne doing the double hernia tango, knees stapled together, rolling. The Bubble shadows him, maintains his distance, wop-slick, Dean Martin. You couldn't call Jack legless, not if you didn't want a dig. Jack was so pissed his boots squelched.

He'd had some bother that afternoon, down the Mildmay, done his wad, stood at the bar shouting his mouth off. Bennie One-Ear was trying to interest him in a barrel of sausage casings, skins in brine. He was getting on Jack's wick, explaining how the profit was as good as hoisting a vanload of ciggies, without the risk. 'There's no security, Jack,' he'd say.

'Fuck security.'

'Be smart, Jack, play percentages.'

'Fuck percentages, you mutt cunt.' Back and forth. Jack trying to keep up with the card at Kempton, the colour on the telly shot to buggery.

In the finish, Jack fucks off out of it, they won't serve him no more. The guvnor says to Bennie, he's never seen Jack go so quiet. He's about to lock up, get out the cards, when Jack staggers in with something sticking out of his cheek. The state of him, a fuzzy-wuzzy from Bongo-bongo land! Like he's bunked off from Stan Baker's *Zulu.* 'Sausage casings, you cunts? I'll fill your fucking sausage casings.'

He's got a bin-bag stuffed with cash-money. He tips it over the bar. 'Enough for you, Bennie, you mouthy cunt? Get 'em in, 'Arry. You gone mutton like the fucking yid?' And he pulls a shotgun out from under his jacket and blasts the ceiling. Plaster fallout dropping in their drinks the rest of the afternoon. They pissed theirselves, the way Jack told it. He gone over the road to the betting shop, in the backroom, straightened the manager, says he's collecting for the Twins. Puts them in for it. On his way through one of the kids who's supposed to be minding the float has a pop at Jack. Don't know him, never seen him before. He ain't got a tool, so he sticks a biro in Jack's boat. Like a fucking porcupine. Blood and blue ink spouting together. A Glasgow kiss done the kid's nose. He's on the deck whimpering. Jack's emptying the till, walks out with the guvnor's blunderbuss.

By the time Tone steers him down Highbury, Jack's choice, he's got a black ring on his cheek, like some quack's tried to mark up the exit wound. His shirt is decorated with phlegm, spew, and five kinds of blood, one of them his own. There's a cocktail of booze soaked into his sports coat. He never wears no tie, but somewhere that afternoon he's picked up two of the cunts. He's sweating like a stallion. All the acid, the waste he won't piss away. He's hot for it. The speed's slowing down and the vodka's got a clear run into his rage centres. Red eyes? No pupil left. Burning coals. He's as twisted as a cyclone. Ready to unwind.

When the old crow, she's drunker than Jack, falls on the stage, the gaff goes quiet. No one wants to give the first catcall. It would be like mocking the dead. She's your best mate's mum, more wrinkles than Club Row. Yellow toothed sheep dressed as fucking rack of lamb. Half of Shirley Bassey's dress riding around her lard arse, mascara wasted like the close of Judy Garland's final performance. She's got her arm around the mike to keep herself up. When she detaches it, the red faced labouring men don't know where to look. You'd think she's made a grab for a dildo. It's a treat for a queeny audience, a drama diva coming apart at the seams. But they've got the wrong crowd in. A couple of murdered torch songs get a ripple of applause, then she goes for the big saccharine close. *Old Shep*. Dead Elvis. Saint Elvis. A dog song. Arthritic knuckles knot around pint pots. Rosary beads are juggled like gallstones. Mildewed sleeves mop up the tears. The boiler's old man is up on his toes, he's off out of it. He'll take Lew Grade's starvation wages. Any drudgery is better than this. He'd rather sit through a millennia of Shirley MacLaine's rebirthing experiences.

Gobsmacked, Tone watched the curds oozing out of the side of Jack's mouth. Meltdown. It was a race with the froth climaxing on the bottle in his fist. The instant before he threw it. Into the band. It missed the singer. She was too far gone to notice. Blinded by a landslip of eye shadow, ill-fitting and mismatched contact lenses. Jack lobbed an empty. They were geriatrics, the musicians. Darby and

Joan, bar mitzvah occasionals. Ruffed-shirt and pacemaker. Dentures clacking against brass. A drummer who chased the beat like an old flame. They didn't want trouble. They downed tools and left her to it. An a cappella nightmare, glass scratching slate. Circumcision of the throat. Vocal chords tight as a ligature. Autoerotic self-strangulation. Dying and coming. The wet squeak of a fork puncturing a rubber chicken.

Jack picked up a metal ashtray. It caught the side of her head. She swayed, tried to remember where she was, fell from the stage. Her shoulder straps gave up the unequal struggle. All of her, scented, hysterical, in and out of her spangles, cascaded on to the lap of a righteous Kerryman. Twelve stone of unrequired lap dancer, Old Shep's shaggy corpse not yet cold in her arms.

The micks have tried to give the old toilet a bit of class for the evening, candles in bottles, a bunch of weeds in a vase, if you're lucky. Jack marched over to the bird and pulled her up, brushed her down. Tried to pour meadowsweets and water into her bosom. All that whalebone and talcum powder. Had his arm in, right to the elbow, before the paddies landed on his back. They couldn't untangle them, a marriage consummated in the black museum.

The Bubble made a strategic withdrawal, went for the motor. Took the plastic sheeting out of the boot and covered the seats. Jack was a mess when they tired of it, the punishment beating. Their clumsy homage to a great trooper. There'd be more home-knitting when Jack got indoors, when his old woman copped hold of what was left of him. He'd be up half the night with a needle sewing his face together. When the Colonel hears about this turnout, he'll shit hisself. An embolism on the spot. Two rules Ron lives by: respect for others and the sanctity of showbiz. What would he make of Jack, flies open, elbows on the formica, shouting for his old woman to get the breakfast on the table? Three-thirty in the morning and he wants the full fucking fry. How could the Colonel repair the damage? A star who has touched the gloved hand of Princess Margaret as good as raped on the floor of a club under his benevolent protection. Diabolical liberty don't begin to cover it.

*

Hessell Street. Take my word for it, you don't want to go down there. Nothing to work with but a name you can't put a face to. Norton. Notron. Not Ron. When the Bubble's nervous, he runs words backwards. Can't hardly speak fucking English in the first place. His old man's been over here since the war and he ain't never got out of the kebab kitchen. A drink of a Christmas morning in the Belgrave Arms, that's the length of it. Not Ron. Tone's got a bad feeling about this one, a geezer defined by his negative capabilities. Ron's antibody. Naked, scrotum-tightening terror's better than a course in the Open

University. He's thinking thoughts so occult you could classify them as philosophy.

Jack's nodded off, dreaming of being asleep. Dreaming of shunting a Jag down Hessell Street, a place he would never go as a mortal soul. 'Like Tangier down there,' he muttered. 'Like the fucking bazaar. Ali Baba land. Food you wouldn't feed your arsehole. We're the cunts. The Colonel's got us in a fucking Punch and Judy show, Tone.'

Amazon Street, a poxy tributary. Hard to believe a white man would live here. Who said Norton was *white*? Who said Norton exists? There's no record of him. The Colonel's got them chasing shadows. He's decoyed them into bandit country. Each street, each stinking alley, worse than the last. Jack jumps out of the motor, up the steps, into a shop that's more like a cave, a hole in the wall. Flies blanketing pinky blue meat. Bringing flesh lumps back to life. A wool of buzzing noise. 'Oi, Sabu. Know where find Norton? Savvy?' He pelts the old man with green tomatoes. He tips out sacks of bright spices, overturns golden yellow heaps – as if Norton should be there, squatting behind the rice barrier.

Norton. He could be any fucking shape or size, any age. You'd never go on Ron's powers of description. The Colonel thought of Eric the Horse from Walthamstow, when he was properly cased-up, as having looks 'synonymous' with Gary Cooper. And this a geezer what can't hardly get his chin on the bar, more arm than a spider, ears like dinner plates, two hairs fighting it out on the top of his head, and a hooter flatter than the fucking fens. Call him Lon Chaney and you'd be flattering him. Ron could never see the man behind the tailoring.

'We've knocked out the drinking money, let's fuck off out of it.' Jack folded his arms, shut his eyes, let the Bubble graft an exit. It was one of those days when the clouds had poodled into each other, no sky worth speaking of, a tin lid on the city. You're sweating inside a poxy tent. That and the stink of alien vegetables, cat piss, cardamon. Tone was claustrophobic, agoraphobic. The lot. That afternoon, he was allergic to life. And it showed. No fucker watching him and his face gave it away. A condemned man waiting for the fake cupboard at the back of the cell to slide away, waiting gratefully for the cloth hood.

Jack was restless. The waking dream was crap. He fancied more pills. He told Tone to cut back through Spitalfields, shoot into the Golden Heart. His fresh scars, the attempts he'd made to dig the cat gut out of his cheek, were gleaming. He looked like sunset over Willesden Junction.

*

Nobody knows Jack's old lady. Jack keeps her well out of it. She keeps out of it herself. The kids, she rules them, runs them. Jack knows his place, kitchen table, and, on occasion, out back with a football and a small red tricycle. Indoors, Jack is a benevolent clown, a familiar stranger. Jack is unbuttoned. He don't need to assert his eccentricity. He don't need to piss in his own grate. The kids tolerate Jack. A good provider, his pockets heavy with change. The old woman can have any gear she wants. 'Pick a label,' Jack says. 'For fuck's sake.' Shirley, down Hoxton, smart salt, would boost to order. She had Vi Kray turned out like Lady Onassis, like Oscar Night in Tinseltown. Shirley *lived* in Harrods, she did, closed the fur department on her own. More expensive commodities had been stuffed down her knickers than you'd fit Pakis in a sweatshop. But Jack's old woman she don't want to know. 'I can dress myself, Jack.' They understood one another, mutual distrust. Different species entirely. They rowed. She threw plates. She did him with a pan. Some nights she gave him a dig as soon as she saw him. He never lifted a hand to her. Or to her kids. She gave him language. He swallowed it. He was forever on the move, Jack. He put hisself about. Cased-up with the city. Or, as it happens, a night or two with some slag he'd been drinking with. A bint who worked down the barber's. Get hisself straight before he dipped for his key. He was human. A man. Put his hand in his pocket when he had to. Pay to have his dick sucked. Same as any other cunt. Go with toms but he never brought it home with him. Conventional. Straight as arseholes. Nothing out of the way. Front or back, no refinements. Thought the world of his family, if he had to, if they was on top of him. But he preferred the town, the liberties of east London, rain on his neck. Sooty rain through an open window. The wind whispering down his ear'ole in a speeding motor.

*

Doubling back down Pitfield Street, alongside the waste ground, Tone's guts started to give him gyp. He knew they was right behind him, up his fucking arsehole. The Bubble had the squits. Now their card had been marked, it was on them. Dirty money killing the hang of his jacket. The hunter had become the hunted. So many faces in the driving mirror, shifting shapes and expressions. And all of them his own. Man of a thousand faces. Tone couldn't find hisself, he aged and he withered. He was wax and linen. He was bone. Oil. Animal. He drew back his lips, tried to, show his teeth. Blood on them. Jack was still out of it.

Eyes closed, asleep, pretending to sleep, in the mime of it, Jack got this strange feeling about the Bubble. The pills did that to him. Paranoid ecstatic. He *knew* that the real job, the poxy oncer, the hangman's fee, was for a vanishing act. Him and the Bubble, one or the other, don't matter. One goes and the other is sorted, cops for it. A vacancy. Mated in the act of it, the butchering. One living to tell the dead man's story. A ventriloquist, mouth stuffed with clay and gravel. Look at the cunt behind the wheel. The Bubble was screwing him. There was no fucking Norton. Not Ron. Norton was another name for nothing. An alias. A nom de guerre. His mate Tone was on an earner to put him down. He was going to join the firm. On a promise. Him and his brother, that headcase Chris. Jack was on his tod in a car filled with brothers. They were coming from up west to meet the Twins.

Jack had to hold hisself back. Strangle the fucking Bubble in the motor and he's giving them what they want. Fuck that! He'll shove the crooklock down the wop's throat and hook up his lights. Jack could ride through hell in a fiery chariot. He'd walk away from it. 'Arright, Tone? Fancy a drink, son?'

You couldn't put the frighteners on Jack. Nothing to frighten. He was a dead man. He was immortal. Turks, Bubbles, Jocks. Wasting their time. The smell of the grass in the summer meadow should have been in his nostrils, but it wasn't. Pitfield Street was the sharp edge of the world. Jack was undescribed by it. Boundaries warped. The hot stench of things cooking in sacks. Pissed mattresses smouldering by unwatched fires.

*

Jack went into Sam's place in Murray Grove like he owned the gaff. The swagger of a man so drunk he has to busk it from memory, the way one leg goes in front of the other, the elbow on the bar, the nod to the twilight punters, the ciggy lifted from an open packet. That's how the pros drink, settle theirselves for a session. On the bar next to them, packet of fags, flick lighter on top. Pint always half done, within a good swallow of the finish. 'Thanks, Jack. Just one more.' The mouthy cunts always caught out, caught sucking at an empty pot. 'Same again, fellers?'

Dressed like a scarecrow in a thunderstorm, Jack had style. He had edge. The inviolability of the dead. Salt sweat running in channels from under the brim of his graveyard trilby, an actor in a bad script. Jack was on the shelf, watching hisself, seeing how he did it. The Alice was finished. Windows boarded up. The gaff was for sale. Optimistic sale boards fixed to the side of a ruin. Dust and rat droppings. A memory hutch. A bell jar of ferns and spectral voices. Jack was a ghost in an Alzheimer's cardigan. One of those numbers with a fold over collar. Tone trailed him, nodding grimly to the faces, shooting his cuffs. The saddest living thing on the manor. Terrified that the narrative thread was about to be cut, that he'd lose it. Mute, hearing the same track forever, the rest of his days. 'Knockin' on Heaven's Door'. Jack was Tone's guide, his author. The Bubble had no other purpose. A car wash jockey. A haircut taking his whack out of a defunct coldstore. He torched warehouses while Solly and his mates, bibs and braces, were scoffing the premiums in Bloom's. He was stiff. He didn't have the backbone for treachery. 'Get them in,' Jack said, 'then check the motor.'

Sam's place had gone, no question. But Jack don't see it. There's a little mob, six or seven handed, over in the corner. Limehouse Willie, Electric Les, and the rest of the Kray furniture. Talking chairs the lot of 'em. On the blower as soon as Jack makes his entrance. "Allo Jack mate. Tone. You lost, son?' The usual patter, eyes like flint. Hoodlum priests in uniform black. Initiates of harm. Good company. Small round table top covered in bottles, beer mats, smoking ashtrays. Traders without a trade. Rabbit merchants. Bent talk. Watch the fists knot.

The Bubble sends Sam over with a tray, but he don't leave the bar. He protects his space. He watches the door. There's two entrances, two sides to this. Which accounts for Sam's popularity. The fact that nobody could find this gaff twice. Motors, ready for the off, hidden behind mounds of black bags. Too flash for bandit country, a waste of public housing, dump bins.

Vodka cola, rum and pep, Russian stout, screwdriver, Irish, gin fizz, any name in the book, any port in a storm. No Euro-sceptics here. Tray after tray. Anything except lager. Baths of it. Cellars of swill. Your choice. They won't let Jack go. One of the comedians demands Buck's Fizz. They send the bird out for fucking orange juice. Jack matches the lot of them, the pensioners of crime. They love each other to death. A pint for the potman, the sweeper, the idiot. Tanking it, Jack and his afternoon chums. The ones who will feed his pieces to the pigs, stomp him down into an industrial meat grinder, who will render his shape as boneless gristle. Mates. All pissed together.

It turns in an instant. Something on the jukebox. Jack the life and soul, gives it a kick. 'No more yoga of the night club.' Bollocks! The heavies won't wear it.

But it takes Jack's fancy. Again and again, he has Sam bung in the silver. Each time the first. The song's in Jack's head. 'No more yoga of the night club.' (Tone hangs on the other line: 'No one told me the Holy Spirit was a woman.' What the fuck does *that* mean?)

'Turn it in, Jack, for fuck's sake.' One of the faces says that the kid who sings it is a poxy minicab-driver from Bethnal Green. 'Straight up, run me out the Isle of Grain for a pony. Lovely feller.'

'What fucking singer, cunt?' There's no singer for Jack, the words are swimming in his head. He knows it's on him. He has his hand down his coat, makes like he's got a shooter. 'Piss off back to those poofs, tell them what I fucking said. Jack is immortal.'

The nutter has the whole mob lined up against the flock. He'd have done them if Tone hadn't stopped him. 'Not here, Jack. Use your head.' They don't need telling, they're out of the door, leaving the wreck of glasses on the table. Jack's shot the Colonel's wad, he's potless. They got to lose theirselves. 'Hit the box and have it out of here.' Tone's bottled it. He'll feel better in the motor, cruising as it gets dark, as the lights come on, and the citizens hide theirselves away in their tidy little hutches. You can stack 'em like egg boxes.

Jack's alone on the street. He's all for giving chase. He wants to nail the scum to a tree. 'Five minutes Tone. Toe to toe. On the cobbles.' He's going to ram them, run 'em off the road. He jumps in the Jag, hoists Tone after him. Unfinished business. He can taste the blood, aspirins crushed in ketchup, a paste of broken glass. He remembers dumping Buller Ward on the steps of the London, his boat in ribbons, seeing him walk away. He knows what Ron's like when the vulture pecks his shoulder. Finish it now. There won't be another chance.

Tone reverses out into the road, going backwards faster than yesterday, when the wheels come off. That bastard Willie has loosened the bolts. The engine's roaring and they've done the suspension. They're skidding to nowhere, the wheels running east ahead of them. Jack is pissing hisself. It's the funniest thing that's happened to him in hours. He goes back into the Alice to celebrate.

*

The Holy Spirit a woman. It plays on the Bubble's mind. Now there's a bitch's face in the mirror strip. Lipstick on his drawn lips. Eyeshadow. He's quite tasty as it happens. Tone is a bird. He's wearing a kind of blue hood. He'd fancy himself if his bollocks hadn't shrunk to the size of frozen peas. If Jack didn't have an arm around his neck. 'No more yoga of the night club.' Jack was trying to sing. 'Remember that slapper, Tone, up Highbury? She had a voice. Like a fucking siren.'

Jack was going. Under the river. White tiles in the headlight beams. All that tonnage of water above him. He can't swim, he floats. What if it's not just the Bubble? What if, inside Jack's white shirt, there nestles a pair of firm alabaster breasts? The urge to stop and look, to touch with his hand, is almost irresistible. Just as crossing water is a kind of death, so travel, in the sealed safety of a motor, is an unsexing, an invitation. You can jump gender, abdicate or assume any sexuality you choose. Eyes shut, drifting. Jack has a woman's soul. The Jag is female. It runs on spirit. Listen to the valves, the pistons, petrol burning in pleasurable agony. Jack is being driven off the edge of the world, down the length and mystery of Sheppey, the Isle of Grain, Medway's ruined military detritus. A choirboy, cheek smooth as blossom, at the wheel. Jack's angel. Jack is the message not the messenger. Flesh cold as mutton. Sheep grazing harmlessly under the curve of the bridge. Jack waking up dead in a meadow. All the city grassed over. Trees breaking the concrete. Alder, birch, chestnut and oak. Whispers on telephones. Wind in the wire. River the colour of his dead father's greatcoat. Sweating in the kitchen. Skillets and side orders of hash. Sunnyside up. Another half, a chaser in a shot glass. Fire in the blood. Headlights making the eyes of the flock shine red. A bottle of cold, clear Russian spirit. Water without the recycled toxins. Yellow rust. Dying of thirst. Eager for the Bubble to piss down his throat. Jack calls the route, through the dark neck to Stoke Newington, anarchists and con artists, kike land. Black hats. March in, down the steps. Front it out. Knives and carpets, a jukebox requiem. Yoga this, you tangerine poofs. Twist back on your own corruption.

They say, quite wrongly, he tried to do a header through the window. It was the rush, the expulsion of animus. Hate giving itself up. Event pursuing elegy. The posthumous shatter of glass reassembling itself. Spirit disembodied. Language jacking it in.

*

Plenty of times Jack had the tights over his face. Domestics. The old woman accompanying him across the pavement. Polished stock of a sawn-off shotgun pressing in his lap. Face not his face, too much his own. Deformed into himself, a tribalised nose. Coming up from the junction, Jack pulls a silk stocking over his head. The rasp of denier. *Dernier cri* smearing his hooter, dividing him. Head too big for the hole, fearful of breeching it. Hat on top. What a sight! What a frightener! Down Kingsland High Street, the mouth of the market. Dead now, rubbish trucks sweeping the syrups, the peels, the pulped exotics. Darkies hassling bagels. Jack loved the smell of fresh white bread baking in the quiet night. Oven sweat. The rush of cabbies calling for cream cheese and salmon scrapings.

He made the Bubble pull over, before they crossed the line. Off limits: Sandringham Road, east towards Amhurst. One of those quiet backwaters. He unbuckled his belt, put an arm around his driver's neck, forced him down. The Bubble was a Mediterranean, a towelhead to all intents and purposes. He'd been inside, knew the score. He could fifty-eight his passenger. He could swallow him. 'Gobble it, you Greek poof.'

Inside, after the first ten years you die. You can't do it. You don't want to. The pictures on the wall are pure decoration. Before that it's complicated. The act itself is easy, but the consequences. You leave yourself behind, leave that place. Never returning in the same shape. Part of you goes back to the other, the punk whose activities you are directing. Imagine. Fantasise. Grey semen slipping down the bristles of your chin. Folk will remember Jack because he was murdered. In the pulse of pleasure. Unable to remember who or what he is. The story.

Tone remembers. The Bubble's hand gripping the resting wheel. All nature calm. Jack has the trousers off him, changed for his own. He has taken a fancy to the slight flaring, the matador cut on the hips.

The swirl of grey cloth over brilliantly polished slip-ons, fussy buck-les. Tone, in his turn, is stuck with Jack's dire drainpipes, wriggling and kicking to get into them. Jack's hand. 'What's favourite, Tone? In the back, you go over and I give you one? Or I have you do a brown eye?' He can feel the Bubble responding to it, the shame. Jack unde-cided which would be the greater humiliation. The way out. The Bubble's cigarette a thread of smoke, unmoving as a candle flame in a windless room.

'Put your foot down, Tone.' Up on the kerb. Light bouncing in high windows. Kept the motor beautiful, he did. On his fucking knees hoovering the fluff, emptying the ashtray, arm under the seat, shaking the carpets. A little Greek housewife. Get him a pinny and a mob-cap. Lovely. Stoke Newington Road, the old cinema, the mosque, the minimarkets, never looked better.

*

'When you go case with a bird, Tone,' Jack was saying, 'when you're on the Job, do you ever, you think about it, let it go?' Night sticky, dust particles, torn blossom on the screen. 'When you're giving her one, ain't you bothered about slipping yourself, losing out, losing your shape?' Now they're drenched with all the lights and colours of the electric garden. The lilies and lily pads of neon. Fascist fireworks. Reds and greens and yellows. Bile and pus with a fire behind it. Names reversed on the slippery glass. Jack's face painted like a tentshow savage. The Jag joins the carnival. 'I never come, Tone. You know that? Not unless I'm coming back.'

Stepping through toys slung out into the garden. He never had a dog. Need to keep the grass down. Sits, splay-legged, on the boy's tricycle. Tips his hat down over his eyes. Keep the hot light out. Jack could never stay indoors, couldn't sit unless they strapped him to a chair. At the kitchen table, pulling out the stitches. Bright scissors and the old woman's tweezers. Film reversed. He was putting hisself back together. Half an inch of cat gut and it kept coming, he needed a fisherman's reel to hold it, wind it in. Yards and yards. Stapling the skin to the bone. Or it would fall apart. He couldn't stand up. A pile of bones for the dog he didn't have.

Jack had lost it. Out of his fucking tree. The Bubble didn't know what the fuck he was talking about. Get him to the club and piss off back to Haggerston, get clear. A meet with the Mills brothers. Take the brothers to see the Twins. On the firm. A prospect. Time to get his future straight. Down Evering Road. How many times that evening? A light in the basement, shaded and red. On to the club. The Regency. They haven't eaten all day. A bit of steak, red on the side. A splash of claret. Settle the stomach.

You could smell it on the street, the testosterone. The fear. The welcome of booze asthma, smoke.

'Some bastard's dreaming me,' Jack thought. 'I can't draw breath.' It hits you at the door, the minders clocking Tone's slacks. Taking care not to catch Jack's eye. The only hat in the gaff, treats the Regency like a shul. Jack standing in a scarlet letter on the pavement, a neon R. Coming or going? Meat caught between his teeth, waiting for the Bubble to make his move. To catch up with the script. Waiting to shove a shooter down his treacherous throat.

*

As they arrived, the brother's with him in the motor, the Bubble and his Chrissy, Jack turned. Looked back. Evering Road. Where else? There was another Jag behind them, another threesome. How many does it take to re-enact a story? How many times? How many nights, how often must he tell it, lights in his face, before he gets it straight? How many recordings? How many copies of his mug shot, his famous look, each one stealing another breath from his life? Older and older. Another day above ground, deeper into death.

The Bubble was transformed. Jack looked at him, opened his eyes. The Bubble was made from wet glass. Slow glass. Light came out of him at the wrong speed. Man's blood, and hope, and human memory. The Bubble was transparent, he had no substance. The neon R was printed on him in beads of red like a giant K. He was a glass suit, the sheen of him. Hard, fast silk. Jack saw himself, his own reflection, in the Bubble. That's what he was, literally, an evanescence.

Death poured from the cups. As they slowed, pulled up outside the basement, and Jack reached for the door, geared himself for the party, he knew that he'd never again put his foot on the ground. He couldn't reach it. Some bastard had had it away with the wheels. The Jag was floating like a balloon, a windsock. The streets were moonlight canals. Jack dropped his keys in the water. The Jag, as they saw it, opening the door of Blonde Carol's gaff, had flattened into a disk. It was hovering. That's how it looked through the bubbled glass diamond. Through the panel at the top of the door. Like a chalk moon caught in a vice, pulled out of shape by malign gravity. Brought to earth.

Jack tipped forward, reaching for the keys, to fish them out, and met his own face rushing towards him. The blue-grey townscape across the dawn meadow. The wind under the bridge. The Bubble was gold light, the best spray job in the manor. He was the spit and double of Jack, the Byzantine Jack. The hologram. Jack touched him with his finger and the finger went in, leaving no impression, not breaking the chill of skin. Two Jacks. Two unlucky hands. He let it go then, let it happen.

John L Williams

Notes

This story is a kind of belated by-product of the second book I wrote – a mutant true crime thing called *Bloody Valentine*. That book started life as a novel set in the Cardiff docklands – once notorious as Tiger Bay – but ended up as non-fiction.

Bloody Valentine's nominal thrust was an investigation into the murder of a prostitute – a crime for which three black men were sentenced to life imprisonment. I had intended to fictionalise the crime but, as I found out more about it, it became obvious that a terrible miscarriage of justice had occurred. So it seemed rather more important to write a book that focussed attention on this injustice than to keep on with the fiction.

In the event the three guys were let out on appeal while I was still writing, and the book, when it eventually appeared, was threatened with a libel suit by a serving police officer. As a result the original edition was withdrawn and pulped, and a bowdlerised edition was reprinted a year later to a fairly muted reception. Which was a shame as, while I think it's a very uneven book, it's also easily the most powerful thing I've yet written.

Anyway, thinking about *Bloody Valentine* a few years on, I found it difficult to get some of the stories I came across in the research out of my head. I was particularly struck by the ordinariness of the lives of the drug dealers and prostitutes who made up part of the world I was investigating. Thus this story: the ordinary life of a Cardiff hustler.

The North Star

by John L Williams

The baby, Jamal, woke up at eight. Maria rolled over once, buried her head in the pillow and tried to ignore him but it was no good, so she fetched him from his cot and brought him into the bed with her. There was plenty of room. Bobby must have left some time in the middle of the night. Though when they'd got to bed it was already the middle of the night, couldn't have been before four.

Anyway, Jamal went back to sleep for an hour or two, so she did too, and by then it was nine o'clock and Donna was up and played with him for a couple of hours so she managed to kip on and off till eleven, which was a result. It had been a hard night.

Maria dug out a fresh pair of black jeans and a pink blouse, then rifled through last night's pockets to see how much money she had left. Forty quid. She was sure she'd taken at least a hundred yesterday. Where had it gone?

Looking at her face in the bathroom mirror, even after a good long shower, she could still trace where most of it had gone. Her eyes were bloodshot from the booze, her pupils dilated from the coke, or at least what Bobby swore blind was coke, tasted more like weak sulphate, her whole face puffy from the tranqs she'd taken to get to sleep. Fifty quid's worth of hangover, any way you looked at it.

Still, she was only twenty two, she could handle it. And she was a mother too and she could handle that, not like some people she knew.

Jamal was sitting in his high chair with a yoghurt pot in front of him and most of its contents around his mouth. Donna was watching *Richard and Judy*. She kissed Jamal and ruffled his black hair and made a cup of tea. Drank that with four paracetamols and she felt halfway human. Sitting on the sofa with Jamal on her knee watching a cooking show, she could feel a memory nagging at her. Something from last night. It wasn't something she'd done, there was none of that guilt or embarrassment lurking there, it was something good, but what?

Getting Jamal ready to go out, zipping him into his miniature puffa, she remembered. It was one of the ship boys, a German boy in from Rotterdam, in the club last night. A little bit of smuggling business he needed a hand with. Her and Bobby had looked at each other, lightbulbs popping up in bubbles on top of their heads. Both thinking the same thing, you better believe it.

Walking down Bute Street with Jamal in his pushchair she tried to recall the details but they obstinately refused to come. So half way down she stopped at the phone and called Bobby. Bobby sounded half asleep, but brightened when Maria mentioned the ship guy, and suggested they meet up at the Hayes Café in a couple of hours, when Maria had done her shopping.

So Maria carried on walking, happy to be out and about on a fine sunny May day. Stopped every couple of minutes for her mates to admire Jamal. Even the old biddies who wouldn't talk to her would stop and have a look at Jamal who was so sweet with his blue eyes and golden brown face and they could see she looked after him well. She wondered if his eyes would stay blue. He was eighteen months now so she supposed they probably would. Weird, but nice; showed there was a lot of her there.

Passing the Custom House she saw John the landlord bringing in a couple of crates of Hooch. He waved and dashed inside, came out with a lollipop for Jamal.

'Col must be proud of him, eh?'

Col was her baby's father. And he was a nice bloke, as it went, though full of all this Twelve Tribes bollocks His main contribution to Jamal's upbringing was to come round and make sure she wasn't feeding him any pork. Not that he'd been coming round much at all lately, he couldn't really handle her scene with Bobby. Rastas hated that kind of thing.

'Yeah. He thinks you're pretty safe, don't he,' she said, tickling Jamal under his chin.

'Yeah, well give him my regards, tell him to stop by if you see him.'

Oh right, she thought, running a little low on the ganja are we? Still you had to hand it to Col. He'd been going on about all this back to the land shit for years and now he was doing a nice little business with this hydroponic gear.

She carried on under the bridge, past the Golden Cross, exchanged hiya loves with one of Col's aunties and thought about going into Toys R Us for a moment. Then she pictured the mountain of toys Jamal already had that he couldn't play with yet. Still, what was the use of having some money if you couldn't spend it on your kid. So she carried on to Mothercare, bought him a couple of new outfits, went into the St David's Centre and mucked about in Boots for a while, buying some nice stuff for herself. Just had a few minutes to get a carton of cheap fags and a bit of food from the market, and it was time to meet Bobby.

The Hayes Island Snack Bar looked like an old park caff that had been accidentally dropped slap bang in the city centre. Bobby was sitting at one of the tables over near the public toilets, a cup of coffee in front of her, brazenly staring down the passers by.

'All right, girl,' said Bobby and Maria's heart leapt. She could swear it really did jump inside her as she looked at Bobby, this stocky black girl with the short locks who was the strongest person she'd ever met. Sat there in a black Adidas track suit looking for all the world like a fourteen-year-old boy, though she must be twenty-seven at least) Maria just wanted to throw herself at her. She wanted to eat her.

Bobby was her pimp.

Bobby insisted on that. 'I'm a pimp, me,' she'd say, flashing her gold tooth, 'Top pimp.'

Maria gave Bobby money.

But it wasn't like Bobby had some stable of bitches, like they say in the down in the hood movies. Bobby was Maria's girl. It's just that that's how it is when you hustle. Someone who shares their life with a hustler, they're a pimp. Maria buys a can of baked beans and gives half to Bobby. Immoral earnings. Hey, one day, Maria thought, she'd like to see someone who had some moral earnings. Colliers. Yeah right. At least with what she did you knew you were getting fucked.

And Bobby had respect. All the lesbians – Christ, she didn't like that word – the lesbian pimps on the scene had respect. The men, though, that was another story. They couldn't handle it. Couldn't handle their woman hustling. Sure they'd take the money all right, but then they'd disrespect you. It pissed her off. She knew she was fit, she knew how men looked at her before they knew, and she knew how they looked at her after. Weaklings. Not like Bobby.

Bobby picked Jamal out of his pushchair. Bobby loved Jamal, was always criticising the way Maria dealt with him. Half the time, people didn't know saw them together they'd swear Bobby was Jamal's big brother. Same colouring. Bobby never talked about her mam and dad; she'd talked about a home though. Surprise.

'You remember the guy, then, last night,' Maria said once she'd got herself a tuna sandwich and a piece of toast for Jamal.

'Yeah,' said Bobby, 'So you going to do it or what?'

The ship guy had told Maria, back in the North Star, luxuriating in the aftermath of the blow job she'd given him in the carpark, that he had a k of the good stuff, prime coke, back on the boat. But he was hinky about bringing it on shore and double hinky about who to sell it to. He was young, no more than nineteen she figured, and she could see that this was a boy jumping out of his depth and hoping he could swim. Mind the sharks boy, she felt like saying, but naturally didn't. Instead she listened to his worries about getting past the checkpoints on and off the boat, and told him it was no problem, bring a girl on and they'll turn a blind eye.

Really, he'd said. Yeah really, she'd said, been doing it long enough.

'But who am I going to deal with,' he'd asked, 'I don't know this town.' Like he knew anywhere.

'Relax,' she'd said, 'I'll bring the gear out for you, and sort you out with a deal, you just cut me a little taste,' and she'd squeezed his dick and half an hour later she'd done him again in the back of a car. When the North Star closed he was almost begging her to meet him again.

'All right,' she'd said, 'See you here, midnight tomorrow.We'll sort your little problem out.'

'Yeah', she said to Bobby, 'He'll be easy.'

Bobby laughed and contorted her face into a parody of sexual ecstacy. Jamal saw her and laughed too, shouting Bobby's name and clapping his hands together.

Coffee finished, Bobby wanted to buy some new trainers, so they trekked round Queen Street checking out the options before Bobby went for a pair of Adidas, white stripes on black to match her track-suit, in a boy's size. By then Jamal was hungry again so they dined at the sign of the Golden Arches and then headed back towards Butetown, making plans for the night ahead.

Bobby peeled off at the Custom House to play pool with the other pimps and the girls on the afternoon shift. Maria kind of missed the afternoon shift, for a start you felt less vulnerable in daylight and for seconds you really felt like you were putting one over on the poor stiffs sweating in MacDonald's, spending your afternoons drinking and shooting pool and smoking with just the odd couple of minutes behind Aspro Travel Agents to earn your wedge.

Still, it worked pretty well for her now too. She could spend all day with Jamal and just go out to work once she'd put him to bed. Donna was always there to babysit. Donna was the only girl she knew that used to pretend to be a hustler, cause it made it sound like she had a sex life. It wasn't that she was ugly really, well she was but that never had much to do with anything, you should see some of the girls out there on the beat and they did all right. It was just she was such an ignorant mouthy cunt. Still, she was good to Jamal.

Eight o'clock Jamal was asleep and Maria spent the last of her money on a cab down to the Custom House. Bobby wasn't there, must have gone back home for her tea, so Maria cadged her first can of

Breaker off Paula, a big girl from up the Valleys somewhere who was already starting to show. 'Only three months,' she said, pissed off.

Half an hour later there was still no sign of Bobby, so Maria thought fuck it and went out on the beat, Shared a spliff with a couple of girls and was just getting fed up with waiting around when a car load of Asians showed up. Normally she wasn't to keen on bulk deals but she'd never had any trouble with Asians. Bloody mainstay of the trade they were, poor geezers over from God knows where to work in some cousin's restaurant for fifty quid a week. No chance of an arranged marriage till they got their own Balti House, no wonder they came down here for a quick one.

So she bent down to the window and bargained a bit. Made a deal. For eighty quid she'd take the four of them back to the flat and do them all.

She was just doing number two when Bobby burst in in the middle of things, blue in the face, saying she needed a word.

Poor bloke inside her didn't know where to put himself so she told Bobby to fucking behave and wait outside, got number two back in the saddle and off in two minutes flat which wasn't bad going as it goes. Then she went out to the living room and found numbers one, three and four looking pissed off while Bobby gave Donna a hard time about something or other. Not keeping Jamal's toys tidy enough probably.

'Now,' said Bobby, 'I've got to talk to you now.' So Maria had a quick word with Donna, got her to do number three for a twenty quid rake off. Sent numbers one, two and four out to the chip shop, and once all the doors had closed asked Bobby what the fuck she was playing at.

'No,' said Bobby crowding her into a corner like she was a tough guy, which was comical really as Maria was a good three inches taller than her, but still, she let Bobby have her fun, 'it's what you've been playing at. Who you've been talking to.'

'What?'

'Kenny Ibadulla knows about tonight.'

'Shit.'

'So how comes, eh? How comes Kenny knows my business, you stupid slag?'

'I'm sorry Bob,' said Maria, realising what had happened and compensating by letting the tears start. She was always a great crier, Maria.

And why did she cry? Because it worked. Bobby was a pushover. She stepped back, said: 'All right, love, who did you tell?'

'Terry. Fucking Terry. Except I never told him, he was just sitting next to me and Hansi.'

'Hansi?'

'The sailor, right, and Terry was there, but I thought he was too out of it to notice what was going on and anyway I didn't think he was talking to Kenny.'

'Yeah, well, maybe this is Terry's way of getting back in the good books.'

Before they could think any more about what to do about the fact that Butetown's most serious gangster, Kenny Ibadulla, had wind of their big score, the bell rang and Maria let in the three punters who sat down and politely offered their chips around. Number three was still in with Donna, must have been a good eight minutes, which outraged Maria's professional soul, so she ate one more chip and took number four into her room and had him back out again just as number three came out of Donna's.

'Any time boys,' she said as she closed the door on the blokes. Bunged twenty to Donna and then sat down with Bobby to figure out what the hell to do next.

Quarter to twelve they went over to the North Star. No sign of Terry or Kenny, though it was unlikely Kenny would show himself. Kenny was a gangster all right but he didn't like to associate with what he saw as lowlife.

Around ten past twelve Bobby was just lighting up a spliff and Maria was dancing with one of the Barry girls to an old Chaka Khan record when Hansi the sailor came in. He was about five nine, dark haired with a rather sorry looking 'tache. He was with three other blokes from the ship, looked like they were probably German as well.

They stood in the centre of the room for a moment, eyes adjusting to the darkness, as the lighting in the North Star was something beyond low, and checking the place out. Hansi saw Maria on the dance floor and waved. Then one of his mates, a six-foot redhead, went over to Maria and the Barry girl and asked them if they wanted a drink. They both said yeah and soon they were all sat around a table drinking cans of Pils. The North Star didn't run to draught beer which was probably just as well, given the overall hygiene standards.

Bobby sat at the bar, smoking her spliff, watching them. After a while she went over to another couple of girls, Sue from Merthyr and Big Lesley, and told them the sailors were loaded and in the mood to go back to the ship for a party.

Around one everyone seemed to be having a good time and the German boys were definitely in the mood for action. So Maria led the way out of the club and, linking arms with Hansi, headed for the hulk of the Queen Of Liberia.

Out in the open it was obvious that Hansi was nervous as shit, but when Maria pulled him closer and whispered in his ear what she was going to do to him when they got to the ship he brightened up perceptibly.

As predicted there was no problem with security when they got to the ship. The watchman was out for the count, a tell-tale can of Tennants Super on his desk. On board ship they piled into an empty mess room, started passing around a bottle of Vodka one of the Germans produced and some spliff that Big Lesley had rolled up. Maria began to notice that Hansi wasn't really all that friendly with the other guys. 'Ozzie', they called him, and from the way he reacted she could tell it was a nickname and not a nice one.

So, after twenty minutes or so, she said let's go back to your cabin and it was with obvious relief that Hansi agreed.

'Some problem with your mates?' she asked, worried that they might have wind of Hansi's deal.

'No,' he said, 'They just don't like me because I'm from the East.'

'Oh right,' she said, and started rubbing the front of his jeans to get his mind back on track.

In his cabin she started taking his jeans off while detailing what she was going to do for him. Experience had told her that talking up her act in advance was just as effective and a lot easier than actually running through her bag of tricks. And so it proved with Hansi. By the time she had him in her mouth he was primed and ready. Thirty seconds later she was rinsing her mouth out in the basin and he was sitting back on his bunk looking a little crestfallen.

'Five minutes,' he said, 'Five minutes and we go again, yes?' At his age, she thought, he probably wasn't joking, time to get things moving on.

'Plenty of time later for that,' she said, giving his hair a quick ruffle, but if we we're going to get out of here while your mates are still busy we'd better get moving.' He nodded and stood up. She hoped to hell he was understanding everything she said.

'You wait outside,' he said and he shooed her out of the cabin. A minute later he came out too, a little black canvas bag over his shoulder.

'Let's go,' he said, and they headed back off the ship. This time there were a couple of official types standing by the watchman's office. They looked dubiously at Maria and Hansi for a moment and said something in German to Hansi but Maria started licking Hansi's ear and he did a creditable impersonation of a drunken sailor walking his girl back to shore, and after a brief hard stare one of the officer types waved them by.

Back in the North Star Bobby was waiting for them. As Maria and Hansi came in she ushered them to a table at the back where the darkness was almost total. 'Is that it?' she said, prodding the bag Hansi held clasped between his knees.

He nodded and she hefted it, testing it for weight, though Hansi never let go of the bag, Then he proffered the bag to Bobby and she dipped a finger in and took a taste from the top, which was all she could get at. Tasted good to her.

'Yeah, that'll do,' she said, 'Now how much d'you want for it?'

'Fifty thousand marks,' he said, puffing himself up a little but his eyes giving him away, nervously looking around the room, realising how little control he had over the situation.

'Yeah, what's that in pounds?'

Neither Bobby nor Maria had much of a clue about exchange rates but they knew what a K of charlie went for and when Hansi came back with, 'Twenty thousand,' after thinking for a moment Bobby almost found herself nodding.

'Fuck off,' she said. 'Five grand tops.'

'OK,' said Hansi, smiling now.

'Half an hour,' said Bobby, 'You stay here with Maria, I'll be back with the money.

Forty minutes later Bobby was back, ten grand in her jacket after a rendezvous with Mikey Thompson, Kenny's only serious rival. Mikey had practically jumped at the deal when she'd set it up that afternoon. Turn it into rocks and he'd be doing some serious business.

'Hansi,' she said, 'Fucker beat me down to four grand.' And she started discreetly counting out the money.

Hansi suddenly looked harder and older than before. A lock knife appeared below table height jabbing into Maria's leg.

'You want me to cut your girlfriend here? By this artery?' he said, 'Or you want to pay me my money?

'Christ,' said Bobby, 'Calm down, mate. Only trying it on.' And she kept on counting till she got to four grand then dipped her hand into her pocket and pulled out another wedge. 'Here's your five grand, like I said.'

Hansi had the money inside his leather jacket before Bobby had time to blink. He stood up, the knife still held inside his sleeve, bowed slightly to Maria and a moment later he was gone.

'Shit,' said Maria.

'Don't worry, girl,' said Bobby, and leaned closer to her and told her how much money they'd cleared.

Maria said nothing for a moment, just thought about the changes five grand could make to her life. 'C'mon,' she said, 'Let's get back to the flat.'

They were almost at the flat door when they heard the footsteps behind them coming up the stairs, Maria had the door open and Bobby was half through it when, for the second time in ten minutes Maria felt a knife pressing against her flesh. It was Mikey Thompson holding the knife and neither he nor his two associates looked too well pleased with life.

Bobby and Maria were bundled into the flat. Mikey made them sit next to each other on the couch and then got right down in Bobby's face. 'What the fuck,' he said, 'What the fuck d'you think you're doing trying to rip me off like that.'

'What?' said Bobby.

'That kilo of crap you sold me. Coke on the top; fuck knows what underneath. I wants my money back, girl.'

'Shit,' said Bobby, looking at Maria.

Maria shook her head in genuine disbelief. She really couldn't credit that Hansi had had it in him to pull off a stunt like this. No wonder he'd looked nervous.

'So where's my money?' said Mikey.

'Mike,' said Bobby, 'It's not our deal. It's this fuckin' sailor. He's the one who's ripped you off.'

'I don't think so, Bob,' said Mikey, 'I don't think it was no sailor came round my house, told me she had a kilo of gear. It wasn't no sailor took my ten grand.' He paused for a moment and stared at Bobby, 'And I'll bet it wasn't no sailor got the ten grand either. How much you holding, Bob?'

Bobby considered holding out for about a millisecond. Then she sighed and said, 'I've got five Mikey, take that and we'll get you the other five back. Just let go of us, right.'

Mikey walked over, took the five grand from Bobby's pocket.

'Yeah, you'll pay it back all right but first you're going to have to learn a lesson.'

'Not here,' said Maria, the first thing she'd said since things went to hell. 'My boy's sleeping. Not here.'

Mikey nodded, 'All right, I knows just the place.'

Mikey led the way down the stairs, Bobby and Maria following, Mikey's guys right behind them.

They were just in the lobby at the bottom of the stairs when a voice said, 'Mikey.'

Mikey whirled round to see Kenny Ibadulla and Terry and another bloke standing there, Kenny pointing a gun at Mikey's stomach. And everyone started talking at once. Five minutes later everyone had some idea what the situation was, and it was clear that it was up to Kenny, as the man with the gun, to dictate what happened next.

'Mikey,' he said, 'You fuck off out of this. You want to be some big time dealer, boy, you does it somewhere else. Now fuck off. You'll get your money.' And at that Mikey and his boys slunk off, doing their best to look like it was their own decision.

Then Kenny turned to Bobby and Maria. 'Now Bob,' he said, 'I got to pay that fucking Mikey five grand. And you know what that means?'

Bobby nodded.

'Right, that means you owe me five grand. And how are you going to get that for me? Your girlfriend going to make it for me? Lying on her back? Or you got some better idea?'

'The ship guy,' Bobby said.

'Right,' said Kenny, 'The ship guy. He's the one to blame, inne? But he's not my problem.' By now Kenny was virtually standing on top of Bobby, letting his size and weight work for him. Then he turned and pulled back, 'You've got till daylight. You haven't got my five grand back by then, you'll be working for me.'

And so Kenny and his boys left and Maria and Bobby sat together on the stairs for a moment, holding each other and shaking. Maria thought she was going to hyperventilate for a moment. The prospect of owing Kenny Ibadulla didn't bear thinking about. Christ knows what the interest payment on five grand would be – a hundred a week at least. Working for herself and Bobby and Jamal was one thing, working for that arrogant fuckhead something else entirely, specially as he most likely wouldn't pay Mikey the money anyway. 'Shit. Shit. Shit,' she said. Then she had an idea.

'C'mon,' she said to Bobby, 'We've got to get back to the North Star.'

It was four o'clock, closing time in the North Star; but luck was with Maria when a couple of sailors came out with Lorna, one of the Barry girls. It was no trouble for Maria to join the party, and ten minutes later she was back on board the ship. Five minutes of wrestling in another messroom with a drunken sailor and she was able to beg off to find a toilet. Ten more minutes of floundering around the ship and she found Hansi's cabin. Took a deep breath and knocked.

He looked horrified at first but Maria pretended not to notice and stuck to her script like the trouper she was. 'Hansi baby, I've come back to celebrate, I would have come straight back with you but I had to dump that dike Bobby.' And before his brain could start functioning, she carried straight on into, 'Hansi I need you inside me,' and started pulling his clothes off.

And it worked. He let her. He let himself believe that he was such a slick piece of work that he could screw the girl over the deal and still screw her all night long with no come-back. Just sail away in the morning.

She had to fuck him twice but the second time she got her result. He fell asleep. It didn't take long to search the cabin. First thing she found was a washbag that weighed far too much. Inside it was another kilo of white stuff. God alone knew whether this one was real or fake but she scooped it up anyway and a moment later she found the five grand stuffed in a sock.

Bobby was waiting for her when she came off the boat. The

watchman waved her by and when she got to Bobby she just
collapsed in her arms. Bobby wrinkled her nose for a moment at the
smell of her, but never let go.

Six-thirty a.m. Bobby knocked on Kenny's door. Woke his wife
up, who shouted abuse out the window, but then Kenny came to the
door and let her in. She handed him the coke, Kenny tasted it, from
the top, the bottom and the middle, nodded and told Bobby she was
cool.

'And what about Mikey?' said Bobby.

Kenny laughed, said, 'Mikey's my problem. Be cool.'

Coke talking, thought Bobby. Everyone's a superman with coke.
And walked back up to Maria's place.

Twelve noon, Bobby, Maria and Jamal got out out of the cab at
Cardiff Airport and checked in for the flight to Tenerife.

Two weeks later they came back.

Week after that Maria was back outside the Custom House and
Bobby was playing pool inside. You know what they say – you have
to hustle in this life.

Maxim Jakubowski

Notes

If you are interested in my views on crime and mystery fiction, the state of the economy and the precise nature of the sex of angels, I refer you to the first volume of *Fresh Blood*, where I ruminated on these subjects in the introduction to my story, 'Blood and Guts, Goodge Street'. Time has passed, but I find I have little to add.

Almost two years, in which the flourishing of British *noir* has continued as expected, but every new voice to hit print is nonetheless a reason for joy. As that man Ellroy says, 'Crime Fiction Rules, OK?'

Two years in which I have accelerated my own return to the art of fiction into fourth gear, with a collection of awkwardly sexual stories which often made for strange companions with their occasionally criminal theme (*Life In The World Of Women*) and my road movie novel, *It's You That I Want To Kiss*, an explicit thriller which saw me being headlined as the King of the Erotic Thriller (or the Wild Frontier) – you takes your choice.

'Femme Fatale Blues' came about while I was gasping for air when writing my next contribution to the Mystery Hall of Shame, a dark tale in which I hoped to combine my love of Cornell Woolrich coincidence and doomed characters with the easy-going amorality of the old Gold Medal novels. Guess why the lady is called Cornelia? At any rate, I needed a breather and came up with this solo adventure for Miss C, also a character in the book. Of course, when it comes from my word processor there is the obligatory death and darkness, but I also see it as a light-hearted *vignette*, with a rather distinctive character. And by my standards, it even has a happy ending, and less than usual rude words and situations.

I have this feeling Cornelia might well survive *Because She Thought She Loved Me* (now available from your favourite bookshop) and become my first serial character.

Enjoy her first appearance on stage.

Take my word for it: she's a fantastic dancer.

Femme Fatale Blues

by Maxim Jakubowski

She danced.

Oh, how she danced.

Bumps and grinds in harmony with REM's 'The Wake-Up Bomb'.

It was the late afternoon shift and the audience was sparse. The suits hadn't yet left their offices, when they'd have just an hour to spare before catching their commuter trains to New Jersey or Connecticut, time enough to down enough alcoholic energy before they had to confront their home life again. Time enough to ogle flesh that was firmer and warmer than the merchandise back in the old homestead.

As she moved, she surveyed the seated spectacle. A few identikit Japanese tourists in assorted grey colours, a bunch of sniggering nerds pretending to each other that sex was not the reason they were there, oh yeah, a couple of serious drinkers who paid little attention to her gyrations on the stage, a kid who must surely be under-age, nursing a beer, hypnotised by her nudity, some regulars.

She knew already which would tip well and those who would feign embarrassment when the song ended and she moved towards them to solicit the obligatory donation, the crumpled dirty green dollar bills she would slip under the red garter on her left thigh, before she would move on to the final song in her set and take the G-string off. Which was, of course, the only thing that interested them.

Lefty the Kleptomaniac visited the joint every week on the same day. He always gave her a ten dollar bill. A generous soul, or else a deep connoisseur of genital anatomy. He had acquired his sobriquet because he invariably pocketed as many of the complimentary match books the club scattered across the tables and the bar. No problem, they just charged him a few bucks more for his drinks.

'Hi, Lefty,' Cornelia said as the music momentarily ended and she bent down towards him. He obliged with a ten. Never said a word.

She moved on to the other punters and, as half expected, only reaped a meagre harvest of cash.

It made no difference. The rules of the game were that you still had to show pussy. Even when the bastards were mean tippers.

She winked at Ade the Film Freak, the big, bulky barman and bouncer, and he pressed the the start button on the CD player to trigger the final song in her sequence.

He was OK; spent all his free time at the movies. Never missed a single new release. Always wanted to know your opinion, if you had seen any of them. His own views were not very critical, but he just loved the conversation. Read all the magazines.

He had once told her she looked like Nicole Kidman.

She didn't see it, personally, but if it made him happy it was just fine with her. If the drinkers appreciated the way her body moved, the uncommon creamy pallor of her skin and the way her sex lips widened moistly apart when she did her act-closing flip and backstand to reveal the pinkness of her insides, it was just dandy with Cornelia.

It was just a job, after all.

Unlike the scherzo-andante-scherzo of a symphony, the punctuation of a good strip act is quick-quick-slow; movement in the final part should be limited, not too frantic. To allow the spectators a good view of her intimate geography. That's what they paid for.

Her music began and she straightened up.

Sarah McLachlan's *Fumbling Towards Ecstasy*.

A long time ago, Cornelia had learned never to look the men in the eyes as she danced on stage. This way she could retain her power over them. Pretend she was manipulating them. Imagine she was maybe on her own.

She just loved dancing so.

As a child she would spend hours twirling in front of her bedroom mirror until she felt dizzy. Later, as a teenager, she would do so naked, feeling the excitement rise slowly through her body until her face was flushed with forbidden pleasure.

She closed her eyes as the music surged.

A quarter turn. Slow. Kicked off the until-now obligatory red high-heeled shoes. Someone in the audience whooped and yelled in anticipation. Cornelia smiled. She knew she was tall enough without heels.

Her legs were undeniably her best feature.

Her fingers moved under the G-string's elastic and she pulled quickly until the velcro snapped as planned. As the flimsy piece of material floated to the floor of the stage, she shyly placed her hands in front of her, denying the voyeurs facing her the sight of what they really wanted.

That morning she had severely trimmed her pubes, and was more naked than usual. Club rules. Which she didn't appreciate. She liked

the way her public hair curled and curled when left to grow naturally. Loved to play with the curls. But the more hirsute you were, the
less there was for the punters to see. Rules of the house.

As her hands moved away from her groin, Cornelia essayed a
mock ballet step and raised her right leg to a brief but impossible
angle, revealing her cunt in all its splendour. The men were now
totally silent, the seductive music filled the air in the low-ceilinged
room. She tip-toed, she jigged, she quivered, she danced with all the
slowness of a princess royal, her long body sliding across the small
stage, followed by a shroud of blinding light. Her movements allied
themselves with the sensuous Arab-like drone of the song's melody
as the waves carried her in their multi-voiced embrace.

Lost in her own world, oh how Cornelia danced!

She glided over to a stool and lowered herself onto it, the small of
her back supporting the weight of her whole body, leaning back and
gently forcing her legs wide, scissoring her legs open and closed and
open again, every time feeling the conjugated stares of all the men
present on her unveiled delta.

She moved off the stool. Turned towards it, bent over, placing her
breasts on the seat, and slowly began to widen further the angle
between her legs.

A few dollar bills fluttered on to the stage.

From the Japanese contingent.

The angle of revelation increased; the men peered freely at the soft
pinkness of her inner corridor and the star-like conic depression of
her anus. Nothing was private. Everything was for sale.

Cornelia, utterly spread-open and on full display, was lost in her
thoughts.

The final harmonies of the song intruded on her consciousness
and she quickly resumed her routine, a shimmer here, another set of
splits there, the backward flip for the whole gynaecological vista,
another bump-and-grind and a quick bow as the record ended.
Picked up the dollars and moved off the stage. The Japanese were
still heartily applauding and jabbering between themselves.

She was now in the changing room, her robe still half open when
Ade the Film Freak put his nose around the corner.

'One of them is offering fifty for a lap dance,' he told her.

'You know I don't do private dances, Ade,' Cornelia answered
distractedly.

'I know,' he answered, with a sigh. 'You could make a fortune,
you know, you get more requests than a lot of the other girls.'

Cornelia knew that. She may not be as obviously sexy as the other
strippers at the club, but there was something about the way she
surrendered to the dance that made men hard in the places that ruled
reason or the lack of it.

'It's still no, Ade.'

He moved back to the club.

Some whores won't kiss; Cornelia didn't do lap dances.

She was taking a shower, scrubbing herself thoroughly, washing away all the abundant sweat with rose-flavoured soap and jets of lukewarm water. Angie, who started off the evening shift, shuffled into the next, narrow shower cubicle.

'Hi, Cornie,' she said. 'I just don't believe you turning down all that easy cash.'

'I don't need it, Angie,' Cornelia answered, switching the water off on her side of the glass partition.

'Everybody needs money,' the other stripper pointed out.

'It's just a means to an end,' Cornelia said, wrapping a towel around her midriff.

'What?' Angie said. 'I just don't understand you. This lap dance lark is a cinch. Rub against them long enough for them to come in their trousers. It's painless. Safe. Clean. In the old Times Square days we had to supplement the cash in the peep shows, where the bastards could cop a feel for just another dollar, slipping their dirty fingers inside you, scratching your tits or worse. I really hated all that, you know...'

But Cornelia, who had heard it all before, was already back in the dressing room, slipping into her white Calvin Klein jeans and short-sleeved black X-Girl T-shirt. Her customary New York summer uniform. She might be a stripper, she knew, but she didn't have to dress like one.

'And it's a first edition, not the later hardback reprint they brought out following the movie?'

'Definitely,' the sales guy at the antiquarian bookshop assured her.

'Great,' Cornelia said.

'O'Brien signed it shortly before his death. There aren't many around, you know,' he said.

'I really love that book,' Cornelia remarked. 'How much?'

'Two thousand dollars.'

'That's quite a lot for a modern first,' she remarked.

'It doesn't come up that often. In perfect condition. Signed.'

'I realise,' Cornelia answered. 'When will you have it?'

'In a week or so,' the salesman said. 'Our West Coast store only acquired it a few days ago. Part of a large collection bought from the estate of some Hollywood honcho.'

'I see.'

'When I saw the book on their inventory, I knew I should drop you a line. It was on your want list.'

'It was. I have the Watermark Press reprint, of course, but this a great upgrade,' Cornelia said.

'We'll put it aside for you. To inspect. As you're a good customer, we won't require a deposit.'

'That's very kind of you.'

Two thousand bucks, she pondered as she walked down 52nd Street back towards Fifth. Forty lap dances. More, in truth: the club would probably take a hefty commission. But she didn't have to demean herself that way, she knew. The book would be evermore tainted if she obtained the cash that way. No problem.

There was a telephone in the foyer of the Ziegfeld, her favourite Manhattan movie house, with its splendid candelabra-laden foyer and deep, comfortable seats.

She inserted a handful of quarters and dialled.

The call was picked up on the sixth ring.

'Cornelia,' she stated.

'Nice to hear from you,' the basso profundo voice on the other end said.

'Any jobs going?' she enquired.

'As ever,' she was told.

'I'm game.'

'Aren't you always?' the man said. 'You freelancers, all you charming dilettantes. What is it this time? A new couture evening dress, jewellery, an overseas vacation?'

'A book,' Cornelia said truthfully.

'Charming,' he said approvingly. Amateurs like her were the best people to use. Nobody would suspect them. This woman was a real find. Six jobs already, and she had never disappointed. Reliable. Discreet. And so cheap. Professionals would want at least four or five times the amount she settled for. Calmly efficient. He kind of wondered what she looked like.

'Usual place?' Cornelia asked.

'Yes,' he confirmed.' Any time after noon tomorrow.'

'How much?'

'Standard. Two and a half.'

'Good,' she nodded as she spoke. 'I'm on.'

'We're on,' the man said and hung up.

Cornelia treated herself to the movie as she was already at the theatre. It turned out to be a mediocre summer big budget catastrophe epic. It would give her something to talk about with Big Ade. Crowds were already milling around the Hilton by the time she walked by down Sixth, a sultry summer night. One day she would leave this town. She was running out of space at her expensively-rented apartment and had no place left on the walls to fix extra bookshelves.

The following day was a Saturday and Cornelia never worked weekends at the club, even though the pay was better. The people there just didn't understand her needs, she reckoned. Soon, she might have to find another dancefloor to parade her wares on. Mick the Knot, who either owned the place or more likely fronted for the real proprietors was becoming too insistent on her becoming more accommodating with her liberal schedule, and looked her up and down too often with a far from hidden agenda on his mind. She didn't wish to stay there long enough to find out how he had acquired his nickname.

She slipped on her running gear, checked her Walkman batteries still had enough juice, selected a few tapes and jogged for an hour up Canal to Second and St Mark's Place and then to Union Square and back, stopping en route for a glass of freshly pressed vegetable juice at a market stall on Astor Place. Dancers had to keep in shape. She cleaned-up and dressed. Nike track suit trousers and a light brown halter top that left her midriff bare, wondering whether she should have her navel pierced. No. Too many of the girls in the clubs did it already. It was nifty, but she thought it looked somewhat vulgar. Something else, maybe?

She took the subway uptown to Lexington and 82nd. The Good Times sex emporium was on the same block as the subway exit. She walked in quite brazenly. Some of the Indian male clerks raised their eyebrows but she walked straight down to the gay section in the basement. They ignored her, she wasn't going to give any furtive male customer upstairs closely examining the explicit images on the hardcore video tape boxes the creeps. Just a woman who wanted to get her rocks off, they guessed. Some did. The row of private cabins was on the basement's right-hand side. She counted, and entered the seventh cabin. The light outside switched from green to red as Cornelia lowered the latch on the door and the cabin darkened.

They probably had monitors at the register upstairs, so she inserted a ten dollar bill, face upwards as required, into the gaping mouth of the machine, underneath the screen. The gay porn menu flashed on. Cornelia pushed a number at random. Two studs with flat top haircuts and improbable biceps were fellating each other, splayed into a difficult physical configuration so that the camera didn't miss any detail. She flicked on to the next movie. Another California standard prototype hunk here vigorously thrust about, furiously buggering another's backside in daunting close-up. All the men in these films were monstrously hung, Cornelia reflected; she'd never come across every-day men so well-endowed. She smiled quietly. Placed her hand under the hard plastic chair in which she was sitting, face to the screen. As expected, the package was sellotaped to the underneath of the chair. She pulled it loose and slipped it into her Gotham Book Mart Edward Gorey tote bag and left the cabin.

There was still over eight dollars worth of sodomy counting down in the top right corner of the screen.

Back at her apartment, she opened the thick padded envelope. Standard: the gun, a photograph, and two pages of typed data. Her clandestine employers were always very thorough. Made the job so much easier. She studied the material she had been provided with.

Yes, tonight would be as good a time as ever, she reckoned. Why delay matters? She studied the information closely. Concealed the package and its content in a safe place behind one of the bookshelves and went searching for a public telephone somewhere down in the Village. The second one she came upon on Greenwich Avenue was free and there was no one hanging around it. She inserted the coin. The number rang.

A male British-sounding voice answered.

'Hello?'

She mentioned his name.

'Yes. Speaking. Can I help you?'

'I'm calling on behalf of Callie Edwin,' Cornelia said.

'Callie…? Oh, God. How is she? Where is she? Please?'

'I don't really wish to speak on the telephone, Mister. Can we meet?'

'Yes. Of course, yes, we can. Meet…' he said, obviously shaken by her call.

'Tonight?'

'Yes, Tonight is fine. Absolutely. What time?'

'Say ten-pm,' she suggested.

'No problem,' he answered. 'Where?' he asked her.

'Do you know the Angelika Theatre, corner of Mercer and Houston, in the Village?' Cornelia suggested.

'Of course,' the British guy said. 'I've been there quite often.'

'There's a very large lobby, upstairs, with a bar…'

'Yes.'

'We meet there,' she said.

'How will I…?' he enquired.

'I know what you look like. I'll find you,' Cornelia told him. 'OK?'

'Fine, but…'

'We can talk tonight. See you.' She hung up on him.

She waited until ten-thirty. By now, the lobby was full. People exiting the early evening performance and crowds queuing for the late-night showings on all five screens. Cornelia wore grey. The most forgettable of all colours. He was standing in a corner, looking nervous, worried about her lateness. But not likely to leave, she knew.

She walked over to the middle-aged guy she had recognised from the photograph. Dark lines surrounded his eyes. He was wearing a lightweight cream-coloured cotton suit and a black silk shirt, open at the neck. Dark brown thick-heeled loafers clashed with his clothes.

'Hello,' Cornelia said.

'It's you?'

'Yes.'

'Who are you? Where is Callie?'

'Later,' she humoured him gently. 'We have all the time in the world to talk,' she added, to put him at ease.

'I suppose so,' the English guy said.

'Come,' Cornelia suggested, touching his arm. 'Let's go somewhere else. I didn't realise it would be so crowded here.'

'Fine,' he agreed.

'Let's walk,' she suggested.

They meandered towards Lafayette, down the Bowery, towards Alphabet City. There were fewer and fewer other passers-by as they moved on at a leisurely pace. Every time he tried to start a conversation, she suggested they wait until later. He complied reluctantly, visibly impatient for news of the errant Callie. Their story would have been interesting, Cornelia knew, but she was aware it was better not to know too much. It was just a job.

Finally, they reached a pool of darkness near the crumbling porch of a derelict building.

'Here,' she said.

He stopped in his tracks and faced Cornelia.

'Here?'

'Yes,' she confirmed.

He looked at her questioningly.

'Callie's sent me. I have a very special message from her.'

'Tell me,' the man said impatiently, a look of hope spreading across his features.

Cornelia quietly pulled the gun from her Gucci handbag.

His eyes froze. But he didn't run. As if he knew he wouldn't stand a chance, anyway.

'So this is it?' he asked.

'Yes,' Cornelia said. 'Callie wants you dead.'

She clicked the safety-catch off.

'I suppose it doesn't really surprise me,' the English guy said with quiet resignation.

Cornelia's gun was equipped with a silencer.

She shot him twice in the heart, and as he slumped mournfully to the ground, she finished him off with a third bullet above his eyes. His body disappeared in the shadows of the deserted street as Cornelia swiftly walked away without a backward glance.

When she reached Houston again, she hailed a yellow cab and had herself dropped off near the Javits Centre. From here, she walked to the edge of the water and disposed of the gun. All according to plan. She caught another cab home near Gramercy Park. By the time she unlocked her front door, it was barely midnight.

On Sunday, she rested.

Packed some bagels from the corner deli and, wearing a large floppy outsize Panama hat to protect her skin, sprawled out in the grass in Central Park and spent the afternoon reading. A paperback. Her first edition of the same book was too valuable to actually read.

She knew the two thousand dollars for the elimination job would follow promptly, reaching her PO Box on Monday or Tuesday in used denominations. It was nice, even after paying the antiquarian dealers' exorbitant price, she would still have an extra five hundred. She decided she would treat herself to something special this time. Money was there to be spent, not worried about.

Her shift at the strip club didn't begin until five in the afternoon on Mondays. It was always a quiet day with few punters, and even worse tippers. Men's generosity was wiped out following the weekend. Still, it meant she could dance quietly, enjoy the way her lithe body moved around the floor and the stage lights shimmered against her unveiled skin.

She thought again of piercing her navel.

No.

Maybe some sort of piece of jewellery there. Like an Indian belly-dancer. Not really her style, she felt.

She left the apartment an hour earlier than usual. Strolled along the busy Village Streets, zigzagging her way towards the club in no particular hurry, checking out the windows and the fashions. In Christopher Street, a sign caught her attention. She walked into the cluttered store.

'I want a tattoo,' she resolutely told the squat, bearded biker-like attendant.

'Easy, lady,' he said. 'That's what we do. Where?'

'Somewhere rather private,' Cornelia said, holding his stare.

'No problem. It's a house speciality. We've seen all sorts,' he added.

He waved her through to the back of the store and indicated a black leather dentist's chair.

Cornelia smiled.

'So, lady, where do you want it. Your butt, your tit, your pussy?' he asked her.

'Pussy,' Cornelia said, although she hated the word.

He pulled a large scroll of paper from a nearby table and handed it over to her.

'A rose is our most popular request. But we can do names, Saints, birds, leaves, any sort of decoration. Take your pick.'

Cornelia looked down at the selection of gaudy illustrations.

The parlour even had skulls, bones and daggers.

'Yes,' she said. 'I see there is one.'

She pointed to the image of a gun.

The large tattooist raised his bushy eyebrows.

'Are you sure? We've only ever done that one on arms.'

'That's the one I really want,' Cornelia indicated.

He sighed.

'One hundred bucks,' he said.

'Fine,' Cornelia said, slipping out of her jeans and panties and moving towards the dark chair.

'It's your hard-earned money,' the big man said, no doubt thinking that students these days did the weirdest things.

'You said it,' Cornelia confirmed, and she opened her legs wide.

Christine Green

Notes

To comment on the state of British crime fiction is a tall order, especially from a writer who rarely reads any. If I read the best I get depressed and if I read the dull, I start but don't finish. It's the reading public who help to shape the trends and the trend seems to be as ever, a mixture of realism and the more traditional. Some of the smaller bookshops stock inordinate numbers of works by dead crime authors and I presume there are still buyers.

For me the fascination of crime fiction are the insights into human behaviour, the 'whys' but not necessarily the 'hows'. The detection of crime is fascinating but the motive remains my prime source of interest plus the desire to understand how events and small acts of violence or selfishness lead to crime and even murder.

My story, 'A Little Peccadillo' is, I suppose, a reflection of my sympathy for all the quirky people. People who are not usually violent but who are so affected by events in their lives that violence becomes a way out, a source of salvation. And that, of course, could be any one of us.

Perhaps that is why crime fiction endures – it tells us more about the human condition in extreme situations and it helps us evaluate not only our crime solving abilities but allows us to vicariously share experiences usually and thankfully denied us.

What more could one genre offer?

A Little Peccadillo

by Christine Green

Graham knew, that Thursday night, his life was about to change.

All day he'd felt a mild anxiety, noticed a gnawing pain in his stomach that could have been hunger but wasn't. Even his office colleagues commented. 'Are you OK, Graham?' asked Anne who sat opposite him. He nodded absently. The office manager, Donald, had peered at Graham over the top of his spectacles, 'I hope you're not going down with the flu.' It was almost an accusation. Graham muttered, 'I'm fine,' as he contrived to look busy by moving papers from one pile to another in a purposeful way. The last two hours of the working day passed by as slowly as a hearse on black ice. Not that Graham felt his usual sense of release as he left the office, he'd felt more anxious than ever and as he drove home he'd had to make a conscious effort not to think about the evening ahead.

The house, in its cul-de-sac cocoon, unlit inside and with bushes and tall conifers standing like shadowy guards outside, seemed to Graham suddenly sinister. The wintery darkness and pale orange light from the one street light contributed to the atmosphere and he'd experienced a fleeting desire to turn the car around and drive away. Where to? That was the one question that made him not dwell on his current desire to shrink from the main task he had set himself that evening.

Once inside he switched on the radio, made coffee and sat at the kitchen table waiting for her to arrive. His wife – Jenny. They had been married for ten years and very often it did seem a day too long. She had one love in her life, her job. Graham tried not to be envious of her success; he knew how hard she'd worked; he also knew exactly how many hours she put in. He always came home to an empty house, always cooked the evening meal, nearly always went to bed alone. The evenings had grown sterile over the years. He tried. He was a great cook but he couldn't fight the bathroom scales and his carefully-prepared meal went uneaten if she found she'd gained a pound during the day. Tonight he was on strike; he wasn't prepared to go to any trouble; he was far too anxious. Or was he excited? His stomach certainly didn't know, it felt both empty and full and he thought it better to feel slightly tense than risk feeling well fed and sleepy. He wanted that hungry edge and he didn't dare go into the dining room where a well-stocked drinks cabinet would tempt him and maybe undermine his resolve.

At the sound of her car entering the garage, Graham shuddered slightly. There was no going back now. He'd made up his mind. Tonight he would tell her.

'Hi,' she called out. 'I'm home.

He heard her go upstairs and knew she was checking her weight. Gain, lose or even the bloody same, he'd already decided she wasn't having him cook for her this evening.

'I can't smell any dinner,' she said entering the kitchen and sniffing the air. At that moment as Jenny moved her head the toss of her long blonde hair reminded Graham of a young filly sensing spring in the air.

'There isn't any.'

Jenny shrugged. 'It doesn't matter. I'm going out.'

Graham stared at his wife. 'You don't usually go out on Thursdays.'

'You don't usually *not* cook dinner.'

'We could have a takeaway.

'I'm going out,' she repeated, giving him a cold hard stare. Even with *that* look on her face, to him she was still beautiful. Like a diamond, he thought, bright and sparkling and indestructible.

'I wanted to talk to you tonight,'

'Oh for God's sake Graham, what about? I've just got time for a cup of coffee. Will it take long?'

Graham felt his resolve crumbling faster than cheese on a grater. 'Not long,' he mumbled. 'What time will you be home?'

'I don't know,' she answered irritably. 'I'm meeting Sally for drinks in the wine bar.'

'You could cancel.'

'Because you want to talk to me?' she sneered. 'Piss off.'

'Don't be such a bitch,' he said trying to keep a calm edge to his voice.

She stared at him for a moment thoughtfully, then her small mouth pouted and she blew him a kiss. 'I've had a bad day,' she said.

That was her way of apologising but Graham knew she was winning. 'You go out then but don't be back late. I'll wait up for you.'

She smiled. 'I'm impressed. It must be serious. An affair at the very least.'

He didn't answer but he was gratified to note that a flicker of anxiety crossed her face. Maybe a few hours to ponder would do her good.

'I'll make my own coffee then,' she said.

'You do that.'

She made herself a cup of instant coffee and went upstairs. Graham listened to her moving about, seeing her in his mind's eye gazing into her wardrobe at her numerous clothes deliberating about what to wear, partly to impress Sally, partly to have the pleasure of men eyeing her up and down. At that thought Graham's stomach knotted with jealousy. The drinks cabinet suddenly had a pull like gravity. He walked into the lounge and poured himself a large neat whisky.

When she came down she twirled before him in a little black dress. *The* little black dress – his favourite. She'd piled her hair high on her head, blonde tendrils framing her oval face, her eye makeup was superb, strong black eyeliner, thick mascara and, best of all, bright red lipstick. Graham guessed she was wearing stockings rather than tights and his eyes rested longingly on her slim ankles above her highest, sexiest black court shoes. Graham resisted the desire to check if she was wearing stockings and instead said, 'You look fantastic.'

She smiled smugly, 'Down boy, I'll see you later.'

Graham wasn't sure if that comment was truly suggestive or her just teasing him. Lately their sex life had been noticeable only by its absence. The bitch was, of course, having an affair.

He watched her leave and then poured himself another large whisky, this time mixed with soda, he didn't want to be paralytic by the time she returned.

Stretching out on the sofa he flicked through the television channels for a programme to divert his mind from Jenny but he couldn't concentrate and after a few minutes he switched off and decided instead to listen to music. After several tracks of a Mozart CD he reverted to silence and thoughts of Jenny. They had been married for ten years but he'd known her for twenty. They'd been sixteen, still at school and so very much in love. He couldn't envisage life without her and yet life with her had become empty and secretive. She was no longer 'in love' with him but he hoped she still loved him – in her own way – which included not having children but a career instead. Graham hadn't minded, not the first few years anyway, but now he experienced the odd twinge of envy whenever he saw a couple with children, because they were after all – a family.

By ten o'clock Graham was restless. He ran a bath and whilst he was waiting for it to cool a little he lifted the loft ladder into position, climbed up, opened the trap door and entered his own private domain. Jenny had been up there only once when they first moved in, she'd seen a spider and being arachnophobic hadn't ventured up again. But Graham entered the loft at least once a week, always when Jenny was out.

For several minutes he gazed around his loft shining a torch systematically over his own private wardrobe. He smiled with satisfaction at the dresses and skirts strung along a makeshift rail with each item carefully covered in polythene. The beam of light rested on neatly arranged shoe boxes, then ranged across plastic containers housing tops and blouses, underwear and a selection of stockings and tights. Everything Jenny wore he owned too. Everything.

He deliberated for a while, then made his selection, placed them carefully in a plastic bag and made his descent. As he descended the ladder he realised the whisky had taken effect and his anxiety had given way to mild optimism. Maybe Jenny would understand, would accept, she might even want to share his little secret.

After his bath Graham walked downstairs naked, poured himself another large whisky, took it upstairs, arranged the clothes on the bed and between sips of whisky he anticipated the sensual pleasures to follow.

He'd chosen black lacy briefs, high cut, with matching suspender belt. The black stockings shone by the light of the bedside lamp and as he caressed his newly shaven legs he marvelled at their smoothness. Slowly he put on the suspender belt, watching himself in the mirror, then came the stockings equally slowly and carefully so that he didn't snag them; then the sensuous delight of running his hands up and down his legs now encased in a delicate softness. The lacy knickers barely covered his pubic hair but his cock lay snug and comforted by their firm hold. The padded bra completed the underwear but as usual Graham felt a tinge of disappointment that he had no breasts.

He took another swig of whisky, then slipped on the black court shoes, just like Jenny's but two sizes larger and paused to admire his now more shapely legs in the mirror. Not bad for a man, he thought. The black dress, gold necklace and earrings completed the outfit. All that remained was the wig and of course the makeup. Over the years he had perfected the art of applying makeup by reading women's magazines and watching Jenny apply hers. 'You are a dab hand with a lip pencil,' he said aloud, smiling. He had no cares at this moment. He was complete.

Maybe he'd been too self congratulatory or just too self absorbed but he didn't hear the front door opening or the sound of her on the stairs. He spun round suddenly aware he was no longer alone. Jenny stood at the door, her mouth open slackly in shock and surprise. When she did manage to speak her voice was high-pitched and shrill.

'You fucking pervert! You evil twisted bastard… you devious…' She seemed to choke on the words.

'Deviant' supplied Graham trying to be helpful.

Her face having paled at the sight of him now flushed a bright pink, her blue eyes darkened, 'You little gutless toad… *Why? Why?*'

Graham couldn't explain several things at that moment. Why, for instance did he desire her so strongly? Why did he feel so stirred by her anger and contempt? He walked steadily and confidently towards her.

'Don't come any closer,' she screamed. 'You revolt me.'

It was then that Graham saw the truth. She wasn't revolted, she was scared and her fear excited him. He put his hand out to touch her breast – oh God, he wanted her so much. Jenny squealed at his touch lashing out with both hands and screaming, 'Don't touch me, don't you dare.' Although he hardly felt the slaps he saw her eyes were brimming with tears and he held her wrists and said, 'I'll explain but you must calm down.

'Explain! Explain! What is there to explain. My husband wants to be a woman and worse he wants to look just like me.' She paused gathering breath. 'Don't ever try to touch me again. I've put up with it all these years. Trying to make the best of our so called sex life waiting with dread for you to make a move… your skinny little body white as a worm… your cock…' She stopped to gaze at his crotch. 'Do you know,' she said evenly. 'I would rather have cleaned drains than have sex with you – no wonder I didn't want to bear your children.'

Graham didn't really know what happened next. He did remember her eyes bulging and a gurgling noise coming from his throat – at least he thought it was his throat. And then there was silence. A silence so profound that in that moment he thought he had ceased to exist.

Jenny had fallen. Her legs were askew and one shoe was half off. He didn't like to see her untidy. He replaced the shoe, straightened her legs, pulled down her dress and then went downstairs to make her a cup of tea.

When he came back with the tea and saw her lying on the bedroom floor he knew she was dead. How she came to be dead he didn't know. He couldn't t remember now exactly what she'd said or what he'd done but he could see marks on her neck. *He* must have killed her, he supposed. Jenny was no more. Her eyes were still open but he could see she was gone.

He sat on the bed staring at her for some time. They were so much alike. The same small features, slight build, although Graham was at least three inches taller and wider across the shoulders. But on a dark night would any one notice?

Gradually an idea formulated – Jenny would be consigned to the loft. Getting her up the ladder would be a problem, although she was slim, Graham wasn't muscular. He needed help he knew, but what?

Head in hands he mused over the possibilities. The whisky he'd drunk must have been exerting an effect because he felt numb, aware that he felt no emotion at the death of the woman he had known and loved for so long. If you really cared about her, he told himself, you'd be topping yourself from the rafters by now. The rafters! Of course. He could haul her up by rope. The idea was easier than the deed but with rope under her arms he finally managed to haul her into the loft. He squatted between two joists to rest and then shone his torch over her. She looked pretty good, considering. He'd been sweating so much he'd have to renew his makeup.

Once Jenny was well wrapped in polythene he managed to squash her into an old tea chest. Of course later on smell might be a problem but he'd cope with that when the time came. Now, his immediate problem was to convince interested parties that Jenny had left him, destination unknown.

First, he thought, convince the neighbours. It was now one-am, so he'd have to be noisy. Next door lived Bill Foster, unemployed video fanatic, awake most of the night and not likely to resist pulling back the curtains to have a quick peek. Graham checked himself in the hall mirror, surprisingly his long blonde wig was still in place but his mascara needed attention and his nose was definitely shiny.

It was only as he opened the front door he remembered that a woman leaving home needed a suitcase. He slammed the front door and began collecting all the items Jenny would have taken with her: handbag, purse, driving licence, passport, makeup, toiletries (not forgetting her toothbrush) clothes, underwear, shoes. He'd filled two suitcases and he had to practice for a few minutes carrying them with a slight sway of his hips. Outerwear was a problem, her jackets didn't fit him but he knew her raincoat did. He slipped that on, opened the front door and shouted in Graham's voice, 'Go on then. Bugger off. See if he really wants you. You'll be back soon enough.'

In her voice as loud and shrill as he could replicate it, he screamed back, 'I won't ever be back you bastard. You'll never see me again and that's a promise.'

'What about your job you silly bitch.'

'Fuck the job. And Fuck you.'

As Graham shouted those words especially for Bill Foster's benefit he slammed the front door loudly and followed that by crashing the front gate. Then concentrating fully on that slight swing of the hips his high heels clicked noisily past his neighbours well-lit front room. For God's sake have a peep, he thought. He paused by Bill's gate ostensibly to wipe away a tear and rest the suitcases for a moment. Sure enough, he was seen.

That's the first hurdle, thought Graham. He walked to the pathway at the end of the cul-de-sac and within minutes was at the back of his house, in his kitchen, drinking coffee. Now what? In broad daylight would he pass as Jenny? Maybe, maybe not. It wasn't a risk he thought worth taking right then, but perhaps at a later date to convince some one she was still alive it would be a risk worth taking, even a challenge. Tomorrow he would ring her office but wouldn't appear surprised when they told him she wasn't there. He'd simply say she'd walked out on him and had probably gone to live with her lover.

It was a week later he reported her missing to the police. They showed a complete lack of interest which Graham found very irritating.

'Took all her stuff did she sir?' said the desk sergeant. 'It happens mate. Try the Salvation Army, they run a missing persons service.'

Graham's days after that were marked by stultifying tedium. Jenny's boss rang twice, one or two of her girl friends rang but they didn't seem surprised she'd gone. Jenny had no family so there were few to miss her. Except of course for Graham. Even cross-dressing had lost its appeal. It meant going up into the loft.

Some evenings when he sat alone and the hours dragged he would remember how previously he and Jenny would sit choosing clothes from her catalogue. She never knew he doubled up on the orders, everything for him being two sizes larger. Once she'd been at home when there was a delivery and he'd written a strong letter of complaint to the company unposted, of course. He'd paid for the clothes so she was more than delighted to have a good wardrobe. He missed the secretiveness, missed the planning and the excitement. He'd thought... what had he thought when he'd killed her? Had he been merely blinded by rage at that moment or had he always harboured thoughts of killing her?

One Saturday night about a month after *that* night there was a knock at the door. A tall, good looking man in his thirties stood there. He wore an obviously expensive leather jacket which vaguely impressed Graham.

'I'm sorry to bother you,' he said in a low, slightly husky voice, 'It's about Jenny.'

'Have you seen her?' asked Graham coolly.

'Could I come in and talk?'

Graham nodded, led him through to the lounge and pointed him to an armchair. He was glad of the company.

'My name's Michael Towers,' he said running a hand nervously through his dark rather floppy hair. This is probably a shock to you but I've been your wife's lover for two years. I've been trying to find her for weeks, eventually I've given up and come to see you. Jenny told me you weren't the violent type so I thought I'd risk it.'

Graham feigned a surprised expression. Then said, 'But I thought she was with you.'

'You knew about me then?'

'I didn't exactly know but I guessed she was seeing someone.'

'And you didn't mind?'

'Of course I minded,' snapped Graham, 'But there wasn't much I could do about it, was there? We had a blazing row and she walked out, bag and baggage, saying I'd never see her again. And I haven't.'

'Have you reported her missing?'

Graham nodded. 'I told the police, they weren't interested.'

Michael Towers sat silently for a while. 'I've got a problem...' he paused, 'I'd bought tickets for a holiday for Jenny and me. It's next week – Bermuda.'

'She didn't tell me.'

'She was going to tell you – it was going to be the time she planned to leave. We were going to live together.'

'I thought you'd be a married man'

'Divorced. No kids.'

'So what's this holiday got to do with me?'

'I thought, unless Jenny turns up the holiday would be wasted. Would you like to go? After all I won't be able to recoup the money.'

'Is that meant to compensate me for you screwing my wife?'

Michael stared at him for moment. 'Jenny did say you didn't have a sex life.'

'Jenny lied. We had a good sex life.' Graham was pleased to note that Michael seemed surprised at that. Then he added calmly, 'Thank you for the holiday offer but I don't have anyone to go with.'

Michael managed a smile. 'My problem too. Perhaps we should join forces.'

'You mean go together?'

'Why not, if you can get time off from work? I mean we both need something to take our mind off Jenny – perhaps she was two-timing us both.'

'I'll think about it,' said Graham.

'Fine. Give me a ring at work in a couple of days.'

Michael wrote down his phone number, they shook hands and by the time he'd driven away Graham had decided a Bermudan freebie holiday was just what he needed.

Two days later he rang Michael's work number.

'Long Street police station. May I help you?' Graham choked out, 'Michael Towers please.'

In the slight pause that followed Graham prayed it was all a dreadful mistake. It wasn't, of course.

'Inspector Towers.'

'Michael, it's Graham.'

'Decided about the holiday have you? Heard anything from Jenny?'

'No I haven't heard from Jenny. Have you?'

'No nothing. She'll turn up when she's had some space. What about the holiday?'

' Yes, why not? A small revenge for Jenny running out on me.'

'On us.'

'Yes. On us',

Graham arranged to meet Michael at the railway station. He was early, so he stood looking at the carousel of paperback books until he felt the hand on his shoulder. He turned swiftly in panic.

'Christ almighty! You look just like her.'

Graham felt an absurd pleasure at his shock. He tossed his pony tail as she used to do and fluttered his well mascara'd eyelashes. What a showman he was. What an actress. In that instant he knew why he'd killed her. He had wanted to *be* Jenny. Only that way could he keep her.

A train announcement seemed to bring Michael to his senses. 'Come on then or we'll miss the train,'

'But what about me?' asked Graham.

'What about you?' said Michael. 'We all have our little peccadilloes.'

In the train with his legs neatly crossed, smelling of Chanel with a handsome man beside him, Graham experienced a tremor of anticipation. He felt... how did he feel? He felt – just like a virgin.

John Baker

Notes

British crime fiction has not been my greatest love, nor my primary inspiration. *Huckleberry Finn* remains my favourite book to this day. What I loved about it so much, and what comes to mind when I think about it, is not the action, not what happens to the characters, but the characters themselves, and the ways in which they interact together. After Mark Twain there was Hemingway and Fitzgerald, and then there was Chandler, and now there is Elmore Leonard. I know George V Higgins doesn't regard himself as a crime writer, and quite frankly I don't give a damn what he calls himself, I'm always ready for whatever he does next.

So it's all Stateside. At least in terms of influence.

The British writers I read for pleasure include John Harvey, Sarah Dunant, Val McDermid, Ian Rankin, Gillian Slovo, and Reginald Hill.

The current story began life as an entry for a competition. It has undergone many transformations since then. Now it's on its own. No creative work is ever really finished, what happens is that the artist comes to a point where he or she can't go any further with it, and then it is abandoned.

Defence

by John Baker

One

Father's Volvo was parked on the quay as we drew into Bekkelagskaia. From the ship's rail I could make out his silhouette slowly growing larger as we approached. He had left the car and was shading his eyes against the sun, looking towards the ship. I had nothing to say to him. I had changed my mind about returning to Norway almost as soon as the ship set sail. One should never go back, I told myself. And yet for me there didn't seem to be a way forward. I wanted Hazel, my wife, and Tor, my son, and they were in the past. I couldn't go back to them. I could never go back.

Father came up the ship's gangplank and shook me by the hand. 'Trond,' he said.

'Far,' I said. There was a smile on his face and disappointment in his eyes.

'Velkommen.'

'Thanks.' His eyes held me for a moment and swung me back into the merry-go-round of childhood and adolescence. The language, though coming instinctively to my tongue, seemed to change my centre of balance. An uncomfortable feeling, like the removing of several layers of skin. I wrenched myself free and looked out over the water to the islands. 'It's beautiful,' I said.

He followed my gaze towards Malmoya and Ulvoya. 'Yes,' he said. 'We have a beautiful country.' It was certainly different to the murky, smog-laden Humber which had been my point of departure from England. The physical beauty was a welcome sight.

We spoke little on the drive into Oslo, and I was thankful for my father's tact, not least because I knew he was bursting with questions. But I needed a breathing space, and he could see that. He was calm on the surface, controlled; we were both calm and controlled.

My mother came out of the house and took my bag. She placed a dry kiss on my cheek and stood back with the same disappointed eyes as my father. The disappointment was genuine: I was their son and I had failed. But it also masked a triumph, for I had returned to them and to their beloved country, and they had always known I would. Not now, but later they would tell me so.

We drank coffee and talked about my journey. They spoke of cousins and old school friends, of the New Norwegian Theatre, and Scandinavian politics. Hazel and Tor were not mentioned, my marriage, my life in England were all avoided as taboo subjects. They were all there, larger than life in the midst of us, but heavily veiled. They would be brought out in the evening, after dinner, when my brother and sister would also be there. I would have to talk about it, confess, answer their questions. But it would be better later than now. There was a kind of safety in numbers.

I spent the afternoon in my room. My old room. The room in which I had spent my childhood. It had nothing to do with me. There were many things still there, things I had left behind years before. But there was nothing I wanted. Books I had never read, toys I no longer recognised. My mother would never throw them out. They reminded her of her little boy, her life as a young woman and mother. They reminded her of her dreams.

I wept on the bed. Weeping had become a habit. I no longer screamed with the pain, the injustice, the incomprehension. I wept quietly, alone. The weeping was a kind of comfort now, though often it was difficult to stop. I had little control over it. It was easy to start and not easy to stop. I wallowed in self pity, in self justification. It seemed all right to do that. It harmed no one, and I hoped that eventually my tears would dry up, that my soul would not be too damaged by the damming up of my feelings.

The events of that day, the day of my arrival in Norway are burned into my memory. I have puzzled long over why that should be so, but I am still not really clear. Perhaps it is because returning to Norway was the first positive thing I did since Hazel told me the one thing I was not capable of hearing. I was welcome in Norway, of that I had no doubt. What I doubted was whether I wanted to be welcome in that way. What my parents, my brother and sister and friends welcomed was not the me I had become during my time in England, but something I had ceased to be. The Trond I had been in their imagination many years before, the child and adolescent who was experienced only in innocence.

I imagined at that time that I would spend only a few weeks in Norway, perhaps a month or two, before returning to England. But I was there nineteen months before the telephone call came, and I might have stayed for ever, tidily wrapped in the trivia of my flag waving family if it had not been for that one event.

The dining table was set with candles. Mother and father sat at the head and foot of the table. The rest of us were placed at my mother's discretion. I to her right, with my sister, Siv between me and father. My brother, Jon, sat opposite me, and my sister's husband, Ola, was next to him. We ate crayfish with Retsina, a ritual dish in the family, used only for special occasions. Father kept our glasses filled with the Retsina, and we each made a border on our plates with the heads of the crayfish.

My diplomatic father asked Ola and Siv about their children, and there followed several anecdotes about the absent generation. Then Siv turned to me.

'And what about Tor?' she asked.

'He's well,' I said trying to keep any trace of emotion from my voice. 'He's not walking yet, but I don't think it'll be long.'

'And Hazel?' The table had become so quiet that I could hear their breathing. I swallowed and clutched at the napkin on my lap.

'She's OK,' I said. 'They're both OK.' I wanted to go on, to keep talking, to maintain the initiative with myself, but at the mention of Hazel's name my mouth dried up. It was all too close to me, the family's expectations too pressing. I stopped talking and looked down at my plate, adjusting one of the crays heads, putting it in line with the others.

Silence hung over us for a few moments, and then Siv drew in her breath. 'You don't have to go into details,' she said. 'But you'll have to tell us something.'

'We've split up,' I said quietly. 'We no longer live together.'

'Yes,' said Siv. 'And Tor is with Hazel?'

'They're still in York, in the same house. I moved out two months ago.

'Two months!' Siv was right to be surprised, I had only contacted them the week before I sailed.

'I didn't say anything about it before. I thought there might be a chance of us getting back together.'

'It's permanent, then?'

I nodded.

Mother moved her hand towards mine, but stopped short before she reached me. Our hands lay side by side on the table.

'Is there someone else?' asked Siv.

'No,' I said.

I couldn't tell them about him. I couldn't even bear to think about him.

'But why, then, Trond?' asked my mother, echoing the question I had asked myself a million times. 'We thought you were so happy, so suited.'

'Hazel needed to live by herself,' I lied. 'It wasn't her fault. We come from different cultures, we have different expectations. It just didn't work.'

'But it worked for two years,' said my father.

'And then it didn't work any longer.'

'And Tor?' he said. 'Will we see him again?'

'Yes. Maybe not for a while. But when he's older I'll have him for holidays.'

My mother breathed a sigh of relief. She wouldn't have been able to cope with her grandson never seeing Norway and not learning to speak the language.

'And there's no hope for you and Hazel?' asked Siv.

'No.' I shook my head. 'I don't think so.

They accepted it eventually. They all of them accepted it much more than I did. It had always been unacceptable to me, and I knew that it always would be. But as the months passed it became more bearable. I learned new techniques for dealing with it, kept it close to myself. Whenever the subject of marriage came up I sidestepped it, spoke in generalities and struggled to stop myself drowning in the turbulent sea of images of Hazel, my wife, Tor, my son; and the other one, the image of *him* who had destroyed it all.

Hazel and I exchanged irregular and pragmatic letters, and after eleven months in Norway I spent a few days in York to see Tor. Hazel invited me to the house, but I didn't want to see him, so arranged for her to bring Tor to my hotel. He was twenty months old, and after clinging to his mother he tottered around the furniture quite independently. He was dark, with Hazel's hair, but a distinctive Norwegian nose. He didn't know me and wouldn't sit on my knee, but before they left he let me hold his hand, and I ruffled his hair and managed to plant a wet kiss on his forehead. They stayed for two hours. Hazel was very pregnant.

I resolved to see him regularly after that, though the experience of meeting him and Hazel together had almost destroyed me. I would have to move back to England to be closer to my son. I couldn't bear him growing up and not knowing who I was.

But it didn't happen. I stayed on in Norway. I know now that I was waiting for that telephone call, but I didn't know it then. For the next eight months my destiny was adjourned. All the time I was intending to return to England, but the forces of my will never came together enough for me to make the step.

Before breakfast on the 7th January 1997 the telephone rang.

'Trond?'

It was his voice. My impulse was to put the telephone down. I felt the beginnings of rage stir inside me.

'Trond?' he said again. 'Don't put the phone down. Just listen to me. Hazel's dead. There's been an accident.'

He was silent. I couldn't think of anything to say. The rage disseminated and mingled with incomprehension and disbelief.

'Trond? Are you there?'

'Yes,' I said. 'How? When?'

'She was in the car. She hit a bus.'

'Tor?'

'He's all right. He was with me. Both of the kids were with me.'

'I want him back,' I said.

There was a long silence. Then he said:

'We'll have to talk about it. Will you come here?'

'Yes,' I said. 'And I want Tor back.'

'Let me know when you'll arrive,' he said. 'The funeral will be on Monday, the thirteenth.'

I put the telephone down and sank to my knees on the floor, my head in my hands. I expected to weep, to scream, anything. But nothing happened. I don't know how long I stayed there, anaesthetised within a dull cocoon of dark silence, before I stood and walked out of the house, ready at last to pick up the remains of my shattered destiny.

Two

I had lived in dread of seeing him, even of hearing his voice. Anything that reminded me of him was enough to throw me into a rage. if I read a book or newspaper and came across his name, I would stop reading. There was violence in me, a dark and over-whelmingly powerful force; a volcano that slumbered uneasily beneath the gentle contours of social manners, but that could erupt without warning into an inferno of destruction. I knew it was there, and that he could unwittingly be the agent of its release.

The voice on the telephone had not affected me in this way, because the message it brought had swamped those baser instincts and feelings. It left me only with the picture of Hazel crushed in the wreckage of her car. Gentle, stupid Hazel, who had destroyed me, and who had now destroyed herself. The picture was a moving image, like a clip from a film. There was a close-up of Hazel, head and shoulders at the wheel, a slight smile on her lips as she glanced into the mirror. Her eyes were bright and quick, like the eyes of a wild animal, and they held no presentiment of fear, saw nothing of what was to come.

The camera panned back and away to the right, and the images faltered into slow motion as the car concertina'd into the oncoming bus, the rear wheels lifting themselves clear of the ground and the nose burrowing deeper into itself. Her dark head shattered through the windscreen, sending a shower of crystals high into the air. And then, still in slow motion, the camera closed in on the body, wantonly recording the helpless, ragged shaking as it was flung from side to side over the crippled bonnet of the car, the legs still pinned under the strangled steering column.

Then there was stillness. Silence.

The picture slowly faded, leaving a shining white screen.

Slut.

After the telephone call I walked. Hazel was dead, laid out somewhere on a slab, maybe in a deep freeze. She would never answer my questions now, never come back. I walked and talked with her in my head, seeing her as she had been on all the other occasions: at our wedding; the long holiday in Norway with crossed skis; cradling Tor in her arms the day after he was born. The adulteress was there too, in her furious love for him and her unreasonable hatred of me. But I could not hear what she said, only the incessant whining of my own pam, the chattering rant of my disbelief. And superimposed on all these flickering images was the one Hazel I had not yet met: the dead one.

I walked along Kirkeveien and stood dwarfed in the snow beneath Vigeland's grotesque human monolith. Hazel was dead and I walked. The Buddha was right to recognise the fact of suffering. It is the only reality. He was wrong about everything else.

I took a short cut through the Slottsparken, past the National Theatre, and along Karl Johans Gate. It was snowing hard, very cold, and my chin and feet were numb. I had not eaten, simply fled the house and the black telephone. I sat under Per Krohg's huge painting of the Christianian Bohemians in the Grand Café and watched their affluent descendants stuffing themselves from the smorgasbord.

The coffee was black and bitter, scalding hot, putting the illusion of strength back into my body. Strength which I wanted to conserve, but which I knew I would squander. I was ready to leave, to walk aimlessly round the city, when a child at the next table reminded me. I had a son. Tor, my English son. He would soon be three years old.

I had quoted Novalis to Hazel on the day he was born: *Children are hopes*. The nurse held him up to the glass and pulled away the shawl from his face. We were not allowed to meet.

A year later I had returned to Norway, leaving him with his mother. The bond between us, stretched to its limit, was torn apart.

After that we had spent two hours together in a York hotel. Before he left he let me hold his hand, and I ruffled his hair and managed to plant a wet kiss on his forehead.

And that was all there was between me and my son. Except that during our first year together he had become more important to me than food. In his absence I had hungered for him, sometimes literally clawing at my belly, my mouth and throat dry with longing. My soul had grown thin and emaciated without him, and whenever I formed his image, so small, so young, so far away, I felt the rhythm of my heart stumble with fear for him.

He needed me, of that I had no doubt. A boy needs a father. No one would ever love him as unselfishly, as impossibly as I did. I loved him totally, as a cow loves grass. And he didn't want me to go. If he had had words he would have argued with Hazel more forcibly than I could. During the long discussions with Hazel before I left, the mention of Tor was taboo. Whatever I said about him was emotional blackmail.

Her mind was made up. She had convinced herself that Tor, as well as herself, would be better off without me. By that time she had build up a protective wall around herself. She no longer listened to my ravings, she was beyond my reach. She could only be touched by *him*.

Later I went to the telephone and dialled the numbers. He answered almost immediately, as if he had been sat by the phone waiting for it to ring. His voice was quiet, subdued, but insistent.

'Hello. Hello. Who is it?' He repeated the number I had dialled.

'It's Trond,' I said.

'Trond? Oh, yes.'

'Listen. I've made some arrangements.' I kept the index finger of my right hand on the notes I had made.

'Are you coming?'

'Yes. I've booked a flight for tonight. I'll stay in the same hotel as before.'

'You can stay here if you like.'

'No. I'll stay in the hotel.'

'What about Tor?'

He was getting ahead of my notes. I had to stay in command of the conversation. 'Can you listen to what I have to say. I'm trying to make arrangements.'

'Sorry. Go on.'

'I'll stay in the same hotel as before. I don't want you to come and see me there, or even to contact me, unless there is an emergency. Do you understand?'

'Yes, but…'

'Good. Next, I want you to give me the name of the hospital and exact address so I can see Hazel.'

'We're moving her out of the hospital. She's going to a private funeral parlour.' He gave me the address and I read it back to him.

'The date and time of the funeral?'

'It's not fixed exactly. I'll have to tell you later.'

'No. You can tell Hazel's parents. I'll find out from them. Leave Tor there, together with all his clothes and toys, and I'll collect him.'

'What do you mean?'

'I'll collect him from his grandparents.'

'And?'

'And what? He'll come back to Norway with me.'

There was a long silence. I thought he had rung off.

'Hello,' I said.

'Yes. I'm still here. Are you serious?'

'Yes. He's my son. You have no jurisdiction over him.'

'Maybe not, but he doesn't know you. He doesn't know what's happening. You can't just drag him away to a foreign country.'

'I want him back.'

'Maybe you do, Trond. But it'll have to be a slow process. He's part of a family here, you can't destroy all his roots.'

'You can't keep him. He's my son.

'But think about it from his point of view. If you really want him back I won't interfere, but you'd have to give him time to get to know you. He's crying for his mother at the moment.' I could see that: Tor, my son, crying for his mother. It was a vivid picture. Part of me rushed away across the sea towards him, leaving a ghost holding the telephone in Oslo. My notes fluttered to the floor, and my mouth dried out, cracking my voice.

'Look after him,' I said helplessly.

There was a short silence.

'Sure,' he said. 'Don't worry, he'll be all right. Come and see us when you get here. We can talk and decide what to do for the best. It would be all right for you to stay here.'

'No,' I said. 'I couldn't do that.'

'Are you sure?'

'Yes.'

'But you'll come and see us?'

I nodded my head.

'Yes,' I croaked. 'Yes. I'll come.

Three

The door opened and we stood facing each other. He smiled tiredly; He was frailer than I remembered, his pale face contrasted with the dark passage behind him, and for a moment I was out of my body and viewing our meeting from somewhere above. The ghost-like figure of him on the inside of the door, and the bulky otherness of me standing opposite him.

'Come in,' he said. His smile, finding no reflection in me, withered away. I followed him into one of the rooms at the back of the house, aware that I was acting a part, conscious that I was unprepared for the role, but that, in the circumstances, I was making a good job of it.

I loosened the buttons of my coat, a prickly sweat breaking over my neck and forehead. There was a smell of urine which became more prominent as we entered the room. Tor, aware of my alien presence, quickly picked up the toy cars he was driving along the carpet, and hid himself behind the man's legs. The baby girl, left alone on the carpet, half shuffled, half crawled towards the sanctuary of her father. I tried not to take their flight personally.

He went down on his knees, enclosing each of the children with an arm, holding them close to his body. 'It's all right,' he told them softly. 'We've got a visitor. Tor's daddy has come to see us.'

They looked up at me, the tall giant, the all powerful stranger from another world. I smiled down on them, stupidly, the bitter-sweet ammonia stinging my nostrils and clinging freely to my skin. I couldn't visualise the image I presented to them: Tor's daddy, Odin, the great father.

'We'll make a drink, shall we,' said the man, standing. 'Will you have tea?' he asked.

'Yes, please.'

'And some juice for Tor and Christine.'

I followed them into the kitchen. 'Shall I take your coat?' he said. He took it to a hanger in the hall, unconsciously stealing the power. Odin, the Sun-being was obscured by the clouds of routine. I was a visitor in an English home. Their home. The awe of their first scrutiny was superseded by the expectation of lemonade.

'Good trip?' he asked.

'Yes, it was all right.'

He lifted Christine and strapped her into a high chair. Tor scrambled onto another chair next to her, and they were served with red juice in plastic cups with lids.

'Have you seen the body?' he asked, setting a tea pot and two cups on the table.

'No. I was going after lunch.'

'You've got the address?'

'Yes. I know where it is.'

'Good,' he said. 'Christine, don't pour it all over the table. It's for drinking.' He took the cup from her and returned it the right way up.

'Do you like juice?' I asked Tor. He ignored me. 'You look as though you do.' He put his plastic cup on the table and pushed it away.

'Oh, I'll drink it, then,' said the man, reaching out for the cup.

'No.' Tor took it back quickly, holding it close to his chest.

'Tor, do you remember Trond?' said the man. But the child wouldn't be drawn. Not only did he not remember, he refused to acknowledge my existence.

'Can I have a drink of your juice?' I tried.

There was no response. Christine sprinkled the table again, and her father mopped it up with a dish cloth.

'More tea?' he asked. But I hadn't yet started to drink the first cup.

'I would have liked to talk,' I said.

'Yes, it's not really possible during the day. You could come back this evening.'

'Yes. About eight?'

'OK,' he said. Hazel's expression. Everything was OK to her. 'The offer of a room is still open if you change your mind. Tor and Christine would like that, wouldn't you?'

Tor and Christine didn't seem too taken with the idea. I shook my head.

'The house is bloody empty these last days,' he said, almost to himself. 'Since, ever since…' There was a perceptible crack in his voice, and I feared he would break down. Christine started banging the table with her cup, and Tor joined in, an almost rhythmic drumming, ancient, as if to resurrect some mysterious power from the beginnings of the world. They gradually increased the pace, rising to a crescendo which promised chaos. The man sat with his head in his hands, his will given up to some inner necessity, and I realised instinctively that if order was to be resumed, it was up to me to do something about it.

The drumming was insistent, like the insatiable rant of war.

'Shhhhhhhh,' I said gently, introducing breath into the situation, as one would introduce rain to a fire. 'Shhhhhhhh.' Tor stopped immediately, his cup poised in mid air, caught in its downward journey. Christine continued drumming for a few more strokes, but with less force, and at my third, 'Hushhhhh,' she stopped completely.

'You'll give him a headache,' I said, indicating their father, who was emerging from his hands.

'I'm sorry,' he said. 'I'm over tired.'

'He's too tired,' said Tor.

'I haven't slept much,' he explained. 'There's so much to do. If someone else was here it would be better.'

I hesitated. Tor had spoken to me. I turned to him and said: 'What about you, Tor? Are you too tired?' He ignored me again. 'Could I help?' I asked the man.

He said nothing, only looked at me through vacant grey eyes.

'All right,' I said. 'I'll stay for a few days.'

I slept during the afternoon, before checking out of the hotel and taking a taxi to Charles' house. I could start to think of him as Charles now, after years of denying him a name, of begrudging his existence.

I had no love for him, did not like him, but he no longer stood between me and Hazel, was no longer a threat.

He was ill. His eyes blazed with fire. He showed me the room I would use, told me to help myself to anything, then crept off to his own room, a tartan blanket wrapped round his shoulders, his whole body shaking with fever.

I explored the house. The house that had been my house, our house. The house from which I had been banished. It had not altered, the furniture was basically the same, the pictures on the walls, even the books on the shelves. Some of the carpets had been replaced, the walls painted, the curtains washed. The signature to everything was Hazel's.

I made the tea on a tray and took it to Charles' room, tapping lightly on the door and waiting for him to call me in. After a few seconds I knocked again and pushed the door open. The room was illuminated by the ceiling light, and Charles was face down on the bed, still fully clothed.

'I've brought some tea,' I said. He turned completely round in the bed, ending face down again.

'Charles? Are you all right?'

'Hazel,' he said, turning onto his back and lashing out wildly with his arms. 'Don't go.'

I placed the tea tray on a desk by the window and sat on the edge of the bed. There was a smell of sickness. His eyes were closed. His face was burning.

'I'm going to get you undressed,' I told him. He muttered something about the freezing cold, but he did not know what was happening. I managed to undress him and made him as comfortable as possible. Then I rang the surgery. I sat by the bed until the doctor arrived. Charles was delirious, calling out for Hazel and his mother, complaining about the weather, sweating freely, and shaking with cold.

The doctor said Charles' fever would continue for some hours, that he would be weak for a few days. He gave me a prescription and left the house, slamming the front door behind him.

Tor awoke and started to cry. I went to his cot and he crouched away from me in the far corner. 'I want Charles,' he said.

'Charles is not very well at the moment,' I said. 'Shall I get you a drink? Or something to eat?'

'I want Charles,' he said. 'And Hazel.'

He started to cry, and struggled when I tried to lift him from the cot. Christine began whimpering from the other side of the room. I took Tor out of the room, closing the door quietly behind us, hoping that Christine would sleep.

'No,' he was yelling, hitting out at my hand and face with his little fists. 'I want Charles and Hazel.' I tried to turn the fight into a joke, pretending to duck his punches, and at the same time talking quickly about how exciting it was to get up in the middle of the night and drink red juice in the kitchen. He gradually quietened down as he realised there was no danger, and the situation might be to his advantage.

'Strong juice,' he said. 'Warm. With sugar in.'

I followed the instructions, pouring it into one of the plastic cups I had seen used earlier. He pointed out that I had used Christine's cup, and that was the best way to spread germs. I transferred it to the other cup, which was identical to the first. I tried to put him at ease by acting the part of a funny man, but he was not to be drawn in that way. He observed me in silence, his face small and white, his eyes betraying nothing of his thoughts.

When I suggested that he should go back to bed, he agreed, but explained that his nappy was wet and I would have to change it. He showed me where the clean nappies were kept, and by trial and error I eventually managed it to his satisfaction. He went quietly to bed, allowing me to tuck the blankets around him; and when I looked into the room ten minutes later he was fast asleep.

Charles was still burning, but he had stopped tossing about and seemed as though he might sleep through the night. I washed and went to bed myself, wondering what the morning would bring.

The next three days were an initiation into fatherhood, or motherhood, or both. Charles tried to get out of bed the first morning and collapsed on the floor. His pyjamas and sheets were wet with perspiration, and I had to change everything before I could start on the children. Their clothes were wet too, my first attempt at putting a nappy on had not been too successful. By the time I had dressed them both, a job that took more than an hour that first morning, I had a pile of wet sheets and pyjamas to fill the washing machine.

Breakfast was chaos. The children had to have their own dishes which were submerged beneath a sink full of dirty pots. There was only a handful of cornflakes left in the box, and I had to fill them up on bread and jam and red juice. Christine dropped everything on the floor, all the time gazing at me with wide eyes, as if unable to believe I had happened to them.

There was no time to think. I was a slave to the day, which roared at me from a thousand different directions. Get the medicine for Charles' illness, but first dress the children, find their outdoor clothes, make a shopping list for cornflakes and food for the rest of the day, master the washing machine, find the soap powder, keep the children happy, give Charles something to eat, drink, read, go to the lavatory, change the nappies again, and again. By the time the children were back in bed in the evening the house was wrecked. I tidied away the toys, swept the kitchen floor, hung out the washing in the dark and refilled the washing machine, took a milky drink up to Charles, who was fast asleep. Then I sat at the kitchen table and fell asleep myself.

I woke with a stiff neck at one-thirty in the morning, dragged myself up to bed, and was awoken by Tor at two-thirty for the red juice treatment. Then we slept until 6am, when it started all over again.

On the day of the funeral Charles and I went together, leaving the children in the care of a neighbour. Charles was still weak from his illness, and I had forfeited so much sleep that I found it difficult to concentrate on the service. There was a dim beauty about it, and an overwhelming sense of accomplishment in the slow descent of the coffin. Like a reluctant soldier, I could have wished that it was not so, but there was a sense of destiny in my participation. Afterwards we exchanged greetings with Hazel's family, with old friends. But there was not much to say. Hazel had gone. We had seen her off.

Charles went back to bed after the service, and I coped with the children for the rest of the day. In the evening I sat with Charles and he asked about the future.

'You wouldn't think of staying on?' he said.

'For a few more days. Until you're fit.'

'No. I mean for the foreseeable future.'

I shook my head.

'It would solve a lot of problems,' he said. 'Tor and Christine are very close, They would both suffer if we split them up. And we could share the load if there was two of us.'

'It wouldn't work, Charles.'

'Do you still intend to take Tor away?'

'That's why I'm here,' I told him. 'I can see it will have to be done gradually. I don't want to cause any more trauma. I can only play it by ear.'

'What's the plan then?' he said.

There wasn't one. 'I don't know. I'll stay for a few more days, and then try to find a flat close by. I want to introduce the idea to Tor gradually. Eventually we'll go back to Norway, or find somewhere in England.'

He shook his head. 'OK. But you don't have to rush anything. You can stay here as long as you like.'

I never seriously looked for another flat. The following week Charles went back to his job with the Council, while I stayed at home with the children. There was plenty to do. The idea of moving out of the house gradually faded away, and I found myself adapting to the role of mother and house-wife. Once I tackled Tor about coming to Norway with me, and he seemed to think about it for a long time. Then he said:

'With Christine? And Charles?'

'No,' I said. 'We could visit them sometimes. And sometimes they could visit us. But we wouldn't live in the same house.'

He didn't like the idea.

'We could live in a house by the sea,' I told him. 'And in the winter there would be lots of snow.

'No,' he said. 'I want to live with Christine. And Charles.'

In the mornings I prepared breakfast, while Charles dressed the children. Then he went off to work. I washed the dishes, cleaned the house. Together with the children I did the shopping. After lunch we played games. I read them stories. Then we made dinner together, in time for Charles coming home from work.

Charles and I took it in turns to wash the dinner pots and put the children to bed. And in the evening we played chess or watched the television. Occasionally one or the other of us would go to the cinema, and once we hired a baby-sitter and went to the theatre together. A year went by like that. I enjoyed being with the children during the day, and I appreciated Charles' company in the evening. He enjoyed his job with the Council, and was happy to relax with me when he came home. During the summer we took the kids to the seaside or into the country during the weekends.

Life was uncomplicated, and yet not without meaning. I had had enough of misery, of living close to madness. Charles and I had our fights occasionally, but we always managed to sort them out. I was constantly impressed by how easy he was to live with. He never sat down if there was something to do. And if everything seemed to be getting on top of me he would make a cup of tea, or take over my jobs for a time.

I didn't make his life so easy. I have always been moody, and too easily slip into depression. Sometimes when he returned from work I had barely started on the dinner, and he would roll his sleeves up and start washing carrots or boiling the rice. Other times the kids would be too much during the day, and I would nag about how easy it was for him, while here I was slaving away at the stove, or the washing, talking in baby-talk from morning till night.

But he was strong. He managed it all. He would smooth away my depression, undermine my bad moods, and generally make life possible. He was a good man.

Four

I destroyed the letter, but I can recall the wording verbatim. It was left on the desk in his bedroom:

Dear Trond,

It would have been painful for both of us to talk about the contents of this letter, and it would have solved no problems. The outcome would have been the same.

Quite simply, I have formed a relationship with someone else, a woman (you don't know her) who needs me, and who I could not consider giving up for anything.

We are going away together (by the time you read this we shall have gone), and I am leaving you with both the children. Tor and Christine. I hope and pray that you will care for them both.

Best wishes
Charles

It was written on blue paper in Charles' large handwriting. On the envelope it said: *To Trond*. And he had propped it up against a stapler on his desk. His cupboard was empty. The drawers of the desk had been cleared. A picture had gone from the wall. The bed had been made.

I walked from the room as though it was possible to leave it behind. To close the door on his bedroom and seal inside the letter and the knowledge of the letter, the act and its implications.

But my will collapsed as I descended the stairs. My legs started to give, and I had to sit on the bottom step. I remember thinking that I wasn't breathing, and having to take in great gulps of air. I thought, without any hint of panic, that I was dying. The physical processes of my body were no longer being driven.

'What are you doing?' Tor asked, sitting next to me on the step, resting his head on my leg.

'Sitting down,' part of me answered, the other part thinking that perhaps it was a joke, that even if it wasn't a joke, Charles would regret leaving us and come back again. Yes, tonight; tonight or tomorrow he would come back. Christine was his daughter. We were a family. He couldn't leave us. He couldn't disappear.

'On the stairs?' said Tor.

'Yes. With you.'

'Christine's in the fridge.' He pulled me by the hand and took me into the kitchen. Christine was sitting in front of the open door of the fridge, drinking yoghurt from the carton. The remains of last night's meal were littered on the floor around her.

None of us have seen or heard from Charles since.

Our house by the sea in Oslo is a large, old, wooden building. During the summer we spent a lot of time on the beach, fishing, playing with buckets and spades. Now it is winter and the children are in bed. Today we walked on the frozen surface of the fjord and I can see its silvery sheen from my window as I write the concluding words of this defence.

I do not dwell. I have found an equilibrium in my soul. The two children with whom I live cannot help but remind me of the two adults with whom I lived in England, but they are faded memories, dead memories. At night they come to me in dreams, strangely intermingled with each other. Hazel turns and in a moment of metamorphosis she is Charles. He speaks to me from the other end of a long room, receding as I try to reach him, slowly becoming my faithless wife of long ago.

They are not bad dreams. They do not enlighten me, but they have nothing of the quality of nightmare. The night is beyond me. What happens in the region of sleep is of another world.

But the days are mine. They belong to me and the children. Tor speaks fluent Norwegian now, and Christine has learnt to run and laugh at the same time. I was beginning to think the period of exile was over.

I would dispute that the human remains found under the floorboards of the house in England are those of Charles. But if there is forensic evidence suggesting that the body parts did once belong to him, then it must also be possible to prove that his death took place after we left the country. I must say, without, I hope, appearing macabre, that the missing head is intriguing. Do the British police think that I kept it as a trophy?

I understand that the terms of the extradition treaty between the two countries state that I will have to face the British legal authorities by the year 2000 at the latest. But I throw myself upon the mercy of the Norwegian government by means of this full and frank statement of the facts.

Charles Higson

Notes

I've written four crime novels. All from the point of view of the 'criminal'. All, in their own way sympathetic towards these law-breakers. And yet I'm as fearful of crime as the next man. I've been burgled enough times to know how depressing it is. I hate violence of any kind. I'm sure all crime writers are the same. They're nice boys and girls who are fascinated yet terrified by the world of crime, by transgression, by the forbidden. Yet they're pathetically law-abiding and timid themselves. Faced with 'real' crime they would be appalled. And crime books aren't real, are they? They're not about 'real' crimes. They're all, in their own way, little fantasies, which is why I have no interest in competing to see who can do the most convincing south London criminal's pub, that whole pitiful jostling over who does the most authentic crime story. That's not the point. And it's all phoney anyway. So I thought for a change I'd try to present an unglamorous, unsexy, lumpen, petty criminal, Ollie Garson, and for a laugh I'd put the boot in. But, even then, I found that as the story of Ollie's hapless night out unfolded, I couldn't prevent a hint of sympathy creeping in, and the story ended up like all my stories – about a man alone. Someone in a nightmare of their own creating, lost, bewildered, with no one to turn to, and always making the wrong decision. That's what appeals to me in crime writing, for want of a less pretentious and over-used term, it is existentialism. A hard look at a universe without a God. So, this car alarm in my story, is it an embodiment of guilt, or of a divine retribution, does Ollie imagine it? I'm not telling.

The title's obviously a nod towards Edgar Allan Poe, like with so much modern fiction, you can't help but draw on what's gone before, use it, re-use it, twist it to your own ends. There's nothing new anymore, just imaginative re-cycling. The car in the story, the TVR Cerbera, belonged to Vic Reeves. He bought one, and had to get rid of it after two weeks, because he was fed-up with waking in the night to find people trying to nick it.

So that's where the idea came from, Edgar Allan Poe and Vic Reeves, filtered though my usual crime book obsessions. And it's no more realistic than any other thing I've ever written.

Or any other of the stories in this book, for that matter.

The Tell-Tale Car Alarm

by Charles Higson

Tim 'Ollie' Garson was a moron; a shit-thick, brainless, dolt. A person for whom the word 'stupid' might have been invented. A twenty-two-year-old with the intellect of a three-year-old monkey which has been repeatedly hit round the head with a spade. It was a happy day for him when it became fashionable to wear trainers with the laces undone, as it ever-after saved him the mental strain of tying them up. This might seem like an exaggeration, but the thing is, you see, he was a thief, and thieves are right down there at the foot of the evolutionary ladder with sponges and sea cucumbers.

A thief is someone, who, when he sees something he wants, just takes it. Pop. Like that. No matter that it belongs to somebody else who has legitimately come by it. There is a fundamental lack of imagination at work in the mind of a thief. Thievery is human activity reduced to its most basic level. You might put it down to economics, argue that those at the bottom of society have no option but to steal, but it wasn't as if Ollie came from a particularly poor family. They lived in a nice little three-bedroomed house on a nice little modern housing estate in Kent. His father did something for a chemicals company (Ollie had never thought to ask exactly what) and his mother was the manager of the local Tesco superstore. His brother and sister weren't thieves – one worked in a bank and the other was at university – so he had no excuse there, not that he was looking for excuses. Ollie was happy. As happy as a pig in shit. Which, basically, is what he was.

Look, maybe somebody with more time than me could work out why the little git was a thief, but frankly, I can't be bothered. Let's just say that somewhere down the line Ollie had decided to be stupid. Yes, he wasn't so much bad as just plain stupid, but life's only so long and there's a limit to how much you can tolerate stupid people. He rarely went to school and when he was there he sneered. He was a bully and he was a coward and he was… He was everything depressing and witless a young man at the arse-end of the twentieth century could be.

He looked like Stan Laurel, so his friends had nicknamed him Ollie. It might be charitable to assume that this was an act of irony, but as his friends were as thick as him, it's safer to assume that they just didn't know the difference between Stan and Ollie and didn't really care. They didn't care about anything, that was their style.

So, there you have him, Ollie the thief, Ollie the housebreaker, Ollie the lifter of car stereos, the smasher of windows, the flobmeister, the graffiti. If you lived in the Ashford area of Kent and came home to find someone had lifted your video, taken a shit on your living-room carpet, ripped up all your family photos and ejaculated into your underwear, you could rest assured it was the work of Ollie or one of his friends in the local criminal elite.

But Ollie saw thieving as a career, and lately he'd been promoted. No more aimless housebreaking and shoplifting for him, he was in the car game now. Not joyriding, you understand, (although he had, of course, done his fair share of that). Not boring old TDA ('taking and driving about' as he and his pals called it). No, he was stealing cars to order for a team of guys in Canterbury. The Lads.

Ollie had been very impressed by their headquarters, an office and warehouse on a smart new industrial estate. The office even had a reception area which was like the poshest dentist's waiting room in the country. It was stuffed full of high class magazines, *Country Life*, *The World of Interiors*, *Elle Decorating*, *Classic Car Magazine*, and a few less classy titles, like *Hello* and *Now*. The Lads scanned these mags for shots of celebrities' homes and possessions, they worked out where they lived, and they nicked it all. Cars were perhaps the simplest and most lucrative line. They had a string of contacts around Europe, the orders came in, they ticked the car off their list and some foot soldier like Ollie went out and took it.

Tonight was Ollie's first job for them and there would be a handy lump of cash waiting for him when he delivered the car.

So there he was, on this chilly February night, skulking around in the dark in the spacious grounds of Richard Slovo's house in the bleak heart of the Romney Marshes. Slovo being the hot, young, dance-music star who had recently been shown in the *Sun* raving about his new TVR Cerbera, in a regular feature called 'Me And My Car'. Ollie was a fan of Slovo's music and had tapes of all his stuff. You would think that this might have introduced an element of guilt into Ollie's shrivelled brain-pan, but quite the opposite, he considered it a real honour to be nicking the car of one of his heroes, Other fans might ask for autographs, but not Ollie, he was going to take the bloke's car, and, for a while, he would actually be driving it. Imagine that, him, Ollie Garson, driving Richard Slovo's car!

And there it was, sitting in the drive, gleaming in the moonlight, magnificent in British Racing Green with a cream leather interior.

There were no lights on in the house. It was three in the morning, but you could never tell with people, especially not guys who made club records. It was all quiet, though, so Ollie walked briskly over to the car. He wasn't particularly scared at this point, fear is largely a product of the imagination, and he'd done this sort of thing a million times before. But there was something – a slight quickening of the heart, a dryness in the back of his throat, a mild churning in his guts. He shivered slightly, but maybe that was because of the cold.

The Lads had given him a special electronic hand-set thing, said it would open any central-locking car and disable the alarm. He tried it now. Pointed it at the car and pressed the button. There was a little R2D2 bleep and a satisfying clunk as the locks popped up.

He got in.

The Lads had also given him a master key to start the engine. Nothing could be simpler. This was cutting edge stuff, high-tech Twenty-first century crime. He was part of the computer age. He was Big Time.

He put the key in the ignition and turned it. The engine rumbled and kicked in. Music came on, a tape in the machine, a tape of Slovo's latest hit. It went throb-throb-throb-whack, throb-throb-throb-whack, over and over, while some bint crooned in French, or Italian, or something,

Great. He had his own soundtrack. This was like the best car chase film you could imagine.

Hand brake, reverse, and he was on his way.

So long, suckers.

The alarm went off.

Shit.

A deafening, brain-rattling, two-toned shriek filled the night.

The TVR skidded round and Ollie jammed it into first. It jerked and stalled. He'd never driven something with such a powerful engine before. He farted. He always farted when he was scared. Now he was scared. The alarm was so fucking *LOUD*.

He looked at the house, a light had come on upstairs. He restarted the engine and bunny-hopped up the drive, the alarm still *wee-wahing* dementedly.

Fuck, they'd be onto the police. He had to motor it. Toe down, swerving out of the drive into the road, fishtailing round, nearly losing it. But he was hanging on. He was on top of it again, barrelling down the road at a hundred miles an hour. The only thing was, he had to stop that fucking alarm somehow.

He saw a gate up ahead and a track going into a field. He stopped the car, got out, and had a look. Far off across the frosty mud he could see a clump of trees. Thirty seconds later he was jostling and bumping over the hard, rutted soil. It seemed to take forever to reach the safety of the trees but at last he was there. He got in amongst the shrubbery and tried to relax, but it was like the alarm was sounding right inside his skull and each scream seemed to tighten something inside him. He turned off the engine and climbed out of the car. The indicators were blinking on and off, front and back. He got back inside and pressed buttons willy-nilly, but he couldn't stop the noise and he couldn't stop the flashing lights, he couldn't even stop the music. Throb-throb-throb-whack, throb-throb-throb-whack. The controls seems to be locked. And the annoying thing was, the alarm wasn't in time the music, which set his brain on edge and caused him to painfully clench and unclench his jaw.

The indicators were shining across the field like beacons, but The Lads would kill him if he smashed them. He had to deliver the car in one piece. So he took off his jacket and draped it over on one of the front ones, then he put his sweat shirt over the other. He managed to cover the back ones by shutting his trousers in the boot.

Now for the alarm. Still echoing across the empty marshes. He had to disconnect it. Yes. Open the bonnet and disconnect it. How to open the bonnet, though? There must be a lever. He looked, saw nothing, fumbled around under the steering wheel, crawled about on the floor, feeling with his hands. Shit, fuck, shit. It had to be somewhere. He should have brought a torch, the silly bastard. A torch. He got out and tried to wrench the bonnet open with his bare hands, knowing full well that he wouldn't be able to, but having to do something. He banged his fists down. Not too hard, in case he dented the car.

'You bastard,' he yelled. 'Open... *open.*'

He went to the edge of the little copse and looked across at the road. A police car was racing along it, lights flashing, although the siren didn't appear to be on. It was difficult to tell with the noise of the alarm blotting everything else out. Surely the cops could hear it, but maybe they just couldn't pinpoint the sound.

Ollie was picking his nose, it comforted him in times like this. He got hold of a fat, sticky, lump and tugged it out. A long, thick tail came with it like a rope of elastic. This tail felt like it was rooted right back inside his skull, somewhere in his brain, and he had to pull quite hard to free it. When at last it came away it yanked out a great rubbery plug which seemed to clear his whole head.

There had to be a lever.

Once more he set to his frantic scrabbling, and at last found what he was looking for, right down beside the driver's seat. He grinned and pulled it and the bonnet clicked up.

He opened the bonnet and peered inside. The engine made no

sense to him, it was like the engine of a spaceship, or something. In his panic he couldn't tell what was what.

Of course. The sound. The sound must be coming from the alarm. He homed in on it, like a bat. Yes, there it was. His fingers touched it and he could feel it warm and pulsing, almost alive. But there was nothing for it, sod what The Lads would think, he didn't have time to fiddle with nuts and bolts and screws, he'd just have to wrench the wires off it.

He set to like a bomb disposal expert in a film, except that he wasn't carefully snipping with little pliers, he was tugging and ripping like crazy. Only it didn't seem to be making any fucking difference. The fucking alarm was still fucking screeching. Shouting, 'Over here! He's over here. This way! Look, there he is, half naked and freezing to death.'

It was no good, he'd have to physically remove the bloody thing after all.

He found a tool kit in the boot and, lighting matches to see what he was doing, sod the risk, he began the laborious task of undoing the four screws that held it in place.

Six screws. Six, for fuck's sake. Why couldn't it just be two? Or a nice little clip, or anything other than six bloody screws.

It was like one of those impossible tasks you get given in night-mares. His hands shivering from the cold, the feeling in his fingers rapidly disappearing, the screwdriver constantly slipping, his body shaking, his teeth actually chattering, like a fucking Bugs Bunny cartoon, or something. Cursing, ripping the skin off his hands, come on, you bastard screws. *Come on.*

But at last it was done. The last screw was out. He jiggled the alarm unit and it came free. He kissed it.

And realised it was still going.

It couldn't be. There were no wires, he'd taken the fucking thing out, it had to stop. But, no, it sounded louder than ever.

In a rage he threw the unit down, went around to the boot again and got the jack. Then he started to hammer that alarm into the dirt. Bang, bang, bang. He belted it with that jack until the jack was bent and twisted, but the alarm unit was unscratched, and still it sang merrily away.

He'd half-buried it in the rock hard frozen ground, so he searched around for some other stuff to completely bury it with, and while he was searching he discovered that the trees were growing round a large, dark, pond.

Perfect.

He prised the unit out of the earth, took it to the pond, and threw it out deep into the stinking water.

And still it wailed and wailed.

Bee-bah-whee-wah-bee-bah-whee-wah…

Well, let it wail.

He crashed back through the trees to check the road, brambles catching at his bare legs, branches whipping his face. Nothing. No police cars, no traffic of any sort. All quiet. He struggled back into his clothes, jumped into the TVR and turned the key.

Nothing, not even a little cough. What had he done under the bonnet? What had he fucking done? The only life left in the car was the indicators and the music, and that was running down, slipping, getting sluggish, the voices deeper and drawn out. Like something from a cheap horror video. He kicked the tape player with the heel of one foot until it whimpered and stopped completely.

All right. Keep calm. Sort it out. Think it through.

It's just that he wasn't used to thinking, and the cold had slowed his already sluggish brain down to near absolute zero.

He could leave the car here. Smash the indicators if need be. Go and get help. Call The Lads. But that fucking alarm. He couldn't leave the car here with that alarm still going, as loud as ever, it was only a matter of time before the cops tracked it down. He had to get it back, properly bury it like he was going to do before he found that bloody pond.

He saw a blue light, in the distance, through the trees, speeding down the road and that decided it. He barged the car door open, jumped out and ran back to the pond.

He stepped in.

It was so cold it burned his legs. He went in up to his knees. How deep was it? He went further, stumbled into a sudden dip and was up to his waist. He gasped as his breath was tugged away. His bollocks shrank to two tiny, hard, white-hot rivets. Goose bumps prickled all over his body.

He felt around with his feet, where was it? Where was it?

Deeper still. It hadn't looked this deep. It wasn't very wide after all. Maybe it was a well? He didn't know about these things. Country things. Ponds and fields and trees. He couldn't swim, either. He was up to his chest now and the stench of the stagnant water clogged his lungs… It was down there, somewhere, beneath the jet black, chilling, pond scum.

He filled his lungs, held his nose and plunged under.

Panic, his body rigid with shock, but there, he could hear it, he felt around, bubbles popping from between his fingers.

He could see nothing, so he groped around with his hands and moved towards the siren call of the sunken alarm, until, yes, there it was. He touched the metal, he pulled.

But it was stuck in the sucking ooze on the bottom of the pond.

He pulled and pulled, his head pounding, his brain beginning to go numb, the alarm louder and louder in his ears. So cold now that all feeling had left him, he was totally disembodied, in a black universe filled only with this terrible noise.

Floating in nothingness. Emptiness. A limitless, dark cage with bars of sound. Already he felt like he didn't exist, like it didn't matter if he existed. That nothing mattered except silence. Blessed silence. If he could just make everything go quiet…

He half-heartedly tried to pull it up again, but he was too weak.

And then he passed out.

And then he died.

R D Wingfield

Notes

This story needs no introduction.

Just The Fax

R D Wingfield

FAX MESSAGE
From: R D Wingfield
To: Mike Ripley
Date: Thursday 3rd April 1997

Dear Mike Ripley,
Many thanks for your letter received today. *Fresh
Blood?* Are you sure you've got the right person?
Flattered you should invite me to contribute a
story to the anthology, but am cursing my luck
that these invitations always come at the wrong
time. Six months ago I would have paid you £100 for
the privilege of writing a short story. I am a
reluctant author and was thoroughly disenchanted
with the grind of writing full-length novels so
resolved that *Hard Frost* was the last and in
future I would only do shorter works like 45-
minute radio plays.
But Bantam, my American publisher, sneakily
announced another Frost book which I had never
said I would write. They then kept bombarding me
with letters from irate would-be purchasers who
couldn't find the new novel in their local book-
store. Bantam wore me down to the extent that I am
now in the process of sulkily churning out a seem-
ingly endless first draft and trying to meet their
deadline. Which means there is no way I can
squeeze in anything else until the new book is
finished, so I must regretfully turn down your
kind invitation but wish the anthology every
success.
Warmest wishes,
Rodney Wingfield

FAX MESSAGE
From: Mike Ripley
To: Rodney Wingfield
Date: Monday 7th April 1997

Dear Rodney,
Many thanks for your fax. Yes, we did have the right person: we know who our heroes are. (See back of *Frost* books for my thoughts!)
Please keep us in mind as we would really like to have you on board. If a short story proves impossible (and I understand completely), then how about a sneak preview of the new book, say a chapter as 'work in progress', a technique we used last year with Denise Danks who also found a deadline pressed up to her right temple?
Failing that, how about a note to the milkman?
If it helps, *Fresh Blood 1* got poll position in the *New York Times Review of Books* on Easter Sunday, something never achieved by an 'import' before now, so we re on a roll…
Aw go on. Yer will, yer will, yer will…
Regards,
Mike.
PS: Whatever, good luck with the next book. I'm afraid I'm now looking forward to it too.

FAX MESSAGE
From: R D Wingfield
To: Mike Ripley
Date: Monday 7th April 1997

Dear Mike,
Many thanks for your fax. Your silver tongued eloquence has wormed its way straight to my heart, but I have absolutely nothing to offer for *Fresh Blood 2*. My 'work in progress' is a heap of ill-typed A4 full of undeveloped characters, bad jokes and half-baked plots. (How is that different from his finished books I hear you ask!). My first draft simply serves to tell me what pitfalls to avoid in the second draft and very few of its ideas are carried forward.
If there's a follow up – STALE BLOOD perhaps I'd love to be asked to contribute to that.
Yours regretfully,
Rodney.

FAX MESSAGE
From: Mike Ripley
To: Rodney Wingfield
Date: Tuesday 8th April 1997

Dear Rodney,
Thanks for your fax. Is this a 'No'?
I think you're weakening, simply tempting us with
your description of your first draft just to up
the price.
Well, we've tried the cheeky approach and the
flattery. Soon, we'll only have the blackmail
gambit left. We could always print these faxes.
Yours from the Four Ale Bar,
Mike.

FAX MESSAGE
From: R D Wingfield
To: The Executors of the Estate of the late Mike
Ripley
Date: Tuesday 8th April 1997

Police Superintendent Mullett stared down with distaste at the
body on the towpath. 'He was a crime fiction critic,' he said.
Frost prodded the body with his foot, hopping back hastily as
more blood oozed out. 'Even scum like that don't deserve to be
decapitated and emasculated with a blunt penknife.'
'He tried to get that nice Rodney Wingfield to write a piece for
Fresh Blood 2 and wouldn't take no for an answer,' said Mullett.
Frost's face hardened. 'That's different. Give us a hand to chuck
him in the canal. We'll say it's suicide.'

Rodney Wingfield.

FAX MESSAGE
From: Mike Ripley
To: Rodney Wingfield
Date: Later the same day…

Dear Rodney, That's great! Many, many thanks for
your faxed story.
We can edit this together no problem.
The cheque is in the… What are you doing…? Oh, is
that a Swiss Army… Nice… And that's the bit that
gets stones out of horses'…?
Aaaaaaaaaaaaaaaaaargh…

About the Authors

John Baker lives in York and is the creator of the twice-married Bob Dylan fan and former alcoholic sleuth, Sam Turner. His romantic character has appeared in two novels, *Poet in the Gutter* and *Death Minus Zero*. He also reviews frequently for *The Tangled Web* and *A Shot in the Dark*.

Christopher Brookmyre won the critics' choice First Blood Award for his debut novel *Quite Ugly One Morning*. Born in Glasgow in 1968, he has worked as a journalist in London, Los Angeles and Edinburgh. His second novel, *Country of the Blind*, is being published to coincide with *Fresh Blood II*.

Ken Bruen is a teacher of English as a foreign language who shares his time between London, Athens and the west of Ireland. His debut, *Rilke on Black,* was widely acclaimed. His second novel *The Hackman's Blues* appears in the autumn of 1997.

Carol Anne Davis lives in Edinburgh and since 1990 she has been writing full time, mainly in the fields of horror and erotica. Her first crime novel, *Shrouded,* appeared in the spring of 1997 and brings new meanings to the usual equation of love and death.

Christine Green spent many years as a nurse, which bore fruit with the creation of medical investigator Kate Kinsella, who has since appeared in a handful of mysteries. She is also the author of the Chief Inspector O'Neill and Detective Sergeant Wilson series, which includes *Die in My Dreams*.

Lauren Henderson came to prominence with her first Sam Jones mystery, *Dead White Female,* introducing the wonderfully politically incorrect sleuthette and sculptor, who has since featured in *Too Many Blondes* and *The Black Rubber Dress*. Lauren, an ex-journalist, lives most of the year in Tuscany.

Charles Higson is a mainstay of the British comedy scene and one of the hippest writers around. His books include *King of the Ants, Happy Now, Full Whack* and *Getting Rid of Mr Kitchen*. When not performing for the hit TV comedy *The Fast Show,* he writes and produces for the likes of Harry Enfield and Reeves and Mortimer.

Maxim Jakubowski worked in publishing but now write, runs the Murder One bookshop and reviews crime fiction for *Time Out* magazine. His recent books include *Life in the World of Women*, *It's You That I Want To Kiss* and *Because She Thought She Loved Me*. He has been called the King of the Erotic Thriller, but it shouldn't be held against him.

Phil Lovesey is a rare instance of a second generation crime writer, being the son of award-winning author Peter Lovesey. He has published several mystery stories in American magazines, but this is his first to appear in Britain. His debut novel, *Death Duties*, is being published early in 1998.

Mike Ripley, in addition to promoting beer, writing for television and co-editing the *Fresh Blood* anthologies, is the popular creator of sleuthing rogue Fitzroy Maclean Angel, whose eighth, funniest and, possibly, final appearance is in *That Angel Look*. He is also crime fiction critic for *The Daily Telegraph*.

Mary Scott is a newcomer to the mystery field, but not to books, having published a well-received short story collection and novel with Serpent's Tail, respectively *Nudists May Be Encountered* and *Not In Newbury*. She is also a frequent contributor and feature writer for *The Independent*, *New Statesman* and *The Literary Review*.

Ian Sinclair is generally considered to be in the premier league of British contemporary writers and poets. His work has always flirted with the borderlines of crime and fantasy. His novels include *White Chappell*, *Scarlet Tracings*, *Downriver* and *Raidon Daughters*. His recent book of essays, *Lights Out For The Territory*, is another look at the secret life of London.

John Tilsley has been a Royal Marine Commando and a mercenary. His first novel, *Be A Good Boy Johnny*, journeyed through the seamy side of Las Vegas and bandit country by the Mexican border. His new book, *Nevada Blue*, continues his exploration of the underbelly of America.

John L Williams has for many years been one of the prominent commentators of crime fiction in British newspapers and magazines. His travel book of conversations with US mystery authors, *Into The Badlands*, is an indispensable volume for all lovers of the hardboiled genre. His first novel, *Faithless*, appeared in 1997 and was widely reviewed as one of the best London and pop culture books of the decade.

R D Wingfield was born in London within screaming distance of the scenes of the Jack the Ripper murders. He followed a career in the oil industry by writing for radio. He is the creator of the popular, and now televised, sleuth Detective Inspector Jack Frost, who has so far appeared in four best-selling novels.

BLOODLINES the cutting-edge crime and mystery imprint...

That Angel Look by Mike Ripley

"The outrageous, rip-roarious Mr Ripley is an abiding delight..."
– Colin Dexter

A chance encounter (in a pub, of course) lands street-wise, cab-driving Angel the ideal job as an all-purpose assistant to a trio of young and very sexy fashion designers.

But things are nowhere near as straightforward as they should be and it soon becomes apparent that no-one is telling the truth – least of all Angel!

Double-cross turns to triple-cross and Angel finds himself set-up by friend and enemy alike. This time, Angel could really meet his match...

"I never read Ripley on trains, planes or buses. He makes me laugh and it annoys the other passengers." – Minette Walters.

1 899344 23 3 – £8

I Love The Sound of Breaking Glass by Paul Charles

First outing for Irish-born Detective Inspector Christy Kennedy whose beat is Camden Town, north London. Peter O'Browne, managing director of Camden Town Records, is missing. Is his disappearance connected with a mysterious fire that ravages his north London home? And just who was using his credit card in darkest Dorset?

Although up to his neck in other cases, Detective Inspector Christy Kennedy and his team investigate, plumbing the hidden depths of London's music industry, turning up murder, chart-rigging scams, blackmail and worse. *I Love The Sound of Breaking Glass* is a detective story with a difference. Part whodunnit, part howdunnit and part love story, it features a unique method of murder, a plot with more twists and turns than the road from Kingsmarkham to St Mary Mead.

Paul Charles is one of Europe's best known music promoters and agents. In this, his stunning début, he reveals himself as master of the crime novel. ISBN 1 899344 16 0 – £7

Shrouded by Carol Anne Davis

Douglas likes women — quiet women; the kind he deals with at the mortuary where he works. Douglas meets Marjorie, unemployed, gaining weight and losing confidence. She talks and laughs a lot to cover up her shyness, but what Douglas really needs is a lover who'll stay still — deadly still. Driven by lust and fear, Douglas finds a way to make girls remain excitingly silent and inert. But then he is forced to blank out the details of their unplanned deaths.

Perhaps only Marjorie can fulfil his growing sexual hunger. If he could just get her into a state of limbo. Douglas studies his textbooks to find a way...

Shrouded is a powerful and accomplished début, tautly-plotted, dangerously erotic and vibrating with tension and suspense.
ISBN 1 899344 17 9— £7

BLOODLINES the cutting-edge crime and mystery imprint...

Fresh Blood edited by Mike Ripley & Maxim Jakubowski

Featuring the cream of the British New Wave of crime writers including John Harvey, Mark Timlin, Chaz Brenchley, Russell James, Stella Duffy, Ian Rankin, Nicholas Blincoe, Joe Canzius, Denise Danks, John B Spencer, Graeme Gordon, and a previously unpublished extract from the late Derek Raymond. Includes an introduction from each author explaining their views on crime fiction in the '90s and a comprehensive foreword on the genre from Angel-creator, Mike Ripley.
ISBN 1 899344 03 9 – £6.99

Smalltime by Jerry Raine

Smalltime is a taut, psychological crime thriller, set among the seedy world of petty criminals and no-hopers. In this remarkable début, Jerry Raine shows just how easily curiosity can turn into fear amid the horrors, despair and despondency of life lived a little too near the edge.

"Jerry Raine's *Smalltime* carries the authentic whiff of sleazy nineties Britain. He vividly captures the world of stunted ambitions and their evil consequences." – Simon Brett

"The first British contemporary crime novel featuring an underclass which no one wants. Absolutely authentic and quite possibly important."– Philip Oakes, *Literary Review.*
ISBN 1 899344 13 6 – £5.99

Hellbent on Homicide by Gary Lovisi

"This isn't a first novel, this is a book written by a craftsman who learned his business from the masters, and in HELLBENT ON HOMICIDE, that education rings loud and long." –Eugene Izzi

1962, a sweet, innocent time in America... after McCarthy, before Vietnam. A time of peace and trust, when girls hitch-hiked without a care. But for an ice-hearted killer, a time of easy pickings.

"A wonderful throwback to the glory days of hardboiled American crime fiction. In my considered literary judgement, if you pass up HELLBENT ON HOMICIDE, you're a stone chump." –Andrew Vachss

Brooklyn-based Gary Lovisi's powerhouse début novel is a major contribution to the hardboiled school, a roller-coaster of sex, violence and suspense, evocative of past masters like Jim Thompson, Carroll John Daly and Ross Macdonald.

"A sharp pistol crack of a book, pure and loving homage to the hardboiled pulps of yesteryear." – *The Daily Telegraph*
ISBN 1 899344 18 7 £7

BLOODLINES the cutting-edge crime and mystery imprint...
The Hackman Blues by Ken Bruen
"If Martin Amis was writing crime novels, this is what he would hope to write." – *Books in Ireland*

"...I haven't taken my medication for the past week. If I couldn't go a few days without the lithium, I was in deep shit. I'd gotten the job ten days earlier and it entailed a whack of pub-crawling. Booze and medication is the worst of songs. Sing that!

A job of pure simplicity. Find a white girl in Brixton. Piece of cake. What I should have done is doubled my medication and lit a candle to St Jude – maybe a lot of candles."

Add to the mixture a lethal ex-con, an Irish builder obsessed with Gene Hackman, the biggest funeral Brixton has ever seen, and what you get is the Blues like they've never been sung before.

Ken Bruen's powerful second novel is a gritty and grainy mix of crime noir and Urban Blues that greets you like a mugger stays with you like a razor-scar.

GQ described his début novel as:
"The most startling and original crime novel of the decade."
The Hackman Blues is Ken Bruen's best novel yet.

Perhaps She'll Die! by John B Spencer

Giles could never say 'no' to a woman... any woman. But when he tangled with Celeste, he made a mistake... A bad mistake.

Celeste was married to Harry, and Harry walked a dark side of the street that Giles – with his comfortable lifestyle and fashionable media job – could only imagine in his worst nightmares. And when Harry got involved in nightmares, people had a habit of getting hurt.

Set against the boom and gloom of eighties Britain, *Perhaps She'll Die!* is classic *noir* with a centre as hard as toughened diamond.
ISBN 1 899344 14 4 – £5.99

Quake City by John B Spencer

The third novel to feature Charley Case, the hard-boiled investigator of a future that follows the 'Big One of Ninety-Seven' – the quake that literally rips California apart and makes LA an Island.

"Classic Chandleresque private eye tale, jazzed up by being set in the future... but some things never change – PI Charley Case still has trouble with women and a trusty bottle of bourbon is always at hand. An entertaining addition to the private eye canon." – *Mail on Sunday*
ISBN 1 899344 02 0 – £5.99

Also available in paperback from The Do-Not Press

Because She Thought She Loved Me by Maxim Jakubowski
'He'll have to die.'
'Yes," I heard myself saying, sealing my fate…'
The course of true love doesn't run easy when your husband is a power-ful pornographer who controls most of the shady side of the Internet. And when a tender love affair runs out of control, desperate measures are needed to stop the darkness engulfing its frantic protagonists.
Because She Thought She Loved Me offers a thrilling descent into the heart of sexual madness, moving in overdrive from London's West End, via the sinister private clubs of Paris, to the no-holds-barred illegal strip-joints of New York.
Maxim Jakubowski continues his daring exploration of the night-side of sex in a suspenseful tale full of memorable characters and sharp emo-tions.
ISBN 1 899344 27 6 – £7

It's You That I Want To Kiss by Maxim Jakubowski
They met among the torrid nightlife of Miami Beach, but soon they were running. From the Florida heat to rain-drenched Seattle, Anne and Jake blaze an unforgettable trail of fast sex, forbidden desires and sudden violence, pursued across America by a chilling psychopath.
Set against a backdrop of gaudy neon-lit American roadhouses and lonely highways, It's you that I want to kiss is a no-holds-barred rock 'n' roll road movie in print, in which every turn offers hidden danger, and where every stranger is a potential enemy.
ISBN 1 899344 15 2 – £7.99

Life In The World Of Women
a collection of vile, dangerous and loving stories **by Maxim Jakubowski**
Maxim Jakubowski's dangerous and erotic stories of war between the sexes are collected here for the first time.
"Demonstrates that erotic fiction can be amusing, touching, spooky and even (at least occasionally) elegant. Erotic fiction seems to be Jakubowski's true metier. These stories have the hard sexy edge of Henry Miller and the redeeming grief of Jack Kerouac. A first class col-lection." – Ed Gorman, *Mystery Scene* (USA)
ISBN 1 899344 06 3 – £6.99

Also available in paperback from The Do-Not Press

The Sandman
by Miles Gibson

"I am the Sandman. I am the butcher in soft rubber gloves. I am the acrobat called death.
I am the fear in the dark. I am the gift of sleep…"

Growing up in a small hotel in a shabby seaside town, Mackerel Burton has no idea that he is to grow up to become a slick and ruthless serial killer. A lonely boy, he amuses himself by perfecting his conjuring tricks, but slowly the magic turns to a darker kind, and soon he finds himself stalking the streets of London in search of random and innocent victims. He has become The Sandman.

"A truly remarkable insight into the workings of a deranged mind: a vivid, extraordinarily powerful novel which will grip you to the end and which you'll long remember"
> – *Mystery & Thriller Guild*

"A horribly deft piece of work!" – *Cosmopolitan*

"Written by a virtuoso – it luxuriates in death with a Jacobean fervour"
> – *The Sydney Morning Herald*

"Confounds received notions of good taste – unspeakable acts are reported with an unwavering reasonableness essential to the comic impact and attesting to the deftness of Gibson's control."
> – *Times Literary Supplement*

ISBN 1 899344 24 1 – £7

Also available in paperback from The Do-Not Press

Dancing With Mermaids
by Miles Gibson

"Absolutely first rate. Absolutely wonderful"
– Ray Bradbury

Strange things are afoot in the Dorset fishing town of Rams Horn.

Set close to the poisonous swamps at the mouth of the River Sheep, the town has been isolated from its neighbours for centuries.

But mysterious events are unfolding... A seer who has waited for years for her drowned husband to reappear is haunted by demons, an African sailor arrives from the sea and takes refuge with a widow and her idiot daughter. Young boys plot sexual crimes and the doctor, unhinged by his desire for a woman he cannot have, turns to a medicine older than his own.

"An imaginative tour de force and a considerable stylistic achievement. When it comes to pulling one into a world of his own making, Gibson has few equals among his contemporaries."
– *Time Out*

"A wild, poetic exhalation that sparkles and hoots and flies."
– *The New Yorker*

"An extraordinary talent dances with perfect control across hypnotic page."
– *Financial Times*

ISBN 1 899344 25 X – £7

Outstanding Paperback Originals from The Do-Not Press:

It's Not A Runner Bean by Mark Steel

"I've never liked Mark Steel and I thoroughly resent the high quality of this book." – Jack Dee

The life of a Slightly Successful Comedian can include a night spent on bare floorboards next to a pyromaniac squatter in Newcastle, followed by a day in Chichester with someone so aristocratic, they speak without ever moving their lips.

From his standpoint behind the microphone, Mark Steel is in the perfect position to view all human existence. Which is why this book – like his act, broadcasts and series' – is opinionated, passionate, and extremely funny. It even gets around to explaining the line (screamed at him by an eighties yuppy): "It's not a runner bean…" – which is another story.

"Hugely funny…" – *Time Out*

'A terrific book. I have never read any other book about comedy written by someone with a sense of humour.' – Jeremy Hardy, *Socialist Review*.
ISBN 1 899344 12 8– £5.99

The Users by Brian Case

The welcome return of Brian Case's brilliantly original '60s cult classic.

"A remarkable debut" –Anthony Burgess

"Why Case's spiky first novel from 1968 should have languished for nearly thirty years without a reprint must be one of the enigmas of modern publishing. Mercilessly funny and swaggeringly self-conscious, it could almost be a template for an early Martin Amis." – *Sunday Times*.
ISBN 1 899344 05 5– £5.99

It's You That I Want To Kiss by Maxim Jakubowski

They met among the torrid nightlife of Miami Beach, but soon they were running. From the Florida heat to rain-drenched Seattle, Anne and Jake blaze an unforgettable trail of fast sex, forbidden desires and sudden violence, pursued across America by a chilling psychopath.

Set against a backdrop of gaudy neon-lit American roadhouses and lonely highways, It's you that I want to kiss is a no-holds-barred rock 'n' roll road movie in print, in which every turn offers hidden danger, and where every stranger is a potential enemy. ISBN 1 899344 15 2 – £7.99

Life In The World Of Women

a collection of vile, dangerous and loving stories by **Maxim Jakubowski**

Maxim Jakubowski's dangerous and erotic stories of war between the sexes are collected here for the first time.

"Demonstrates that erotic fiction can be amusing, touching, spooky and even (at least occasionally) elegant. Erotic fiction seems to be Jakubowski's true metier. These stories have the hard sexy edge of Henry Miller and the redeeming grief of Jack Kerouac. A first class collection."   – Ed Gorman, *Mystery Scene* (USA)
ISBN 1 899344 06 3 – £6.99

Outstanding Paperback Fiction from The Do-Not Press:

Charlie's Choice: The First Charlie Muffin Omnibus by Brian Freemantle – *Charlie Muffin; Clap Hands, Here Comes Charlie; The Inscrutable Charlie Muffin*

Charlie Muffin is not everybody's idea of the ideal espionage agent. Dishevelled, cantankerous and disrespectful, he refuses to play by the Establishment's rules. Charlie's axiom is to screw anyone from anywhere to avoid it happening to him. But it's not long before he finds himself offered up as an unwilling sacrifice by a disgraced Department, desperate to win points in a ruthless Cold War. Now for the first time, the first three Charlie Muffin books are collected together in one volume. "Charlie is a marvellous creation" – *Daily Mail*

Elvis – The Novel by Robert Graham, Keith Baty
"Quite simply, the greatest music book ever written"
        – Mick Mercer, *Melody Maker*

The everyday tale of an imaginary superstar eccentric. The Presley neither his fans nor anyone else knew. First-born of triplets, he came from the backwoods of Tennessee. Driven by a burning ambition to sing opera, Fate sidetracked him into creating Rock 'n' roll.

His classic movie, *Driving A Sportscar Down To A Beach In Hawaii* didn't win the Oscar he yearned for, but The Beatles revived his flagging spirits, and he stunned the world with a guest appearance in Batman.

Further shockingly momentous events have led him to the peaceful, contented lifestyle he enjoys today.

"Books like this are few and far between." – Charles Shaar Murray, *NME*

ISBN 1 899344 19 5 – £7

The Do-Not Press
Fiercely Independent Publishing

Keep in touch with what's happening at the cutting edge of independent British publishing.

Join The Do-Not Press Information Service and receive advance information of all our new titles, as well as news of events and launches in your area, and the occasional free gift and special offer.

Simply send your name and address to:
The Do-Not Press (Dept. FBT)
PO Box 4215
London
SE23 2QD
or email us: thedonotpress@zoo.co.uk

There is no obligation to purchase and
no salesman will call.

••

Visit our regularly-updated Internet site:

http://www.thedonotpress.co.uk

Mail Order
All our titles are available from good bookshops, or (in case of difficulty) direct from The Do-Not Press at the address above. There is no charge for post and packing. (NB: A postman may call.)